A Dangerous Passion

There was a nerve-wrackingly long moment before he said, "I'd see you out of this dress."

"Wh-what?" Ailís whispered.

"Aye. Out of it entirely." Only the quick drop of his hands back to her shoulders kept her from sliding into a jellied heap at his boots. "Pink doesn't suit you. When next we meet I'd have you in silver, like the moonlight."

Ailís heard the hoofbeats ahead on the road, echoing the pattern of her heart, growing louder.

"Patrols!" the Hound's companion shouted from his place at the front of the team. "In force, too."

The bandit's gaze slewed from Ailís to the road and back again. "Go," Ailís urged him, some sense returning to her head. She pushed at his chest, tensed and granite-hard beneath her palms, to shove him away.

"Dammit, man, now!" the second bandit snapped.

Instead of feeling An Cú move, Ailís suddenly found herself flat up against his chest.

His mouth covered hers. Hard, hot, demanding, and gone before she could gather her thoughts around the incredible sensation. Then his hands were gone, too, and she staggered, almost going down. . . .

Scandalous Secrets by Patricia Oliver

Years ago, Lady Francesca St. Ives was divorced, and cast out of her family amid scandalous rumors. Now, she has returned home to make a new life for herself—without the aid of a man. But a little girl who needs her help—and the child's handsome, intriguing father—may slightly alter the lady's plans...and her heart....

0-451-19886-7/$4.99

The Barbarian Earl by Nadine Miller

The unscrupulous Earl of Stratham has offered his illegitimate son Liam a generous inheritance—if Liam marries the noble Lady Alexandra Henning. But an arranged marriage is an affront to Alexandra's romantic sensibilities—unless Liam can find the way to her heart—and perhaps open his own as well....

0-451-19887-5/$4.99

The Scottish Legacy by Barbara Hazard

Clear-headed Lila Douglas never believed in love at first sight—until she fell hopelessly in love with her dashing second cousin, Alastair Russell. Ever since, she's dreamed of future meetings that end with happily ever after. But can her romantic fantasy withstand reality—not to mention a most unexpected rival?

0-451-19888-3/$4.99

The Irish Rogue

Emma Jensen

A SIGNET BOOK

SIGNET
Published by New American Library, a division of
Penguin Putnam Inc., 375 Hudson Street,
New York, New York 10014, U.S.A.
Penguin Books Ltd, 27 Wrights Lane,
London W8 5TZ, England
Penguin Books Australia Ltd, Ringwood,
Victoria, Australia
Penguin Books Canada Ltd, 10 Alcorn Avenue,
Toronto, Ontario, Canada M4V 3B2
Penguin Books (N.Z.) Ltd, 182–190 Wairau Road,
Auckland 10, New Zealand

Penguin Books Ltd, Registered Offices:
Harmondsworth, Middlesex, England

First published by Signet, an imprint of New American Library,
a division of Penguin Putnam Inc.

First Printing, November 1999
10 9 8 7 6 5 4 3 2 1

Copyright © Melissa Jensen, 1999

For my Christor's parents.
Barbara, I adored you in Kilnaboy and cherish you now.
Neil, quite simply, I couldn't have written this
without your help.
Go raibh míle maith agat.
Tá mé i ngrá libh.

Chapter 1

Ailís O'Neill had ample experience with creatures of the night. The rest of the household was not so practiced, however, and the chorus of shouts and shrieks had reached symphonic proportions by the time she rushed past the drawing room with her net. Doors slammed along the hallway. The downstairs maid was scuttling under the massive hall table. And Fergus, the usually stoic footman, came bolting from the dining room, worn coat pulled up well over his ears.

"In there, Miss," he grunted, flicking a thumb over his shoulder before continuing at high speed toward the back stairs.

Ailís stepped into the room and closed the door behind her. Her mother was seated at the head of the mahogany table, teacup in one hand, the daily *Freeman's Journal* held over her dark curls with the other. "Honestly, Ailís," she sighed as her daughter entered, "why could you not have liked flowers?"

"You know I like flowers very well indeed." Ailís scanned the dark paneling, net at the ready. "The next series might be local plant life, as a matter of fact. For now . . . Ah! *Tost,* Donnagán. I am not going to hurt you."

Anne O'Neill flinched slightly as the bat came swooping across the table, narrowly missing her cup. "I can almost accept that you bring these creatures into the house, dearest, but must you give them family names?" Ailís crept stealthily around her mother's chair, then cursed under her breath as the bat careened upward toward the ceiling. "Really, Ailís, your language!"

Ordinarily, Ailís would have been far more patient in her pursuit. But she was concerned that the little animal might injure itself in its mad flight, so she made a determined sweep with the net. The bat, in the process of turning, went straight into the silk mesh. Crooning softly to still its fluttering, Ailís drew the net back and caught it below the rim. A clearly unhappy Donnagán was well caught.

She shoved her spectacles back to their proper place at the bridge of her nose and made certain the bat wasn't tangling itself dangerously in the mesh. Bats weren't particularly bright creatures for all their appeal. "Now tell me, Mama, that he does not resemble Cousin Donn to a turn. A bit more handsome, perhaps, but it's the same face."

Anne withdrew delicately from the proffered net. "Oh, Ailís." She did, however, take a brief look. "I suppose there is something of a similarity around the eyes."

"I was sure you would see it. But this fellow is a great deal more handsome, actually. My apologies for the insult," she said to the struggling bat. Then, striding to the door, she opened it and called for Fergus. He did not look at all pleased to have charge of the animal, but accepted the net with grace. "Be certain to lock my chamber door behind you. We cannot have him escaping again."

Once footman and bat had disappeared up the stairs, Ailís returned to the table. The *Journal* was folded neatly on the linen cloth now, and Anne was pouring herself more tea. "Your nose is yellow, dearest, and there appears to be a mauve spot on your left sleeve."

Ailís touched the tip of her nose and her fingertips came away with a faint golden tint. Sighing, she withdrew a paint-smudged handkerchief from her pinafore pocket and rubbed at the pigment. Lately, she seemed to be wearing more paint than her paper. "I was having some difficulty with the ears. They are the defining feature of the long-eared bat, after all, and I need to get them just right."

"Of course you do. Dare I hope you are almost finished?"

"By tonight." Ailís filled her own cup and sipped absently. The ears were a challenge, but she was more concerned with the second image she would be painting. She had composed the picture in her head countless times, but was still having difficulty in putting all the components together. "I need to send the painting off tomorrow. They will be expecting the series in London."

"Oh? Is the book to finally be published, then?"

"I've no idea. I send the pictures and hope they'll suit. I don't ask about the publishing." Ailís accepted a slice of toast and hastily changed the subject. She did not want to discuss the long delay in the printing of the guide to Irish wildlife she was illustrating. "Is Eamonn up and about yet? I've a bone to pick with him about the racket he made coming in last night. He clattered his stick all along the hall."

Anne glanced at the mantel clock with some exasperation. "Your brother has taken to sleeping away the morning more days than not. Practicing for life in London, I assume."

"I'll wake him, then. We can't have him growing any lazier than he is already." Ailís tempered the words with a smile. Eamonn was an industrious man once he'd rolled out of bed, a trait he had not yet lost in his new incarnation as a man of the world. "It's the company he's keeping, out all night and lying abed half the day."

"Yes, well. Speaking of which, I don't suppose . . . er . . . Donnagán could stay caged for the day. We're to have company for luncheon."

"Hmm? Oh, I'm afraid not. I have a vole in the cage at the moment and Donnagán seems quite content to hang from the wall sconces."

"This might seem like a silly question, Ailís, but why can you not simply have one animal at a time?"

"I try, but Tommy Cleary brought me the vole yesterday, and I couldn't refuse the opportunity. They are so rare in Ireland, and he went to such trouble to find one." She waved away the marmalade, mind whirling with possibilities for how she would paint the bat. She would have to consult her list, see what would suit best.

"About luncheon, Ailís."

"Oh, I'll just have a tray sent up. I haven't time—"

"Of course you do. You've quite perfected your painting, but your social skills seem to have slipped somewhat of late."

Ailís stifled a smile. Her mother, tiny and tough, the very picture of Celtic blood from the top of her dark head to the tips of her capable fingers, managed nonetheless to put one in mind of blue-blooded royalty. Proper manners, Anne decreed, were what separated man—and woman—from the furry and feathered creatures with which her daughter spent so much time of late. And whose traits, she lamented with increasing frequency, she was very much afraid Ailís was starting to acquire.

"I am sorry I hurried out of Lady Lorcan's garden party, but I'd other matters to attend."

"I am less concerned with your departure, dearest, than with your parting words. I cannot think what purpose you meant to serve by telling the lady's son that you'd spent more enjoyable afternoons with a squid." Anne's lips twitched, but she continued sternly, "That does not speak well for either your manners or the company you keep."

Ailís gave an amused shrug. "In my experience, squid tend to keep their multitude of extremities to themselves. Philly was doing his best to get all ten fingers onto various parts of me."

"Oh, dear, was he? I wish you had told me, Ailís. Or Eamonn. He would have seen to the matter."

No doubt her brother would indeed have seen the lecherous Mr. Philip Lorcan right out the door and headfirst into Stephen's Lake. And her mother might well have applied a tiny foot to his departing posterior. Elegant and urbane as the O'Neill family had become, generations of hot country blood could not be blotted out entirely.

"Philly Lorcan is naught but a bumbling puppy. I'll simply stay out of his way as much as possible in the future. It isn't a hardship for me, avoiding Dublin's foremost and finest."

"No," Anne sighed. "I am afraid it is not a hardship for you at all. If I assure you that today's company is a far step above Mr. Lorcan, will you tolerate an hour of tedium at the luncheon table? Sweeney found some lovely salmon at the market this morning."

Oh, it was tempting. As far as Ailís was concerned, nothing compared to the cook's baked salmon. Handed down through generations of Donegal Sweeneys, the recipe produced a dish sweet enough to make a hardened warrior cry. During the

O'Neills' year of residence in town, far weaker guests had been reduced to begging for the recipe to take home to their own cooks. However, white-haired Sorcha Sweeney, with a beaming smile, had resolutely refused, brandishing her vast wooden spoon when necessary as she made her escape. Ailís adored her.

"And who might this illustrious company be?" Salmon or no, Ailís was more than weary of fashionable Dublin.

"Oh, merely a friend—or perhaps two—of Eamonn's. Supporters of his stand for Parliament. You'll have the rest of the morning to yourself. He . . . er . . . they are not expected till one."

Ailís gave her mother a sharp look. The wide brown eyes, so much like her own, gave little away. "It's Lord Clane you're speaking of, isn't it?"

"Now, Ailís—"

"I'll be having a tray in my room, then. You know how I feel about that man."

"Oh, Ailís, really! The earl is your brother's friend, not to mention far more distinguished company than we're daily accustomed to. We should be honored to have him in the house."

"So you say. I might disagree."

Anne rolled her eyes. "I cannot fathom why! He has been nothing but pleasant to us all."

"He has, but I'd still just as soon dine with my vole."

"Forgive me for saying so, love, but I would not be surprised to hear that Lord Clane thinks you something of a shrew. Your behavior toward him has been, shall we say, somewhat less than amicable."

"I am always civil."

"I will not argue with that, dearest. Without resorting to profanity, it's difficult to be uncivil when speaking in single words."

Ailís closed her eyes wearily. "I have nothing to say to Lord Clane and he has nothing to say to me."

"He tries, Ailís."

"He speaks of the weather and all we've had recently is rain!"

"You love the rain."

"Not in the city," Ailís replied grimly.

These unpleasant little exchanges had become woefully familiar in the past month since the lofty Lord Clane had come back to Dublin and started hanging about. True, he was a friend of sorts to Eamonn—had been his captain in the Connaught Rangers. In fact, if her naturally dramatic brother were to be believed, the earl had saved his careless hide at Badajoz.

Still Ailís could not like the man.

It was difficult to say precisely what rubbed her most wrong about him, a circumstance that irked her nearly as much as Clane himself. He was pleasant enough, if somewhat reserved. That she attributed to his station and upbringing. Anglo-Irish or not, he was the epitome of the proud aristocrat. There were enough of those about Dublin to be familiar and a bit amusing. No, it wasn't his bearing that annoyed her.

Nor was he unpleasant to be near. He certainly smelled better than most of his peers. He looked better, too. In fact, if one were to be objective, the earl was a stunning creature. Tall, broad of shoulder, and firm-jawed, he had the near-black hair and clear, sun-touched skin of an Irishman born to the land. He had, too, a deep crease to the right of his mouth that appeared with rakish speed whenever he smiled. The smiles were rare, and wry as often as not, but they were created by a perverse God to set female hearts thumping.

As best Ailís could tell, it was the eyes that made her feel twitchy whenever he was about. They were the blue-green of Dublin Bay, and just as clear. They were also disconcertingly sharp when they fixed on her. It was, she'd decided after a mere hour in his presence, rather like being studied by a powerful, well-fed cat. The speculation in the gaze might be imagined, but it was dangerous if it was there.

She was well used to speculative glances from men. She had little experience, however, in avoiding them. Usually, she stared boldly back until the fellow's eyes dropped. Or she simply turned away with disinterest and went about her business. Lord Clane's gaze never dropped, and Ailís couldn't help feeling that turning her back on him would be as wise as a vole turning away from a prowling tom.

She glanced down at her hands to find that she was gripping a dull butter knife with unnecessary force. She hurriedly loosened her fingers and shoved the thing under the edge of her empty plate. "I can't be bothered to make nice with his lordship today, *Máthair*. I have a bat to paint."

Anne managed a very good scowl and Ailís very nearly felt cowed. But her mother had never been much of a scowler and, at nearly six-and-twenty, Ailís was fairly resistant to maternally inspired shame. "One hour, Ailís. That is all I ask. You will have ample time to paint your bat."

A suspicion that had been niggling at the back of Ailís's mind sprang to full life. "You are matchmaking."

"I am not—"

"You are, and I won't have it. It isn't subtle any longer, *Máthair,* and you know I've no intention of marrying anyone, let alone a puffed-up, pinch-lipped aristocrat with more money than brains, and padding in his coat!"

Ailís thumped her fist against the table for emphasis, setting cutlery jingling and her spectacles sliding down her nose. She shoved them back into place and glared at her mother.

"Well, my love, that was impressive." Anne had the gall to smile. Indulgently, no less. "Believe me, Ailís, if I were to do the unforgivable, and try to put my daughter in the path of a man who might love, honor, and cherish her as I was for more than twenty years, I most certainly would not choose a—what was it?—puffed, poked, and padded man!"

"Pinched," Ailís corrected, crossing her arms over her chest.

"Pinched. Of course. Well, I must say, I would be willing to wager nearly all I possess that Lord Clane does not pad his coat. And I would hardly call him pinch-lipped. He has a lovely mouth with a lovely smile and that lovely dimple."

"That is not a dimple. It's a crack made when he tried to smile once." Ailís couldn't help but be annoyed that her mother had fallen victim to that cursed smile. She was beginning to suspect that she herself was the only woman in Dublin who did not want Lord Clane grinning at her. "Is Eamonn part of this dismal little plan, too?"

"There is no plan, Ailís. There is simply luncheon and common courtesy."

"Aye, and I'm the Queen of Connaught." Suddenly weary, she slumped back in her chair. She loathed arguing with her beloved mother. And she usually lost. "I don't like him, Mama. I can't help but think he's after something, and I've no doubt it's something we—Eamonn, at least—wouldn't want to give."

"Are you perhaps being a bit dramatic?"

"Perhaps. Part and parcel of being an O'Neill if I am." Ailís raised a tired hand and rubbed at her nose. "Something smells wrong. Why would a man like Clane be in Dublin at all? There's little society to be found here since our parliament was dissolved by the Union, and less sport. And as for his wanting to gad about with Eamonn—"

"Your brother might very well be standing for Parliament, for Ireland," her mother said gently. "Clane was born here, of old Irish stock. Isn't it possible he simply likes his homeland, likes Eamonn, and wishes to support him?"

Oh, it was possible. Anything was possible. After all, Ailís had, only minutes before, been chasing a long-eared bat in broad daylight through a Dublin townhouse. And she needed to get back to her work more than she needed to concern herself with the Earl of Clane.

"I'll think about luncheon," she offered, "but I will not accept a lack of padding inside those ghastly dear coats of his."

"Oh, Ailís," her mother sighed, "sometimes I am forced to believe you are a foundling."

A sudden clattering in the hall forestalled further discussion of either Ailís's social proclivities or her faery origins. It seemed the O'Neill men had decided to get out of bed.

Great-Uncle Thaddeus came through the door first, grizzled hair and hoary white brows slightly wilder than usual, gold-tipped cane gripped tight in his bony hand. Dressed as always in the pristine satin breeches and embroidered tailcoat of the previous century, he stalked across the worn carpet with the stately poise of a sixty-year-old aristocrat. Not a bad feat at all, considering the fact that he was eighty and had been born in a thatched cottage in Tullamore to parents barely of the gentry class. The O'Neills' present social status was due far more to the impressive determination of Thaddeus and his brother— Ailís's grandfather—than to ancestry.

Thaddeus's cane, soundless now as it moved along the carpet, was a vanity piece. Carved of glossy ebony, topped and tipped with elaborate gold, it had been a gift from the old Duke of Ormonde some thirty years before. Thaddeus had carried it every day since, and not needed it once.

Behind him, employing a plain and sturdy ash stick, was an obviously dragging Eamonn. Ailís noted the tight lines around his mouth, the shadows under the hazel eyes, and the whiteness of his knuckles where he grasped the cane. He hadn't been relying on it much of late—the bone shattered in Spain had been mending well—and she watched worriedly as he made his slow way to the table. For only being nine-and-twenty, he was moving like an old man.

"Rough night?" she asked quietly as he lowered himself into the seat beside hers. "Running about, were you?"

He gave a wan grin and shoved whiskey-brown hair from his forehead. "Sprinting the Fellows' Square at Trinity, of course. Broke the record, too." The jesting fell short, but Ailís let it pass. Lately Eamonn didn't like discussing his nocturnal activities, and she didn't press. "Did I wake you?"

"You did," she replied tartly, forcing her light tone to match his. She chose not to mention that she had only taken to her own bed a half-hour before his return. That was a moot point. She had been quite happily asleep when he'd come rattling in, and she sensed he needed the ribbing more than coddling. "Where did you hide the elephant?"

"Oh, he's tucked happily away in the attic. I'll have him out again before *Máthair* notices the thumping." To their mother, he said, more loudly, "Have we coffee this morning? My eyelids turned to lead sometime during the night."

Anne's eyes softened to warm bronze at his lopsided smile. "Serves you right, love, for tipping that last tankard." She lifted the quilted cover from the coffee pot. "Would you care to tell your mother what number was the last?"

"And sully my boyish innocence before you? I think not." Eamonn sighed thankfully when she tipped a generous measure of coffee into a cup. "I daresay Uncle Thaddeus would have a bit, too."

"Ah, aye. 'Twas the concert at the Rotunda." Ailís turned to her uncle, who had filled his plate at the sideboard and was now tucking happily into his black pudding. "Will it be a good review in tomorrow's *Journal,* Uncle Taddy?" When he did not respond, she raised her voice a notch. "Uncle Taddy?"

"Hmm? What?" He looked up and blinked at her. "Oh, thank you, nay. I'll make do with the eggs. Wretched night, you know, quite turned my stomach."

Ailís exchanged a quick smile with her brother and shouted, "I take it you won't be writing a good review of the performance, then."

"Not if Mozart himself rose from the grave and begged. All plinking and squeaking. Not a whit of talent among the whole blasted orchestra." Grumbling to himself, the esteemed music critic for the *Freeman's Journal* went back to sawing at his breakfast.

"I don't suppose you were there," Ailís asked her brother.

Eyes slightly brighter now with amusement, Eamonn shook his head. "I wasn't. But from all reports, there is a grand amount of talent in that orchestra. Lady Morgan claims they're the best lot in five years."

"Well, I daresay they'll survive a bad review. 'Tisn't as if there's much else to do of a night here. *Uncle Taddy?*"

"Aye?"

"What do you have on next?"

He rubbed at the crown of his head, sending his hair into greater disarray. "Opera in Kildare Street. *Orfeo ed Euridice,* I believe. Thursday." His seamed face broke into a sweet smile. "Would you care to accompany an old man to the opera, my girl?"

Ailís grinned back. "I would be delighted."

"Well, grand. Has to be better than last night. All plinking and squeaking, you know."

"Perhaps I'll go, too. Clane will be there, no doubt." Eamonn stole a piece of uneaten toast from Ailís's plate. "He's taken a box." He apparently missed her reflexive scowl. "He was asking after you yesterday, by the way. Most interested in your painting."

Ailís knew better. What had undoubtedly happened was that Eamonn, in his brotherly way, had been going on about her talent. Clane, in his cool politeness, might have asked a bland question or two.

She had a feeling that Lord Clane found her work, what little he knew of it, slightly amusing and decidedly inconsequential. There was no question that ladies of his acquaintance, if they had any artistic bent at all, made use of their paper and watercolors to paint flower gardens and the occasional peacock.

Ailís made up her mind right then to develop a headache before luncheon. Should she be forced to converse with the earl over salmon about her inconsequential pursuits, she would be sorely tempted to set him straight on the matter. And that, she knew, was completely out of the question. Discreet endeavors, after all, lost a great deal of their efficacy in the absence of discretion.

Chapter 2

"Interesting family, the O'Neills."

Christor Moore silently agreed with his companion. The O'Neills were an interesting family, indeed. He rested his forearms on the brass rail in front of him and gazed thoughtfully across the theater's upper tier to where the four occupied their own box. The old man appeared to be asleep, his chin buried in the folds of his lacy jabot. Mrs. O'Neill and her son were head-to-head in quiet discussion.

Ailís was the only one paying any attention whatsoever to the scene below. In fact, she had been rapt since arriving. It had taken Christor less than five minutes to decide that she was not watching the opera at all, but the audience. Candlelight glinted off the lenses of her little silver spectacles as she turned her head from side to side in a steady perusal of the persons in attendance.

Christor might have been watching the crowd, too, had he not had his eyes fixed on the O'Neill box. On stage, Gluck's florid opera was being taken to new lows by a consistently, enthusiastically flat soprano and awkwardly fat tenor. The colorful audience in the pit, unconcerned with the social restrictions that kept the loftier attendees yawning and rigid in their more expensive seats, whistled and hooted and occasionally sang along. Or rather, sporadic bursts of Irish pub tunes competed with the performance.

"Young Eamonn is making quite a name for himself here in town. War heroes are scarce in Dublin, and he seems to be making the most of it." Jonathan Lyndhurst leaned closer to Christor, bracing his own elbows on his knees. "I would say Harrington's seat in Commons will be his for the asking."

Eamonn certainly looked at ease with his position as hero and gentleman. In his well-cut coat and breeches, hair just avoiding the messiness of current London fashion, he was every inch the up-and-coming public figure. He could have been any one of the bright young men confidently ensconced on the parliamentary back-benches. And there was no doubt he would appeal to the populace. The strong, handsome face and imposing frame were Irish to the core; the clever tongue and cool mind testimony to Anglican education. And the ash cane always to be found in his fist or resting near to hand was as clear a symbol of patriotic bravery as the shiny medal Christor imagined was tucked away with O'Neill's 88th Division uniform.

His gaze slid yet again to the young woman on Eamonn's right. Where Eamonn was all midland solidity, Ailís O'Neill brought to mind the storm-swept northwestern coast. Anne O'Neill, Christor knew, was descended from Donegal Gaels, and she had passed that mystical, vivid aspect to her daughter.

One had to be standing very close to see the auburn and gold threading through the mahogany hair, the faint scattering of coppery freckles over the straight nose. Christor had seen both. He had also discovered that the bold, wide-set eyes were not truly brown, but a dark amber mingled with hazel and gold. Now, from a distance, she was all vividly dark hair and brows and pale skin. From a distance, the fire was hidden.

"The uncle has been in Dublin a good sixty years," Lyndhurst went on. "Trinity man, as was his nephew. I have no idea why Thomas O'Neill returned to Tullamore. Being something of a gentleman farmer suited him better than the law, perhaps. I imagine Eamonn could give you more insight into his father. No matter, really. Thomas left a sufficient legacy for his wife and children to maintain the house here in town. I daresay they're living well enough."

Ailís's pale green muslin dress was several years and quite a few country miles out of style. Christor had never taken much of an interest in fashion, but even he knew that the high bodice and higher fichu would be laughed out of an elegant assembly. It was a pity. Miss O'Neill possessed a lush form which was effectively concealed by the deplorable gown.

Anne, too, was dressed with bland simplicity. Clearly the money which might have been spent on clothing was going to

fund Eamonn's political aspirations. The little house in
Fitzwilliam Lane was impeccably clean, but the silver was battered from use and the carpets worn thin in spots. No, the
O'Neills were not living particularly well. Comfortably perhaps, but by no means elegantly.

"Catholic originally, of course. Fortunate for O'Neill that
his great-uncle and grandfather converted. I daresay we'll
never have Papists in Parliament, with good reason." Lyndhurst leaned back in his seat and crossed silk-stockinged legs.
"I've heard the sister teaches English to Catholic farmers outside of town. Amazing, isn't it, Clane, how a mere ten miles
from Dublin, they're still speaking Gaelic."

Christor grunted noncommittally. Lyndhurst prattled on, "I
imagine Eamonn knows the language, but I've never heard
him use it. From what I've gathered, Miss Ailís is rather fond
of spouting the ghastly stuff at the occasional fete. Shame, really. She's a pretty creature."

"Ay-lish."

"I beg your pardon?"

"Her name is pronounced Ay-lish, not Ay-lis." Christor gave
a faint smile. "It's Gaelic."

Lyndhurst grunted. In the twenty-odd years Christor had
known the man, he had never taken a correction gracefully. At
Samuel Whyte's Academy in Grafton Street, where Wellington
had been an indifferent student many years before, Lyndhurst
had stubbornly refused to acknowledge that Londonderry, far
to the north, had once been simply Derry. At Eton, where
Wellington had, contrary to popular belief, not been much of a
force on the playing fields, Lyndhurst had never conceded a
cricket goal.

Christor had followed Wellington into a military career.
Lyndhurst would never have been able to tolerate regimental
control. He had instead chosen what would no doubt be the
General's future career—assuming Wellington survived this
infernal war—and entered politics. Christor was certain he
would get a great deal of pleasure in having gotten to that
point first.

Lyndhurst was a bully. He was also an old acquaintance and
a powerful force on the House of Commons floor. Christor had

always found it far easier to accommodate the man than con-
front him. Now, with his own responsibilities to Lords, his
feelings had not changed. Completing this favor for Lyndhurst
would go a long way toward easing the opposition to his own
planned reforms.

It would also, with luck, answer some of his own silent
questions.

"I have been home less than a month," he announced, reluctantly turning his gaze from the lovely Ailís to his pink-faced,
paunchy companion, "but I believe I can set your mind at ease.
There's no reason to suspect O'Neill has any connection to
this An Cú character you've described, or has any intention of
becoming so. You can endorse the man for Harrington's seat
with no fear of Commons being infiltrated by filthy road bandits."

"You are amused by all this."

Christor stifled an unamused chuckle at the accusation. "Far
from it. I fully comprehend your concerns. I would imagine
society finds it most inconvenient to be preyed upon by a
modern-day Robin Hood, not to mention expensive and rather
embarrassing that no one seems to be able to capture the fellow."

Lyndhurst snorted. "Oh, he'll be caught soon enough. I've
no doubt of that."

Privately, Christor disagreed. An Cú—the Hound—had been
evading capture for some years now, much to the distress of the
Anglo-Irish wealthy whose pockets he emptied. There had been
a lull of several years when the nighttime roads near Dublin
had been quiet. As best Christor could tell, people had assumed
the fellow had moved on, or died. But the robberies had begun
again and Dublin Society returned to helpless indignation.

Adding insult to injury was the fact that the bandit and his
accomplices were well known for their habit of robbing only
Anglo travelers, and for spreading their booty among the local
poor, making the Hound something of a folk hero. A great
many people had not supported the dissolution of the country's
Parliament and union with Britain. And the Irish were not
known for taking discontent submissively or touting their heroes quietly. The frequent draping of Dublin statues with black

cloaks and masks *à la* bandit stuck in many patrician craws. Military units were deployed on a regular basis—always, it seemed, on the wrong nights. An Cú remained free.

"I admire your certainty that he will be captured," Christor offered. "But I still don't understand why you were so concerned about O'Neill to begin with."

Lyndhurst frowned and ran a hand through his thinning, pale hair. "We have people keeping an eye on things here in Dublin. There's been some odd murmuring about that household. Nothing we can pin down, but I need to be sure. Be a good fellow, Clane, and stay close to O'Neill. I cannot afford to have my judgment proven faulty after he is elected."

Across the theater, Eamonn was now cleaning his sister's spectacles with his handkerchief. Christor had seen him do it before on several occasions. Apparently Ailís did not object to seeing spots. "You know, even if he were a member of this group—or An Cú himself—he would hardly be likely to mention it offhand to me."

"To Christopher Rhys Francis, Sixth Earl of Clane, probably not. But to Captain Christor Moore, Dublin lad and blood fellow of the Devil's Own 88th Division Connaught Rangers, who knows? Give me another fortnight, Clane. You yourself said the London Season nearly turned you into a raving madman."

It had indeed. But Christor could not help feeling that to use friendship forged by war for the cause of a nervous Tory Member of Parliament would turn him into something far worse.

The fat tenor and flat soprano were beginning their final, deafening duet. Within a few minutes, the audience would be filing its way out into the Dublin night. "Very well. But I want your assurance that, if I remain certain of O'Neill's circumstances after the fortnight, you'll support his election and leave him alone."

Lyndhurst grinned and thumped a fist onto Christor's shoulder. "Gladly." He rose then and reached for the box's curtain. "I will see you at Daly's Club then, Tuesday next? We can have a hand of faro and you can give me your report."

Christor nodded and waved the man on his way. If nothing else, he would get a decent bottle of Irish at the lively club.

Dublin Society, he decided, was altogether too English. He had swilled enough port and sherry to float an armada. After a sennight back in town, he'd become used to leaving his social engagements feeling slightly dowly. Beyond that, this entire business with the O'Neills was not sitting well in his gut.

As Orfeo moaned and lamented, the O'Neills were beginning a cheerful collection of their belongings. Ailís's dark head vanished. She resurfaced after a moment, brandishing a gold-tipped cane which she passed to her uncle and a palm-sized silver object that went discreetly into Eamonn's hand. A flask, Christor decided, and smiled. The man would have to learn to keep a better grip on his grog if he were to sneak it into the interminable sessions in Commons.

Imagining the taste of prime whiskey on his own tongue, Christor left the box and went to intercept his quarry in the lobby.

He knew the moment Ailís spotted him. Her soft mouth tightened into an unmistakable grimace. There was little doubt that, had she been able, she would have bolted out the door at a dead run. She was trapped, however, by the simple fact that Eamonn had one hand on his cane, the other at her elbow, and was moving with all the speed of a three-legged turtle.

Christor had no idea what he had done to earn the girl's obvious dislike. He had been in her presence not much above a half-dozen times and could not possibly have offended her. His most incendiary topic of conversation to date had been the uncommonly warm evening they were having. It had been just temperate enough that Mrs. Kenrick had opened her salon windows a full four inches, rather than the customary two.

No, he could not imagine what prompted Ailís's disfavor. But it would have taken a far stupider man not to comprehend that her headache on the previous Sunday had been an attempt to avoid his presence. He had been the only guest present at luncheon. And she had looked perfectly hale and hearty when, just as he was taking his leave, she'd come hurrying down the stairs in hot pursuit of a bat. Only his quick sweep of his hat through the air had kept the creature from going right out the open door. With admirable coordination, Ailís had captured the thing in a net. With something less than sincerity, she had thanked him before disappearing back up the stairs, shoulders rigid.

He would very much have liked to see her painting of the bat. If the work were anything like the artist, it was certain to be bold, slightly odd, and decidedly pleasant to view.

Eamonn spotted him approaching then and released his sister's arm to give a friendly wave. Mrs. O'Neill's smile, when she looked over, was equally welcoming. Thaddeus appeared to be engaging in some agreeable inner contemplation, his wrinkled face wearing a happy if undirected smirk. Ailís looked as if she had smelled something unpleasant.

The crowd had thickened into a determined river flowing toward the door. Christor's size helped somewhat as he maneuvered, salmon-like, across the floor, but not enough. At one point, he found himself being borne cheerfully along by a trio of drunken Trinity boys, on their hurried way, most likely, to the stage door where the pretty chorus singers would exit.

Fortunately, the O'Neills had not moved at all by the time he finally reached them. Rather, three had not. Ailís was nowhere to be seen. Christor darted a quick glance over his shoulder. No, she wouldn't have left the theater without her family, no matter how distasteful his presence was. Wherever she had gone, she would be back.

"Good evening, Mrs. O'Neill." Christor bent over the lady's hand. A faint, pleased flush appeared on her cheeks, but she nodded with all the grace and poise of an experienced grande dame. "Eamonn. Did you enjoy the performance, Mr. O'Neill?"

Thaddeus was still gazing at nothing in particular. Christor saw him blink suddenly and assumed Anne had made a discreet tug at his arm. "Eh? What's that? Ah, good evening, young man. What did you think of the performance?"

"A truly impressive display of vocal stamina," Christor replied deftly.

"*Arianna,* eh? Nay, I cannot see much of a similarity to Monteverdi." Thaddeus gave him an indulgent smile. "But then, I am the trained critic here."

"You are indeed, sir, and I will eagerly await your commentary in the *Journal.*"

Eamonn, lips twitching, stepped forward. "If you haven't other plans, Clane, come along with us. Sweeney can always be counted upon to produce a smashing late supper."

Christor quashed the image of a lamb opening the paddock gate for the wolf and looked to Mrs. O'Neill. She gave him a warm smile. "We would be honored, my lord."

"The honor would be mine, madam." He glanced casually at the empty air at Eamonn's side. "Was Miss O'Neill not with you?"

"Oh, Ailís." Eamonn chuckled. "Left a glove or something in the box and rushed off to retrieve it. She'll be back soon enough."

Probably not as soon as she might, Christor thought with amusement—and a bit of exasperation. If she had left anything in the box, he was King Brian Boru.

"Perhaps you ought to go after her, Eamonn," Anne suggested. "'Tis a terrible crush in here."

Eamonn rolled his eyes, but good-naturedly prepared to go off in search of his errant sibling. Christor seized the opportunity. "Allow me." He gestured discreetly to the younger man's cane. "It will take but a moment."

"Good man, Clane. She'll move a sight faster if you're with her."

No doubt Eamonn simply meant that some brotherly impatience wasn't as likely to scoot Ailís along as a nonfamilial escort. Christor expected that she would certainly move as fast as possible if he were to appear. A wise man with any concern for his pride would take heed and stay away. He had always fancied himself an intelligent fellow. And he was as careful to avoid humiliation as anyone. But there was something about Ailís O'Neill that beckoned to him. Perhaps once he had figured out what it was, he would lose interest and be on his way. The lady was clearly eager for him to do just that.

She was not in the box at all. Instead, she was standing alone in the center of the upper hall, tapping one scuffed slipper against the carpet. Had there been a clock present, Christor knew she would have been counting the pendulum swings until she felt it safe to return. He wondered how much time she had allotted for him to chat with her family and leave.

"Miss O'Neill."

She turned slowly to face him. "Well, good evening, my lord."

Well, bloody hell would have been better suited to her expression.

He crested the stairs and strode toward her. "Your mother was concerned that you might have been delayed by the departing crowd." There was no one else in sight. "I offered to come see if I could be of any assistance. Did you locate your glove?"

She glanced down at her arms, both covered to the elbow by white kidskin. "It . . . was not a glove, my lord, but a . . . comb."

Christor glanced at the glossy crown of dark curls, nearly auburn now under the light of the wall sconces. He could see several pins tucked randomly into the mass, but no evidence of a comb. "You found it, I hope."

He could almost hear the workings of her clever mind. As little as he knew of Ailís, he had every confidence that she could come up with a perfectly plausible explanation for standing in the hallway, doing absolutely nothing when she was meant to be retrieving some possession from a box twenty feet away.

She did not disappoint him. "It occurred to me just as I reached this spot that perhaps I didn't have the comb to begin with. It's more than likely I left it on my dressing table."

"Ah. Well, I would be happy to have a look with you. Just in case, you know." He waved toward the row of curtains. "Now, which box was yours?"

He thought she might abandon the absurd charade and flee. Instead, after a moment, she grudgingly pointed to a portal and he gestured her ahead of him into the box.

She promptly moved the few feet to the rail and stared down into the fast-emptying gallery. So she wasn't going to give her whole heart to the charade. Christor shook his head wryly and tipped one chair a bit to the right. He would not waste his time on a fruitless search, but he certainly wouldn't reveal that he was on to her ploy. Not yet, at least.

"I am afraid I don't see anything, Miss O'Neill."

She flicked her gaze back to him briefly. "Nay? As I said, I probably left the thing at home."

"Are you quite certain? Why don't you have a peek at the floor there."

This time, she looked him fully in the eye. "I'm sure you have better matters to attend to, my lord, than a comb which won't be found here, no matter how dedicated your search."

"And deny myself the pleasure of your company? Good heavens, what an unappealing thought."

Ailís had a cleft in her chin. Funny that he hadn't noticed before. But it was impossible to miss now, thrust forward as it was. Apparently sarcasm, even that with sincerity behind it, was not lost on the lady.

"You must sorely miss the society of London," she announced, "to be courting the company here. Perhaps you ought to go back."

It occurred to Christor as he joined her at the rail that he must have taken leave of some of his senses. There was no other explanation for the fact that he had an undeniable desire to be near Ailís O'Neill—when she obviously wished him to be anywhere but there. Damned if he could understand it.

"As a matter of fact, I have no interest in being in London, Miss O'Neill. I am quite content to be in Dublin."

"For how long, my lord?"

That was a very good question. And one for which he did not have an answer just yet. Eyes fixed on hers, Christor leaned against the rail. "What is it, Miss O'Neill? Have I inadvertently offended you somehow? I don't think Napoleon wanted me out of Spain half so much as you seem to want me gone from Dublin."

Another woman might have blushed, stammered, denied the assertion. Not Ailís. She drew herself into an almost military posture, bringing the top of her head even with his chin and, he couldn't help but observe, her noteworthy breasts within inches of his coatsleeve. "Perhaps I just don't like you, my lord."

"Fair enough." Oh, she was fair indeed, fair enough to have made his tongue go thick in his mouth. "I don't suppose there is anything I can do to change that."

"You can keep away from my brother."

Startled, he found himself speechless for a moment. Then, "Why?" he demanded.

"Because you'll do him ill, Lord Clane," she replied, "and I won't have him battered any more than he already is."

With that, she pushed past him and started toward the curtain.

"Miss O'Neill . . ." Christor reached out to block her way, to simply make her stop and explain the harsh words. His hand caught her arm, his fingers coming to rest in the warm hollow at the crook of her elbow.

He had stripped off his own gloves during the performance and had not put them back on. Now, where his fingertips met her skin, they tingled. He heard her soft intake of breath, felt her twitch. She turned to face him again and he half expected her free hand to come smacking into his jaw.

She stood very still for a sweet, fleeting instant.

"Good-bye, Lord Clane."

An instant later, she was gone, leaving him holding empty air. He could hear her footsteps padding quickly away down the hall. "Good God," he muttered.

Blinking, shaking his head to clear it, he managed to wander out of the box and toward the stairs. He needed to reach the O'Neills before they left, to make his excuses. He would not be partaking of their cook's smashing moonlight repast that night.

Nor would he be finding a dark corner outside Leinster House from which to watch Fitzwilliam Lane. He could always do that later, should he find a reason. For now, he was going to seek out some whiskey and his own library chair. He would have peace and quiet in which to ponder what had just transpired between himself and Ailís.

Ailís's brother would do what he wished in the next hours. Christor was all but certain that wherever the man went late at night, it was not to meet with members of the Irish robber band that so irked Jonathan Lyndhurst and his fellow nervous Tories.

Eamonn O'Neill, Connaught Ranger hero and future Member of Parliament, was not a member of the original An Cú gang. Nor had he made any overtures toward joining. As founder and leader of that merry crew, Christor would have been the first to know.

Chapter 3

Ailís handed over the sturdy carton with some sadness. She had become rather attached to the vole during its time in residence. Órla, as she had named the creature after her sweet but unfortunately whiskered great-aunt, had taken to poking her little nose out the bars of the cage whenever anyone entered the room and wiggling it happily. Auntie Órla always did just the same on the arrival of visitors. It was a familiar sight, her nose nearly pressed into the window glass as she eagerly awaited an hour's worth of gossip. Her lumbago kept her from getting out of the house much, so guests were a special treat.

"Have you anything for me, Tommy?" Ailís asked the freckled adolescent as he tucked the box under his arm.

"I haven't, Miss Ailís, nay, but Gran asks if you'll stop by after the church."

"I will, Tommy. You'll let the vole loose now?"

"Aye, back of the hedgerow. 'Twas where I found it. I saw badgers, too, not three days back. Will you have one o' them?"

Ailís pictured yellow teeth and fierce claws. "Not just yet, I think. Perhaps a blue hare if you come across one."

The boy nodded, but looked disappointed. He had probably been looking forward to a good badger stalking. "Aye, a hare, then. And mayhap you'll be wanting a badger after."

They walked side by side along the rutted path to the village church. Country girl though she was, Ailís was always surprised when the city opened into field land. Just past Eccles Street were the acres upon acres of potatoes and cabbages. Now, a mere five miles from her own front stoop, she might as well have been in the middle of County Tipperary. Dublin seemed an ocean away.

"I looked for your brother at the theater on Thursday. Was he not there?"

Tommy shrugged. " 'Tis Séamus, that, in and out of town as he will. Thinks he's a fine gentleman, he does, gadding about in his green coat."

"Well, tell him to have a care. I don't want him ending up in irons." Séamus Cleary had a clear-sightedness beyond his years, but he also had a young man's fire in his belly. "I'll be in to see your gran, Tommy, and I would be happy for a hare. *Go raibh maith agat.*"

He grimaced, then answered her thanks in Gaelic before scampering off to release the vole. Like many children in the country, he was learning English in his tiny school. He wanted to use it. His brother spent as much time as possible in Dublin, and Ailís could see the longing to follow Séamus in the boy's eyes. She could only hope that he wouldn't be following into trouble.

The tiny, ancient stone church was nearly full when she entered. There were at least thirty men there, all in their well-mended Sunday best. Old Lugh Conall, seventy if he was a day and bent as a windside rowan tree, was there. Beside him sat his son and grandson. Ruarc Sláine had come from Clonee, another ten miles to the west. Malachy MacNisse from Dunboyne, miles again from Clonee, was still on crutches. It had been two months since his plow horse had kicked him and Ailís assumed the break was still healing.

These rough, mostly illiterate farming men came every Sunday, some from good distances, to learn English. They gave up their precious day of rest and, in some cases, deep grudges. Finbarr Scannal and Cian Branagán, who had not spoken a single civil word to each other in thirty years—due, Ailís had learned, to some argument over the ownership of a hammer—were presently debating the correct use of the word *stomach*.

A chorus of greetings followed Ailís to the front of the church. Several men inquired after her health and her family; several more unabashedly handed her posies of wildflowers. She had grown to know them all over the past months, to respect their earthy intelligence and admire their dedication in learning an impossible language. She'd never felt nearly as proud in her life as on the afternoon when the group had turned to the door and, in perfect unison, said, "Good afternoon, Miss O'Neill."

She noted that Felic Augaire had brought his wife. In fact, there were a handful of women scattered among the group. Ailís had encouraged the women from the beginning. It seemed that some of the husbands, brothers, and fathers were finally beginning to relent. With luck, more would follow.

It was time to commence with the day's lesson. As thirty pleasant, eager faces looked to hers, Ailís took a deep breath and began. *"Cánachas,"* she said clearly. "Taxation."

Three hours later, she was sitting down to tea with Father Peadrán and Tommy's grandmother in the Cleary cottage. In deference to the old woman, they spoke Gaelic. "A good session, I think," the equally elderly priest announced, contentedly spreading fresh butter over a thick slice of brown bread. "They've come a long way with you, Ailís."

"I just wish there were more coming," she replied.

Mrs. Cleary set a pot of honey beside the bread. "They'll come, *cailín.* 'Tis but a matter of time."

Gazing into the lovely, deeply lined face, Ailís saw what she did in so many country faces: endless patience and simple goodness. "Aye, perhaps. And you, ma'am? Will you come one Sunday?"

"Nay, nay. I've not the mind for funny words. I get the few I need from the boys, when they've the time to spare."

Ailís could well imagine that Tommy and Séamus had little time—or inclination—to spare on teaching their grandmother English. And Father Peadrán was the only other option. He was always the first, however, to decline. Beyond the fact that his thick Galway brogue made his English difficult to understand, he had a tendency to sprinkle it with the Latin he'd learned at the seminary. It had been Séamus Cleary who had first suggested that Ailís come do the teaching. She hadn't been certain at all that she was qualified, but had been more than willing to try.

"You've had no problems from our using the church, Father?"

His sky-blue eyes twinkled beneath wild brows. "Not a peep, my dear. The squire and his Anglo cronies are only too delighted to hear there's English being taught here. Never was too bright, our Squire Woodhall."

"And you? You've still no qualms?"

The priest's gnarled hand reached across the table to cover hers. "I'll not countenance breaking of the Commandments, nor the encouragement of it in God's house," he replied gently. "The Church is for spiritual guidance, but I've a firm belief in my people knowing the way of things in the earthly realm. Vote or no, they've a right to know what those fellows in London Town are about *de die in diem*. Nay, Ailís O'Neill, I've no qualms."

He tottered off a half-hour later, leaving the women alone. In a rare moment of rest, Mrs. Cleary was seated at the rough table. Hers was a hard life, Ailís thought, and unlikely to get easier. "Tommy said you asked for me, ma'am."

"Oh, aye. I did that. 'Tis Séamus, it is. I fear for him, Ailís, and I haven't a hint of what to do." The old woman clasped her hands tightly on the table, whitened knuckles her only outward sign of distress. But behind her eyes emotions blazed. "You'll help me, will you not?"

"If I can, Mrs. Cleary. Of course."

"Aye, well then." She rose from the table, crossed to the battered shelves, and pulled an object from beneath a cloth. Ailís got a glimpse of gold, but couldn't imagine what the thing was. "I found this beneath his bed a sennight past."

Ailís gaped at the very ornate, very large earring the old woman plunked onto the table in front of her. "I . . . er . . ."

" 'Tis an *ear bob*."

"Aye, I see . . ."

"A *lady's* ear bob! And a flash one, at that. 'Tis gold."

It was gold, with a profusion of small gems and, as Mrs. Cleary asserted, not of a subtle sort. Ailís studied it curiously. She did not know anyone who wore such a gaudy jewel. The only women she could imagine . . . Her gaze flew upward to meet the older woman's.

"Aye. You see it, too. My Séamus has taken up with . . ." Mrs. Cleary glanced briefly at the little wooden statue of the Madonna standing above the hearth and lowered her voice to a shaky whisper. *". . . an English doxy!"*

"I . . . how do you know she is English?"

All reticence vanished. Mrs. Cleary prodded the earring with a gnarled finger and snorted. "Look at its size! There's not a woman in Ireland with ears to bear something the size of that. English, she is. A great horse of a thing, I'd say, and she'll be the ruin of my boy!"

"Now, Mrs. Cleary—"

"Flowers it will be at first, then sweetmeats, then jewels like this. And what then? Séamus will be forced to gambling, he will, then thievery." She fixed Ailís with pleading eyes. "Will you talk to him, Ailís? Please."

"Could you not . . . ?"

"On such matters? Oh, nay! I couldn't possibly. But you, you're a girl of modern times. Perhaps you can find a way . . ."

To talk to a red-blooded young country lad about . . . about . . . Ailís, who took great pride in the fact that she seldom blushed, felt the heat rising in her face. She opened her mouth to refuse, but Mrs. Cleary was looking at her with such hope—such trust—that she closed her eyes and sighed.

"I'll think on the matter, ma'am. If there is anything I can do, be sure I will."

"Ah, you're a grand one, Ailís O'Neill. You've taken a load from my heart."

Resigned, Ailís watched as the old woman bustled about the room, filling a basket with fresh eggs and butter, a thanks and payment in advance, as it were. It seemed she was going to have to find a way to approach Séamus Cleary about his relationship with an elephant-eared trollop. Somehow.

Later, as Fergus drove her home in the family's battered coach, Ailís decided she had no choice but to involve her brother. Much as she hated to ponder the matter, she expected Eamonn knew a thing or two about women who wore such baubles in their ears. And he'd known Séamus for eons. The two had rolled home drunk on more than one occasion, rattling the china and all but stripping the paint from the walls with their breath.

Aye, this was a task she would pass on to Eamonn. If she ever saw him. He hadn't been home of a night for a sennight now, and even she had been fast asleep when he did return. If

he did return. For the last several mornings, hard as it was for
Ailís to believe, he had been gone before she rose. Matters of
business, their mother reported vaguely.

He would be attending the Farnham ball that night. Ailís had
not intended to go. She loathed the necessity of dressing up
and pretending interest in any number of conversations where
the most important topic was the new coat of paint on the Rotunda. Eamonn, however, thrived on these gatherings. It appeared she would be accompanying him. And as it happened,
she could do a bit of work there as well. Such gatherings, tedious as they were, provided just the material she needed.

Unfortunately, Clane would no doubt be there, too. It was
just his sort of affair, rich and dull. What a pity, Ailís thought,
that she could not send a little message and have Tommy
Cleary detain him in a root cellar somewhere for the next year
or so.

As much as she might have liked it, she couldn't punish the
earl for always being about, or for setting her pulse to racing
when he stood too close. She did not like Lord Clane.
Pompous, preening dandy. Oh, she'd done well enough at
snubbing him in the theater box—until he had touched her.
The instant his fingers had touched the sensitive spot inside
her elbow, her brain had turned to porridge. At that point, the
best she had been able to manage was an abrupt and pitifully
weak exit.

This was no time for her to go soft-headed over a man, especially one she disliked. For nearly twenty-six years, she'd
escaped the mooning and moaning that had captured nearly
every one of her friends. At first she had listened with interest
as Maggie, Síle, and Susan Foyle rhapsodized on pounding
hearts and watery knees, when Barbara O'Brien had listed the
countless charms of rakish Dagán Dooley who could ride Tullamore to Mullingar in less than a day and drink a full bottle of
Irish on arriving.

Ailís had very nearly decided to have a look around for a
beau herself. Then her cousin Muirne had run off with Calum
Ricard, a boy she had hated since they'd crawled about Tullamore floors together as infants. Lightning, Muirne had called
it, striking her like a bolt. Ailís wished Muirne the best, but as-

sumed the worst. Strike most things—people included—with lightning and they would go up in flame. Flames always went out eventually.

It hardly mattered that Clane exactly matched her image of the dashing highwayman An Cú and his epic brethren: brawny, dark, with the bold blue eyes found only in Ireland. The broad cheekbones, blunt jaw, and massive hands were Irish, too. Perhaps she would have liked him better—not well, but better—if those hands weren't far more likely to hold a snuffbox than a blunderbuss.

Nay, Lord Clane wasn't a man for action. More's the pity, Ailís thought dryly. Even if she could orchestrate Eamonn's shoving a decorated doxy in the earl's direction, he would probably just let the creature plod right past him. Dull as dirt, respectable as a Humberside curate, Clane would no doubt prefer a gift of a flannel waistcoat to that of a lively and willing trollop.

She had no idea why that thought made her smile.

Christor was ready to commandeer Eamonn's stick and apply it to Philip Lorcan's backside. The offensive pup was all but slobbering onto Ailís's bosom, now displayed to great advantage. Odd, how mere days before, he'd been lamenting her unfashionably modest dress. At present, he was tempted to tug one of Mrs. Farnham's velvet draperies from the window and wrap Ailís securely from head to toe.

She was an entirely different creature tonight. Swathed in a flimsy column of white muslin, her hair drawn into a classical collection of shiny curls, she resembled a figure from the Parthenon. Demeter, most likely, the goddess of fertility and harvest. And Lorcan was clearly more than willing to do some reaping and sowing.

Eamonn seemed wholly unconcerned with the spectacle. His only response, when Christor had suggested that Lorcan's attentions were perhaps a bit excessive, had been, "Oh, Ailís can manage Philly. I've offered to pummel him a bit, but she wouldn't hear of it. She has a gentle heart and iron will. We all know better than to argue with our Ailís."

Christor would agree about the iron will. He wasn't so certain of the soft heart. In fact, he was beginning to think her all ice and steel inside. She had returned his greeting earlier with raised brows and curt nod. Then she had promptly sailed off, almost right into the arms of Colonel Ellsworth. She had remained in that gentleman's company for a good quarter-hour.

She had smiled. She had laughed. She had, more than once, rested her hand on Ellsworth's sleeve. Christor had managed to watch the display with relative detachment. The arch-conservative colonel was a portly fifty, with a hawk-eyed wife and slew of indolent children. Hardly worthy competition. But he had made Ailís laugh: a clear, enticing sound. Christor was torn between the urge to glower at the fellow, or to approach him for advice. He'd felt very much the same when Ailís drifted from Ellsworth to the Marquess of Carricknock to the Lord-Lieutenant himself.

His feelings for young Lorcan were considerably less indulgent.

"I say, Clane, they've struck up the music in the next room. Go and have a dance with some fair young thing." Eamonn tapped his stick lightly against his injured leg. "I'd have a go myself if I weren't certain to embarrass myself."

"Oh, I think not."

"Go on, man! Maria Farnham has been casting hopeful looks your way all evening." Eamonn chuckled at Christor's wince. "Aye, so she's a bit clingy. Her parents are desperate for her to marry a title. Dance with Ailís, then. She's a lovely sight on the floor when someone coaxes her out. Of course, it looks like Philly's having a go at her . . ."

Pride bedamned. Christor had a thick skin. He was certain he could take a few more barbs from Ailís. He was not going to stand back and watch as she danced with Philip Lorcan. Drawing a fortifying breath, he strode off to tempt fate.

As it turned out, Lorcan himself was the only persuasion needed. "I believe I hear the beginnings of a country dance, Miss O'Neill," he was saying as Christor approached. "Nothing like a country dance, I always say, for strengthening a delightful acquaintance. I can't abide those sets which last a mere three minutes. No, give me a good quarter-hour . . ."

As grim as Ailís always appeared in his presence, Christor took heart at her expression now. She looked as if a long stroll through hell would be preferable to a quarter-hour on the floor with Lorcan. "Miss O'Neill," he said, smoothly sliding in front of her companion, "I believe you promised me the first dance."

"Now, I say, Clane!" Lorcan objected. "I was just—"

"Do excuse us, sir. So kind of you." Christor offered Ailís his arm. She hesitated a mere second before accepting it.

"From pan to fire?" he murmured as he led her into the adjoining room. Had he not been admiring her fine eyes, free now of the spectacles, he would have missed the quick blink. He surely would have missed the nearly imperceptible curve of her lips. In fact, it was gone so soon that it might not have happened at all.

It hardly mattered that she did not say a word as they joined the set. He had almost made her smile.

Christor enjoyed dancing. He always had. And Eamonn had been quite right in saying Ailís was a joy to behold on the floor. She had a lively, easy grace and confidence as she moved through the steps. If her flashing smile was now for familiar gentlemen in the set, Christor wasn't overly bothered by the fact. She could dazzle them all she wanted. Each pattern brought her back to his side.

"You seem in good spirits this evening," he commented as he took her hand in a turn. He should have known better than to push his luck.

"I trust you won't see my good spirits as a change in my regard, my lord."

"Certainly not, Miss O'Neill."

She eyed him warily for a moment, then nodded. "I did not wish to dance with Mr. Lorcan. He is persistent, and you were convenient."

She stepped away again and Christor found himself paired for a tense minute with Miss Farnham. The lady, as Eamonn had so aptly phrased it, clung. And simpered. He was delighted to send her back into the hands of her partner.

"I am delighted to be of service," he muttered as Ailís did an enticing little circle around him.

"Of course you are," was her dry reply. Then she nearly smiled again. "As it happens, I have had a very good day."

"And what made it so very good, if I may ask?"

"Well, among other things, I was alone for much of it."

That, apparently was all she planned to say on the subject. And she made no attempt to inquire after his day, which was just as well. He had spent a good part of it in a dark pub, swilling watered ale and listening to a pedantic solicitor—An Cú's contact within Four Courts—meander through countless details of pounds, pence, and the increasing military presence on country roads. All in all, it had been a fruitless and deadly dull encounter.

Eight years earlier, a pampered youth of twenty-four and yet to experience the education that war provided, Christor had created An Cú. He had chosen a handful of young men, none with his sort of background but all with brains and fire in their guts, and they had become the most efficient group of philanthropic road bandits since Robin Hood and his merry men had conquered Nottingham. They had disbanded when Christor went off to the Peninsula, agreeing not to revive An Cú unless all agreed there was a dire need. For years, there had been no need. Christor had quietly provided monies from his own fortune; Séamus Cleary had dispersed them.

Now there was a problem. Someone was riding the night roads again. Someone who was effective enough to make Dublin Society anxious, someone who, for whatever reason, had Lyndhurst watching—even mistakenly—the O'Neill household and giving the nervous M.P. sleepless nights.

Christor knew it was time for him to step back in and get involved. That was what had brought him back to Dublin and that, if he were not mistaken, was going to give him his own nocturnal discomfort sooner or later.

At the moment, however, he didn't want to be thinking about night roads, or the robber band he had created so long ago. He wanted to enjoy the brief interlude with Ailís, while she was neither snapping nor scowling at him. He had a very good idea that it wouldn't last.

"I read your uncle's commentary on the opera," he told her. Discussing her family seemed safe enough. "It was very eloquent."

"It was indeed. Uncle Taddy is always eloquent. Did you enjoy *Orfeo*?"

No, he had not. He had found it rather dreadful, beginning to end. But Thaddeus had given a glowing report. The last thing Christor wanted to do just then was say anything which might be taken as an insult to the old coot. Discussing her family had seemed safe enough.

"I am not overly fond of Gluck," he stated.

"Nay? Handel, I imagine, then."

"I do enjoy Handel, but . . ." Nothing ventured, nothing gained. "I would just as soon listen to the pipes and *bodhrán* drums."

This time, as she winged away, she kept her eyes on him. Then, slowly, her face broke into a full, dazzling, unmistakable smile. And it was directed at him. By the time she returned to his side, he was grinning like an idiot.

"You know, Lord Clane"—Ailís's hand was warm in his as he guided her through the last turn—"I am very good at admitting when I've been mistaken." The music swelled to a finish and she dipped into a graceful curtsy. "But I'll eat my shoes if you've ever been within ten feet of a *bodhrán*. Now, if you'll excuse me, I think I'll be off. I need to speak with my brother, then I need to go home to work."

Christor paused, still half-bent in his own bow, blinking at her departing back. "Well, hell," he muttered after a long minute. And went after her.

She was with her brother. Eamonn was leaning against the mantel, looking quite comfortable. Ailís, despite the fact that Christor could not see her face, was clearly not pleased. Head thrown back, hands on her hips, she appeared to be giving her brother a mighty blast of temper. Christor stopped an arm's length behind her. O'Neill raised one brow a fraction, but did not reveal his presence.

"I came, I chatted, I even danced with your pompous English friend. Now I'm ready to be gone. Will you come with me?

"I will not," was her brother's mild reply.

"Fine, then. I'll go on my own."

"Sure and I'll let you go traipsing off into the night. Do be serious, Ailís. You'll wait for me."

"While you jabber away with your political cronies? I think not. I'm not ready to go to sleep just yet." She tilted her head then, and Christor noticed that she had a tiny mole at the nape of her neck. "I am going home now. And you, Éamonnán, cannot move fast enough on that leg to stop me."

She probably would have gone right out the door and down Baggot Street had she not come up short against Christor's chest. "If you can abide my pompous English company for another five minutes, Miss O'Neill," he said blandly, "I would be happy to see you home."

"I . . ." She actually blushed. He'd begun to wonder if she were capable. "I don't think . . ."

"You'll see her straight to the door, Clane?"

He turned to Eamonn. "Of course."

Ailís fixed first Christor and then her brother with a fierce glare. "Have I no say in the matter?" she demanded.

"No," the men retorted in unison.

She grumbled, and shrugged off Christor's hand when he moved to assist her with her wrap. She allowed him to guide her out the door, however. She didn't bother bidding Eamonn good night.

Nor did she say anything during the short walk to her home. Christor was content with the silence. He really had nothing to say at the moment. He had decided that, rather like a wild forest creature, Ailís just might get used to him if he simply was near her frequently. And he was planning on staying very close to the O'Neill household for the time being.

At present, he took as long as possible to get to Fitzwilliam Lane. Ailís started to charge ahead at first, but soon matched his leisurely pace. It was obvious that she was lost in her own thoughts. As long as he did not intrude, he thought she might stroll along at his side indefinitely.

Unfortunately, they reached her house altogether too soon. She looked up when he stopped, blinked, then skipped up the stairs.

Christor followed her to the stoop, and waited until she'd gotten her key into the lock and opened the door. "Good night, Miss O'Neill."

She glanced backward over her shoulder as she entered the candlelit hall. One dark curl had come loose and he resisted the impulse to draw it away from her shadowed face. "Good night, my lord."

He braced his hand against the door to keep it from closing. "As it happens, Ailís, I am not English. I am very nearly as Irish as you are."

She regarded him silently for a moment, then shook her head. The tumbled curl slid enticingly toward her breasts. "It's not a matter of birth, nor even blood." She reached up, touched the spot just below the simple green pendant she wore. "It's in the heart."

She closed the door with a firm click.

Christor rubbed the back of his neck as he went back down the stairs. Damned if he could understand this adolescent resistance to her obvious aversion to him. The last time he had followed a woman about like a lovesick hound, he had been fourteen and she had been a twenty-year-old buxom housemaid. Who, he'd learned broken-heartedly, was warming his father's bed. The last time he had pursued a woman simply for the sake of winning out over disinterest, he had nearly ended up unwillingly married when his charm finally worked and she decided he was a splendid creature after all.

Mad, he mused as he wandered past the row of neat houses and reached Merrion Street. He had to be mad. There was no other excuse for the fact that he could not seem to keep Ailís out of his head. She flitted in and out like a blasted wraith, albeit a lush flesh-and-blood one, and refused to leave.

Yes, he needed to decide just what it was about Ailís O'Neill that drew him. Until he did, there was no question of being done with her.

"My lord. Lord Clane!"

Startled, he spun about to see her running from her house, heedless of the puddles left by the afternoon rain. He paused in the middle of the street, hopelessly curious as to what she would sling at him this time. It must have been an inspiring insult, to send her flying out after him.

She all but leapt from the curb and came to an abrupt halt in front of him. "I couldn't let you leave without saying—" She broke off suddenly, brow furrowing. "What is that?"

Christor had heard it, too. "Merely a carriage."

As it turned out, it was not merely a carriage, but a heavy black coach-and-four that came looming out of the darkness down Merrion Street. As they watched, it picked up speed, the team's hooves clattering against the cobblestones. There was no question that the thing was moving at an unnatural speed—and wasn't going to stop.

Chapter 4

Ailís watched, mesmerized, as the coach blasted through the darkness. Without her spectacles, the vehicle's edges were blurred a bit and there was every possibility that she was imagining the sparks flying from the cobblestones beneath the team's heavy hooves. It was still a terrifying sight.

The thought that she was about to be mown down by a coach from hell formed in her mind an instant before the impact.

Clane's arm banded around her ribs with enough force to send her staggering backward. Stunned, off balance, she nearly went flying onto her posterior. She reached out by instinct and managed to get one arm around his neck even as he lifted her off her feet and bore her out of the street.

The coach thundered by, sending up a spray of mud and stone. Ailís buried her face in Clane's shoulder. When she looked up a long moment later, the vehicle was disappearing rapidly into the night.

"Saints preserve us," she whispered.

"Well put." Clane's deep voice resonated in her ears and against her breast. "Are you hurt?"

"Nay. I think . . . Nay."

Ailís drew a steadying breath. And belatedly realized that she was flat up against the earl's chest, his arm still wrapped like steel around her back. Despite the fact that she could still hear the horses' hooves clattering in the distance and her heart was pounding fit to rival any *bodhrán,* she felt perfectly well. In truth, she felt quite safe and very nearly comfortable. She was not used to feeling comfortable around this man and promptly developed the familiar skittery stomach.

When she took a shaky step backward, he let her go. "You are certain, Ailís?"

"Oh . . . aye." She pressed a trembling hand to her waist before looking up. "And you?" One side of his face was streaked with mud and, she thought, blood. "It looks as if you've been struck."

He raised a hand to his brow. His fingers came away dark. "A stone, probably."

"Bloody idiot, driving like the devil was on his heels." She glared banefully at the vanished carriage. "Come inside and I'll have a look at your face."

Clane withdrew a handkerchief from his pocket and swiped at his forehead. "There is no need. I will see you into the house, then . . ." He glanced down the street and Ailís had a very good idea he meant to go after the carriage.

"You'll come in and sit until I've seen to you. The carriage is long gone and there's no use in going after it. With the mist and dark, I'm sure they simply didn't see us. We haven't your fancy London street lamps here in Dublin and there's a drunk bumped into the gutter each week because of it." When he did not respond, she tugged sharply at his mud-streaked coat-sleeve. "Come along, my lord. I won't have you bleeding all over the cobblestones."

He allowed her to guide him into the house, but hesitated when she shepherded him into the parlor and pointed to a chair. "I am filthy, Miss O'Neill . . ."

She gave him a shove toward the seat. "As if it matters. This furniture has seen far worse than you. Take off your coat if you must, but I want you seated when I return."

She left him in the middle of the parlor, handkerchief pressed to his brow, and hurried to the kitchen. Sweeney was still up, thank heavens, and had the fire going. Fergus was seated with the cook at the rough table and both clambered to their feet as Ailís bounded in.

"Jesus and Mary!" Sweeney bustled around the table. "What happened to you, Miss?" she demanded, eyes round in her plump face. "Fergus, go wake the missus!"

Ailís glanced down. Perhaps she was not nearly so muddy as the earl, but her skirts were spattered and creased and she could only imagine the state of her hair. "Oh, nay. I'm fine, really. Don't wake *Máthair*." She made her way to the water basin and soap. "Lord Clane was walking me home and we had a bit of a run-in with a blind coach driver. Will you fetch the medicine basket for me, Sweeney, please?"

The cook moved amazingly quickly for her impressive bulk. She all but upset the basin as she turned Ailís to face her. "Where are you hurt?"

With the best reassuring smile she could muster, Ailís gently shrugged off the woman's hands and went back to washing her own. "I'm not. It's not for me, but for his lordship. He has a little cut and I'll see to it. If you'll just fetch the basket from the pantry . . ."

Apparently satisfied that Ailís was, in fact, unharmed, Sweeney trundled off to retrieve the household physic basket. Ailís emptied the wash water, collected a clean cloth, and carried the basin to the hearth. Fergus slipped from his seat to join her.

"Are ye certain ye're well, Miss?"

"I am perfectly fine, Fergus, simply dirty."

"Aye, well, there's news, then."

"News?" Ailís filled the bowl with steaming water from the hearth kettle and turned to face the grizzled footman.

"Aye, and of the best sort." Fergus's peat-brown eyes were alight with excitement. "He's struck again, Miss. An Cú."

Ailís's hands faltered, but she scarcely noticed the hot water slopping over her wrists. "Are you certain?"

"Heard it from the milk man, I did. 'Twas night before last, outside Baldoyle. He stopped three carriages, one belonging to Squire Keller. By dawn today, there were a dozen new milk cows standing in barns near Raheny."

"Oh. Oh, Fergus." Giddy, Ailís set the bowl on the table and braced her hands beside it. So the whispered rumors were true. An Cú was back in full action.

She had no idea who he was, who he truly was. The bandit had taken his name from *Cúchulainn,* the Hound of Culann, the great mythical warrior of ancient Ireland. The new Hound had founded his group some eight years back, waylaying English carriages and distributing the spoils among poor Irish farmers. Few knew his face; fewer knew his real name. But he was widely lauded and loved, this Irish Robin Hood, and tales of his midnight rides had become almost as numerous and varied as those of his namesake.

Now he was back, after years of silence. There had been rumors for weeks, but no confirmation. Now . . . Ailís's knees felt weak.

Sweeney reappeared with the basket. "Did Fergus tell you, then?"

"Aye. It's wonderful news."

"It is that. We'll have new tales for the fireside now." The cook proffered the basket, gaze sharp. "You'll see to the *Sasanach,* Miss Ailís, and have him out of the house? We can't have him lingering about, not if we're to speak of our Hound."

"Nay." Ailís shakily tucked the basket under her arm and lifted the water bowl. "Nay, indeed we cannot."

Clane was seated when she entered the parlor. He had indeed removed his coat and was sitting on it, the clean lining against the chair. Ailís paused in the doorway. Well, she admitted silently, her mother had been right. Lord Clane did not pad his coat. He had been given his full share—and that of another man—in the breadth of his shoulders.

The toplofty Earl of Clane, in his waistcoat and shirt, cravat loosened to display a column of strong, lightly tanned throat, no longer looked like an indolent, tailored-tip-to-tail aristocrat. He looked, Ailís decided as she approached, just as she had always envisioned An Cú. She grimaced inwardly at her fancy. Just because the earl had the striking dark hair, blue eyes, and blunt features of the true Irish, simply because his height and solid form made him wholly unlike most of the slight, sharp-edged aristocrats she had met, he still was not a noble bandit.

Ailís had dreamed of meeting An Cú for some years now, since the moment she had learned of his exploits. Now the desire was even stronger. She needed to meet the man if only to see for herself that he looked nothing like the Earl of Clane.

"Here now, let me look at your face." She deliberately cleared her head of its silly thoughts and pulled his hand from his forehead. "Well, it could be worse."

The cut, what she could see of it through the blood, ran diagonally through his right eyebrow. It wasn't terribly deep, nor more than an inch long, but it looked painful enough. She dipped the clean cloth into the water and wiped away the dried grime and blood. A fresh red line appeared, but the flow was sluggish.

Clane did not flinch, and his hand was steady when he reached for the cloth. "Perhaps you ought to allow me."

Ailís turned and dipped into the water again. "Sit still," she commanded. "This will only be the worse for you if you twitch about."

Taking care not to look too closely at the rest of him, she pushed her face close to his brow and cleaned away the rest of the dirt. "It won't need stitching, I think, but I'm afraid you might have a bit of a scar to show for the night. Try not to fret over it. You may tell your friends you were wounded in saving the life of a damsel in distress."

His hand snared hers as she reached for the jar of comfrey ointment. "Don't think me ungrateful for your attention to my male pride, Miss O'Neill, but for some reason I feel compelled to inform you that my face is the least of my concerns. Now, will you sit down, please? You have had a shock, after all."

She tugged her hand away and muttered, "Your attention to my female sensibilities is a waste of breath. Now be still."

"I have full faith in your—" He broke off and winced as she applied the comfrey salve, but did not protest what was certainly a painful sting.

Despite herself, Ailís was impressed. Considering what he was, Lord Clane had some grit to him. Her own touch gentled as she rubbed in the ointment. "Thank you," she said softly as she finished.

"For what? No one who has ever met you would doubt the strength of your nerves for a moment."

"Well, I suppose I ought to thank you for that, too, but I meant for what you did in the street. Not many would have moved as quickly as you did, and I'm grateful for it."

She turned back to the basket again, averting her face. Christor stifled a smile. He knew he had just received as much of a favor as this particular damsel was willing to bestow. He was more than satisfied.

He was also feeling decidedly uncomfortable and neither the wound, which was negligible, nor Ailís's soft presence, which was not, had anything to do with it. No, he was far more concerned with the possibility that someone had just tried to run him down. Christor did not believe in coincidence on a good day. On a bad day, when flailing hooves and heavy wheels were involved, he would sooner believe in the man on the moon. Unlikely as it was that his connection to an old series of highway robberies had been discovered, he hadn't survived as he had by taking chances. Beyond that, there had been something vaguely familiar about that carriage. He just couldn't identify it—yet.

He knew he should probably stay away from Ailís O'Neill now, for her own safety. He also knew it would be easier to walk on water.

She was busy with her nursing implements and he drank in the sight. If one ignored the streaks of dirt, Ailís looked very much like a woman who had just stepped out of bed after a good romp. One little sleeve was half off her shoulder, her hair had come loose to riot halfway down her back, and there was a soft flush to her face.

"I have bandages if you . . ." Her voice trailed off as she turned again. She stared at him, eyes wide. One small hand reached up to cover some of the pale skin visible above her bodice. It was, Christor thought, a charming if futile move. Both of his hands might serve to cover the soft swells. One of hers did little other than to stir his blood.

Her eyes widened further. Realizing his own expression probably resembled that of a hungry wolf, Christor dropped his gaze.

She had kicked off her shoes.

"I don't think a bandage is necessary." There was nothing delicate about Ailís's feet, except perhaps the white silk stockings covering them. Her feet were square, solid, and not particularly small. He imagined them sliding up the outsides of his own calves. "Well, hell," he muttered and shifted in his seat. "Will you sit down now, please?"

She looked ready to protest, but after a moment chose the sofa farthest from his own chair and dropped onto the cushions. When she tucked her feet under her muddied skirts, Christor heard himself sigh.

She still looked somewhat wary, yet managed to infuse her voice with familiar insolence when she demanded, "Would you care for something to drink, my lord? Now that I am seated?"

His eyes slewed around the room, over faded green brocade and empty japanned tables. It was a place for sipping tea or overly sweet lemonade. He needed something stronger. "Thank you, no. I am . . . quite content."

"Grand. Shall I have Fergus summon you a hack, then?"

For a moment, amusement won out over arousal. "Why is it that each of our meetings is characterized by your eagerness to end it? If you would set your unquestionably formidable mind to it, you might discover that I am not such a bad fellow."

Ailís stretched one arm along the back of the sofa and regarded him seriously. "I daresay I like you better than I did, my lord, but I do not trust you."

"Trust me? At what?"

"At anything," she replied bluntly. "You've no reason to be in Dublin, not with your sort of society crowding itself into London. And I've said before that I don't like you hanging about Eamonn." She made no mention of his all but drooling over her.

"Yes, you have said that." Christor leaned back in the chair, but was careful to keep his legs crossed. He was fast discovering that amusement didn't last long in Ailís's presence. "As for my sort of society crowding London, I would say that is as good a reason for not being there as any."

"Mmm. I might agree with you if I wished to. But why Dublin?"

Christor gave her a thin smile. "You know, my dear, you insist on asking me questions, yet refuse to believe my answers. Conversations with you tend to be an exhausting exercise."

To his great surprise, her lips twitched into a brief smile. "Fair enough. Shall I summon Fergus for the hack?"

"Must you?"

"Well, it has been a tiring evening as it is. I wouldn't want to add to the strain now, would I?"

Damn, but the girl had a tongue on her. Christor, despite the fact that she was insulting him right and left and would undoubtedly continue to do so, found he was enjoying himself. "If I give you an answer, will you at least ponder a moment before discarding it?"

She negligently surveyed a neat fingernail. "Aye, I'll do just that."

"Good. I happen to like Dublin. I like the sounds of the streets, especially the lilt of country voices when the street vendors arrive in the morning. I like the slightly grubby trees in Stephen's Green and the fact that the walnut I climbed as a boy is still there." He could see he had her attention now. "I enjoy walking through Temple Bar and over Carlisle Bridge across the Liffey. I delight in the fact that no one here feels compelled to wear pink striped waistcoats or quizzing glasses. And I positively wallow in the fact that no one here gives a damn what the Earl of Clane eats for breakfast."

There was a moment of heavy silence. Then, "Well. Perhaps I was mistaken."

"Oh?"

Ailís tilted her head, fixed him with her bold, gold-flecked eyes. "Aye. You've a fair sense of this town and that counts for something."

"But?"

"But . . . true as that all may be, there's more, I know. You've another reason for being in Dublin and that's the one I don't like. I know your secret, Lord Clane."

A disconcerting moment passed before he dismissed the possibility. There was no way she could know. "Would you care to tell me what that is?"

This time, when she leaned forward, he was not distracted by the view. "You are here on behalf of your English Tory cronies to have a go at Eamonn. It's not subtle, my lord, nor acceptable. He went off and fought for your addled king, for money and power he'll never know. And you see where it left him. Wounded, weakened, and without a shilling to show for it."

"Now, Ailís—"

"You think that if you can coax him to stand for Parliament as a Tory that he'll support English rules and English taxes. Well, I'll tell you, my lord, Eamonn isn't half so malleable as he might seem, nor so simple in his character. He won't be helping you to keep Ireland docile and content like a well-fed cow, not if the people feel differently. And he'll get his seat with or without you."

Christor was impressed. Ailís had a very good grasp of politics, and of the position of Ireland. She also had the heart of a true—and savvy—patriot. He wished there were more hearts like hers, along with more quick minds.

It was time to disabuse her of some of her notions. What a shame he knew he had to do it slowly.

Leaning forward in his chair, he willed her to meet his gaze squarely. When she did, he held the contact for a count of five. Then he said, *"Rugadh in Éirin mé, Ailís Ní Néill. Is Éireannach mé.* Beyond that, I am a Whig."

"Aye, well, it's grand and all that, but . . ."

Ailís felt her jaw dropping. He had spoken to her in Gaelic. A simple pair of phrases, to be sure, but with a simplicity that no one with Ireland in her heart could deny.

I was born in Ireland. I am, he'd declared with such quiet conviction, *Irish.*

"You have the tongue," she replied, awed, in Gaelic.

"I do," he answered in the same. "And the blood. The first Earl of Clane was born to the land, a descendant of King Brian Boru, he liked to claim. His wife was Irish, as was the next countess and the next. My grandmother, yes, came from England, but her son married a girl from County Cork." He smiled then, the crease beside his mouth deepening, and switched back to English. "My mother's name was Maeve Katherine Ryan and she gave me my first *bodhrán* when I was three."

Ailís's stomach had done several little flips during his speech. It shivered into place now. "But you were an officer in the 88th. You sit in Lords and Eamonn said you stood for Commons before your father died. No Irish Catholic can do that. No Catholic at all."

"I never said I was Catholic. And no one ever asked."

"You are . . . ?"

"The product of smart men and smarter women." He shrugged. "We don't fight holy wars any longer. Men choose religion to suit them and go to battle for money." Ailís jumped when he slapped his knees and rose abruptly to his feet. "There is no need for you to bother . . . Fergus, was it? I shall walk home."

Ailís's own knees were a bit shaky as she clambered from the sofa. "Do you truly play the *bodhrán*?"

"That, I suppose, is a matter of opinion. My father always used to say the racket I made reminded him of a lame horse on a muddy road. My mother was kinder in her opinions, but then, mothers usually are." Clane gathered his coat from the chair and put it back on. Ailís was forced to admit that he wore mud and creases rather well. "Would you care to judge for yourself?"

"I . . . judge what?"

"Whether I sound like a lame horse, naturally. Would you be so kind as to allow me to play for you, Miss O'Neill?"

He took a few steps across the carpet until he was an arm's length away. Ailís tilted her chin upward to look fully into his face. The expression was perfectly serious, but his eyes were doing that beastly dance again. Beastly in the literal sense. The proper, arrogant Lord Clane had a great cat—or a wolf—behind his Dublin Bay blue eyes. It was, she discovered with some dismay, rather exciting.

"What is this, my lord? No man ever made peace by pounding a drum."

"Perhaps I will have the distinction of being the first."

"Oh, aye, and ask nothing in return?"

"Now, I didn't say anything about playing without remuneration."

"Fancy that," she shot back. She would have stepped back, too, away from his unpadded shoulders, unpadded thighs, and untempered grin, but her own legs were already up against the sofa. "I expect I'm daft to be asking, but . . ." She spread her hands in question and waited.

"I want to see your paintings."

"My . . . paintings? You are jesting with me."

"Not at all. *Bodhrán* for bat. It seems a fair trade."

It seemed an odd one. An extremely odd one. A disconcerting thought flashed through her mind before she dismissed it.

He couldn't possibly know. "Why are you doing this, Lord Clane?"

"Críostóir," he said affably.

"What?"

"My name, *Ailís Ní Néill. Críostóir Rhys Próinsias Muiris.* A mouthful, but I daresay you can pronounce it if you try hard enough."

"Críostóir," she shot back, unable to resist any challenge to her Gaelic. Then, realizing he had never doubted her, she scowled and muttered, "It's a good name, Lord Clane, but I'm still not certain of the man it graces."

"Give it some time . . ." His hand snaked out to capture one of hers. Ailís promptly tugged, but he tugged back. In the blink of an eye, she was nearly flat against his chest for the second time that night. "You will be."

If there was one sight more intriguing than the Earl of Clane from a distance, it was the Earl of Clane from much too close. Ailís could clearly see the red line bisecting his eyebrow and a small, blossoming bruise on his bold chin. It was coming closer, that chin, right beneath his curving lips.

She had the hazy thought that she ought to move. But his fingers were circling the back of her hand, his thumb firm against her palm. Like the rest of him, his hands were large and powerful looking. Powerful feeling. She was not moving anywhere if he chose not to let her go. Beyond that, she was not quite certain that she wanted to move. And important decisions, after all, should not be made without complete certainty. So she waited, trying very hard to feel helpless and righteously indignant, for his mouth to drift those mere inches closer.

Gently, firmly, he drew her arm upward and pressed his lips to the sensitive inside of her wrist.

His eyes never left hers. Fiercely blue-green, they held her captive as surely as his grasp. When he released her hand and stepped back, it took her a moment to realize he had let her go.

Then he looked—and moved—away, collecting his hat from the side table and striding across the room with enviable grace. He stopped in the doorway and turned back to face her. "Good night, Ailís."

"I . . . Lord Clane . . ."

"Christor," he corrected blithely. "Ah, by the by, your mother has kindly invited me to supper tomorrow night. Does she have an aversion to drums?" Ailís shook her head mutely. "Well, good. Until tomorrow, then." He gave a short bow and was gone.

Her knees, bless them, supported her until he was out the door. Then they turned liquid as water and she went into a graceless heap on the sofa. Despite the fact that her mind had become every bit as useless as her legs, she couldn't help but note the fact that her arm was just as he had left it: raised in the empty air, wrist up.

Chapter 5

He returned without the *bodhrán,* and a full six days late. Ailís watched irritably from across the parlor as Christor greeted her mother. Anne, clearly unconcerned with the fact that he had not appeared at her carefully planned dinner party earlier in the week, held out both hands and smiled as he approached. Ailís could not hear the greeting, but she doubted there were any recriminations involved.

She was not feeling quite so forgiving. As far as she was concerned, a promise was a promise. She had been prepared to show Christor her illustrations for the guide to Irish wildlife, had even brought them downstairs to spread over the parlor table. But he had not come. Instead, he'd sent a note, begging forgiveness and stating that pressing business prevented him from attending. It was always pressing business, Ailís knew from years with a careless brother and his cronies, that prevented gentlemen from keeping their engagements. She'd been rather disappointed in Christor. Surely he could have come up with a more eloquent excuse.

What she could only just admit, and grudgingly, was that she had been disappointed for herself as well. He had managed to shatter her comfortable dislike with a few Gaelic words. Then he'd effectively turned her inside out merely by pressing his lips to her wrist.

Ailís had every confidence she would sort out all the new feelings. The process would take rather longer than expected, however, if Christor kept changing—and changing his plans on her.

She had been looking forward to seeing him at one of her mother's simple, intimate suppers. Now, in the midst of a well-attended soiree, with her mother glowing, Eamonn smiling indulgently from his place at Ailís's side, and the earl himself radiating complaisance and self-assurance, she merely felt cross.

She spared his companion a fleeting glance. Mr. Lyndhurst wasn't particularly interesting. He was merely one more Anglo-Irish genteel politician who was either too poor or too low on the Parliamentary ladder to remain in London. No doubt his attentions to Eamonn were a desultory attempt to rope in one more Irish Tory. Ailís had great faith in her brother and no interest whatsoever in Lyndhurst.

Christor, on the other hand, was impossible to ignore. In stark evening black, his waistcoat a sedate ivory, he was every bit the aristocrat. His hair was fashionably touseled, his collar points dramatically sharp, his face . . . smudged.

She blinked in surprise, then peered intently at his forehead. The cut on his brow appeared to be healing well, the bruise on his chin faded, but they were now joined by one rather colorful bruise at his left temple and another, fainter one on his cheekbone. On inspection, the immaculate, aristocratic Lord Clane looked a bit rough around the edges. Ailís saw him wince when Lady Morgan swept past him with a light, flirtatious rap at his forearm with her fan. Had it been another woman, Ailís might have thought the wince one of distaste. But everyone was smitten with the lovely Sydney Morgan.

It seemed the earl might have a hidden bruise or two as well.

"You and Lord Clane haven't been at each other in the sparring ring, have you?" she demanded casually of Eamonn. Her brother, absent from home all day, had appeared just before supper with his own faintly bruised jaw. Ailís had not asked about the mark at the time. Eamonn had always sported his share of bumps and smudges through the years. Now she was highly curious. "You both look as if you've been mucking about in my paints."

"Nothing so noble." Eamonn chuckled. "According to Clane, he had a bit of a brawl with his mount. The beast took first blood and ultimately won."

Interesting, Ailís thought. She knew the reason for the scarred brow. The injured head and arm were more recent.

"And you, Éamonnán? I'd be hard put to believe Kells gave you that bruise. For all you paid, that horse is dull as two short planks."

Eamonn fingered his jaw. "Oh, I . . . er . . . stumbled on my way to bed last night. Too much ale, I'm afraid."

He was lying. Ailís had been awake when he came home well after midnight, putting the finishing touches on her picture of a weasel. She would have heard had Eamonn fallen into anything hard enough to cause a bruise. She had heard almost nothing at all and the quiet had been more notable than any crash would have been. Her brother moved with all the stealth of a blind bull when he was drunk.

He was gone till the wee hours nearly every night lately. And he never spoke of them in the mornings when he was present for breakfast. Drinking and elbow rubbing with his political friends? Gaming? Ailís had no idea. This secrecy between her and Eamonn was distressing, to be sure, but only because they had always been so close. She had no reason to be concerned. Not yet, at least.

Her gaze drifted back to Christor. He was looking straight at her. Even from a distance, she could see the warm glint in the blue eyes. Her pulse promptly did an annoying little dance and she could feel the heat rising in her cheeks. Irked, she turned her attention to the far wall, but not before she saw his lips twitch in response. The smug lout knew precisely what effect he had on her.

Had he been mistaken, Ailís would have felt her own dismissive amusement. Men, after all, could always be counted upon to suspect more interest than a lady actually felt. Unfortunately, this particular man was absolutely right. As unwelcome as the feeling was, she had begun to find him a bit fascinating.

It was time, she decided, to regain control of the situation. If he couldn't be bothered to keep an engagement, she couldn't be bothered to care. One Society buck was rather like the next, and the next who came along would do quite nicely.

"Ah, Miss O'Neill!"

Her deliberately brilliant smile froze on her face when she turned to find the Honorable Gerald Fitzjohn all but leaning onto her shoulder. Philip Lorcan was right behind him. The pair were as dissimilar in appearance as they could be: Gerry flame-haired, lanky, and bearing a strong resemblance to the big setter dogs he collected; Philly fair, stout, and no taller than she despite his built-up heels. In character, they were distressingly alike. Both were forever hanging about, spouting appalling poetry and practicing ridiculously fashionable boredom. Both were about as appealing as week-old brown bread.

For his part, Gerry tended to keep his hands to himself, but his feet had a way of straying under a lady's skirt with regularity. To date, Ailís had been unable to determine whether it was by design or simply due to the fact that his limbs were too extensive for him to keep track of all of them at once. Now, with Philly leering beside him, fingers twitching visibly, Ailís decided to give Gerry's feet the benefit of the doubt.

"Good evening, Mr. Fitzjohn. Are you enjoying yourself?"

"Always guaranteed of a splendid evening here," he replied eagerly. When he nodded, his overlong ginger hair flopped like a pair of canine ears. "Your mother never throws a dull bash."

Discreetly surveying the sedate gathering, Ailís gave a silent sigh. Gerry's asinine comment aside, she was nearing the end of her short social tether. It was not that she would have preferred a party filled with loud music and louder guests. On the contrary, she found the standard crush a crashing bore. But it was far more difficult to slip away from a quiet fete. And she had every intention of disappearing as soon as possible.

"We've prevailed on your mother to allow some dancing," Philly announced, edging closer. "Since I was deprived of the pleasure at the Farnhams', Miss O'Neill, I trust you will stand up with me now."

"And with me after," Gerry insisted. "You must say yes, Miss O'Neill. Not another lady in the room I'd give a ha'pence to partner."

Ailís glanced once again around the guests. There were several lovely creatures in attendance. And several rich ones. She was confident enough of her own attractions, but honestly could not fathom what her great appeal was to these silly fellows. She was pleasant to them only when it suited her, and she certainly never flirted. She also knew her lack of fortune kept her well protected from the designs of pockets-to-let suitors.

The problem, she decided, was that Dublin society was so terribly limited. Any group that could list Maria Farnham as a prime catch was clearly in need of some fresh blood.

Maria Farnham, she had recently noted, had attached herself to Christor's coatsleeve. In terribly limited Dublin society, an unmarried man in possession of both title and fortune was a rare commodity. An unmarried, titled, wealthy man who looked like the Earl of Clane was liable to cause a frenzy of batting eyelashes and unsheathed claws.

He smiled down at the girl and her furious lash-batting stopped abruptly. For a long moment, Miss Farnham bore a striking resemblance to a bat caught in bright light. Then she recovered enough to give her own self-satisfied smile and dig her claws more firmly into his sleeve. Ailís saw Christor wince again. Had she not felt so annoyed with him, she might have been sympathetic.

As it was, she was beginning to feel a bit sorry for herself. Gerald and Philly had taken to bickering over who would get the third dance. "You cannot have two in a row," Gerry announced firmly. "Rules say."

"No such thing," Philly countered. "If Miss O'Neill wishes to have me twice over, there's no reason she can't."

Ailís closed her eyes wearily. Idiocy, she decided, knew no bounds. Nor could she make any sort of easy flight. Christor was coming toward her now, Maria and Lyndhurst in tow. Eamonn, lounging at her side, was no help. From his expression, he was finding the whole situation highly amusing. More importantly, he was blocking her best escape route.

Ailís endured the requisite greetings. When cornered, one had two choices: fighting like a tiger or graceful surrender. For the time being, she would opt for grace. "Good evening, Lord Clane," she offered, discreetly mashing Gerald's encroaching toes with her heel. "I am delighted you could attend."

"Thank you, Miss O'Neill. I am flattered."

She knew she was fair competition for Miss Farnham when she gazed up at him from beneath her lashes. "When you did not keep our last engagement, I feared some ill had befallen you. I trust you have exchanged your horse for one easier to control."

He thoughtfully ran a fingertip over the bruise on his cheekbone and smiled. "I prefer animals with spirit. The tame are not nearly so enjoyable. Knowing what I do of you, I would assume you agree."

She returned his smile with a sugary one of her own. "Actually, my lord, I don't. I prefer reliable behavior."

"The devil you do, Ailís." Eamonn, typically oblivious of the current running between his sister and friend, poked affectionately at her arm. "You haven't had the least interest in domesticated animals in years." She resisted the urge to poke back with somewhat more force than he had employed when he continued to no one in particular, "Ailís delights in bringing wild creatures into the house. Says they're better company than the human alternative."

Lyndhurst yawned. Miss Farnham gave an appropriately disapproving frown. Christor inclined his head and said solemnly, "Perhaps Miss O'Neill needs more excitement in her life. I fear the city can be infernally dull for an adventurous spirit."

In that moment, Ailís could not decide if he was mocking or if, just perhaps, he truly understood her. The latter was a distinctly interest-piquing possibility. Considering the alternative: pondering the walls, the bland refreshments, and the rest of the company, she was ready to be piqued.

"Dull?" Philly pushed his rotund self forward and declared, "Not a bit of it! Doesn't Dublin have the best mills in Ireland?"

"Dashed good cockfights in Carlisle," Gerry added.

"Ah, and do not forget the occasional drunken rumpus at Trinity," was Eamonn's dry contribution.

"All the province of men." Christor's eyes fixed on Ailís and she felt the familiar, cursed rising of heat in her cheeks. "I daresay the ladies would appreciate their own lively entertainment."

"The day ladies attend anything at Trinity," Lyndhurst drawled, "will be the day swine fly."

Ailís prided herself in a very good drawl of her own. "I have heard there are some very clever pigs in town, Mr. Lyndhurst."

"The criminal An Cú is back in Dublin."

Six pairs of eyes slewed to Miss Farnham's complacent face. She had been uncustomarily silent during the exchange. Ailís had not been fooled. Decorum and modesty never had anything to do with Maria's still tongue. For not possessing a precisely sharp wit, the girl was not stupid, especially when it came to men. She could be counted upon to speak when she had something attention-worthy to say, and not before.

This announcement certainly qualified.

"You don't say!" Gerry's puppy face creased in interest. Maria nodded.

"What rot." Philly snorted. "Fellow doesn't exist. An Cú is merely a figment of lowly imaginations."

"Oh, I wouldn't be so sure," Eamonn murmured. "He is a fairly well-known figment."

"Who?" was Christor's addition.

Ailís, who had caught her breath at the mention of the Hound, let it out in an exasperated hiss. Here was yet another tick against the Earl of Clane. No man with half the Irish blood he claimed should be ignorant of An Cú.

"I hear he nearly put a hole in Peter Bertram last week," Eamonn announced.

"Who did?" Christor demanded.

"Oh, he's a nasty, bloodthirsty beast!" Maria sidled another inch closer to him. "He has robbed four carriages this week alone, Mr. Wharton's last night. No respectable person is safe on the roads now that he has returned."

"Is that so?" Christor's scarred brow rose. "I had thought all bloodthirsty highwaymen had been eradicated a good many years ago."

"Not this one. I overheard Papa speaking with Colonel Ellsworth only this morning. Apparently An Cú and fifty of his men raided a dozen stables in town several nights ago, stealing horses." Maria's voice dropped to a breathy whisper. "Captain Carter had the blackguard cornered in Temple Bar, but he shot ten soldiers before vanishing into thin air like a phantom."

By now, Ailís's heart was lodged in her throat. An Cú nearly trapped. She could only imagine what the Sasanach Captain Carter would have done had his troops caught him. It would have been loud, bloody, and very public.

"Curious the news wasn't all over town the following morning," Lyndhurst mused.

Nay, Ailís thought. It wasn't. When Irish malfeasants evaded the hapless authorities—and they nearly always did— Dublin never heard of it. When one was captured, everyone knew.

"I still call it a load of nonsense," Philly insisted. "No such person."

"I would be inclined to agree." Lyndhurst offered a bored smile. Apparently he had the interest span of a gnat. "Such crude, impotent figures are created to entertain the common folk and frighten good society. It doesn't work. Everyone knows better and no one cares."

Ailís would have very much liked to snort aloud, but quashed the urge. Beside her, Eamonn gave a thoughtful hum. "I would say this character has people caring a great deal. He's certainly an epic figure among the ladies."

Oh, and he was. Ailís allowed her eyes to drift shut for a moment. She imagined shoulders broad enough to make the massive portals of the former Parliament House a tight squeeze, hair dark as a Tullamore midnight, and eyes the blue of the Irish Sea. He would have an irresistible crease beside his wide mouth. . . . Nay, that wasn't right. Warriors did not have dimples. But it was such an appealing picture. . . .

Christor watched the catlike smile slip across Ailís's lovely face. It annoyed the hell out of him. She was clearly moon-eyed over this wild-hearted bandit who had cut down ten of His Majesty's Best in Ireland before vanishing like smoke into the night. And Miss Farnham called An Cú bloodthirsty. Christor was beginning to think that it was Ailís who had the penchant for violence—and for the heroic Hound.

If only she knew, he thought crankily.

The fifty men who had accompanied him had, in truth, been three. The quick strike on a dozen stables had really been a plodding search of a dozen for the mysterious black coach.

They had not found it. They certainly had not stolen a single horse, merely loosed a few when Captain Carter had suddenly stormed up with his soldiers. Nor had the escape been in the least phantomlike. Christor, Séamus Cleary, and the Scannal brothers had spent a miserable two hours in a freezing, wet culvert that smelled of cats, waiting for Carter to call off the search.

Most importantly, the only person who had been shot was Christor himself. It had been a glancing blast across his forearm, a mere scratch, but it had burned, bled, and even now hurt like the very devil. The discreet bandage his valet had arranged was little protection against the rapping fans and clinging fingers of Dublin's ladies.

He glanced at Ailís's fingers, absently stroking the stem of her glass. She was not a clinger. Save for that brief period in the street when she had held on to him, and he unfortunately had had little chance to savor the sensation, she kept her hands very much to herself.

Christor had a feeling that sharp-tongued, suffer-no-fools Ailís O'Neill might cling to An Cú. The most sensible of women, he had discovered, could turn into starry-eyed fools at the thought of being swept off their feet by a highwayman. Then again, he was forced to admit, most men would gladly contemplate a night with the huntress Diana. He also remembered how the mere mention of Amazons had always turned Samuel Whyte's adolescent pupils into blushing, stammering idiots.

There was something about human nature, it seemed, that thrilled at danger. Absurd. As a result of far too much experience, Christor knew that combat was dirty, gruesome, frequently ineffective, and about as romantic as mud.

Around him, the others were still chattering about the Dread Hound. Ailís was still silent, lost in her own inner contemplations.

"I take it you believe in this An Cú, Miss O'Neill," he said mildly.

"Hmm?" She blinked at him. "Aye, certainly. I've far more reason to believe in him than doubt."

"And are you among the women who find him a dashingly romantic figure?"

He would not have expected Ailís to like that question. Clearly, she didn't. "It's not a matter of romance, my lord," she snapped, a telling—and charming—blush staining her cheeks.

"I should say not," Lyndhurst muttered. "All this rot about noble thievery is nothing more than fanciful antagonism against civilized life."

"Fanciful antagonism?" Now Ailís rounded on the unfortunate fellow, dark brows lifted into dramatic arcs. "That, sir, is a ridiculous phrase!"

Christor wondered momentarily if he ought to step in. Lyndhurst, after all, took any criticism rather poorly. Wisdom, however, kept him from interfering. Ailís, no doubt, would take his intrusion even less well. So he gently moved his injured arm from Miss Farnham's reach and waited.

"Ireland is part of His Majesty's realm, and by its own choice, Miss O'Neill," Lyndhurst commented dryly. Christor didn't particularly care for the condescending tone. He assumed Ailís liked it less. "A band of illiterate country farmers waving pistols at innocent people and depriving them of their well-deserved possessions is, at best, a fatuous, infantile act of defiance toward their betters. At worst, it becomes a capital crime and a dashed nuisance to the local authorities."

"*Infantile act of defiance. Betters.* Why is it, Mr. Lyndhurst," Ailís demanded, "that whenever an imperial country tromps into another and plunks down a flag, it's considered fair play, yet when unhappy people protest, it suddenly becomes criminal? It seems to me you wouldn't be labeled a criminal should a fellow member of whichever London club you frequent—one who was elected by some—decided to empty your pockets by changing all the gaming rules or cheating and you took your money back by force."

"Please, Miss O'Neill. That analogy." Lyndhurst shook his head indulgently. He appeared to be far more amused by Ailís than offended. Bad choice, Christor silently chided. "I hardly think the intelligent members of White's would approve such a fellow's admission."

"Precisely, sir. The intelligent members might not. As for the rest . . ." Ailís shrugged. "Now, if you would all excuse me, I believe my mother is in need of me."

She sketched a brief curtsy and strode away—in quite the opposite direction from where her mother stood. Christor watched her go, his admiration rising with each of her firm steps. What a pity she was not the O'Neill standing for Parliament. Oh, Eamonn was sharp enough, but Christor was convinced that should Ailís be allowed onto the Floor, she would have the entire Tory party jibbering and chasing their own tails within minutes.

"Miss O'Neill, wait!" Hair flopping, young Fitzjohn went trotting after her. "My dance!"

"And mine!" Lorcan cried, hot on his crony's heels. "I have the first, you know . . ."

Christor turned back to the remaining trio, and neatly sidestepped Miss Farnham's grab at his arm. "Interesting discussion, Lyndhurst."

"Not in the least. I must say I am quite disappointed in Miss O'Neill. One would not expect a young lady of breeding to support the antics of a common criminal."

"Ah, but such a dashing, romantic criminal," Christor said blandly. When Lyndhurst merely snorted, he asked, "Are you staying after all? You did say you had a previous engagement at . . . your club, was it?"

"I did, yes." Lyndhurst shot him a confused look. "And . . . er, I really ought to be going."

"Allow me to walk you out." With only the slightest twinge of guilt, Christor addressed Eamonn. "I entrust the lovely Miss Farnham to you, O'Neill. You will make certain she does not lack for amusement."

Neither party looked precisely overjoyed, but Eamonn gave a gallant bow. "It would be my pleasure."

"Splendid." Christor nodded his approval, then promptly hustled Lyndhurst toward the door. The familiar footman left his post for scant seconds before returning with two hats. "Thank you, Fergus, but I shall be staying." When Fergus vanished again, he said, "Give my best to our confederates at Daly's, Lyndhurst."

The man nodded. "Found something on O'Neill, have you?"

"No, as a matter of fact, I haven't. But I did promise you a thorough inquiry." Christor saw no reason to disclose that his interest was wholly directed in Ailís's direction. He didn't think Lyndhurst would find raging lust particularly helpful to the parliamentary cause. "I shall contact you soon."

"Good man." Lyndhurst cheerfully donned his hat. "I do appreciate thoroughness."

"I am certain you do." Christor was already back to thinking of Ailís. He had the strong suspicion that she was making a stealthy escape from her mother's party. "Good night, Lyndhurst," he announced, and all but shoved the man out the door.

He peered back into the drawing room, quickly withdrawing when Miss Farnham spied him and popped to her feet. He had seen what he needed to see, and could make very good use of the back hallway.

Ailís had just gone out the rear of the room. She would no doubt slip past the guests and musicians in the parlor and head for the back stairs—if not for the Wicklow hills. Christor had every confidence that he could intercept her before she escaped. The decision might not bode well for his health, once he caught her, but he was willing to take the chance.

Danger to life and limb aside, he was in the mood to corner his own fiery woman warrior.

Chapter 6

"Fanciful antagonism," Ailís muttered as she pushed through the door between the rear hall and the sewing room. "Fanciful antagonism, indeed!"

She shoved the door shut behind her with such force that it banged against the jamb and bounced back open. Ignoring it, she stalked across the room and dropped heavily into a muslin-draped chair. She rarely entered the sewing room; in her opinion, needles had been created to keep women from taking up larger sharp objects—like rapiers. She certainly never employed any of the various embroidery paraphernalia her mother enjoyed.

Anne, in her infinite motherly wisdom, had ceased sewing lessons after the third. She had always been very good at knowing when to count her losses. She certainly would not come looking for her daughter in this room. She would, however, likely take Ailís to task for having so rudely abandoned their guests. It would not be the first time.

"Insufferable man," Ailís grumbled, recalling Lyndhurst's indulgent smirk. "Chinless spawn of the Mayfair sty."

Worse, perhaps, than his condescension to her was his opinion of An Cú. *A fatuous, infantile act of defiance toward their betters,* Lyndhurst had called the nighttime strikes. *A crude, impotent figure,* he had called the bandit. *Crude, impotent figure.* Ailís's hackles rose at the memory. She would very much like to see the two men squared off on a dark country road. There was no doubt in her mind that the dashing, strapping, broad-at-the-shoulder and sharp-at-the-mind Hound would make mincemeat of the sniveling, bantam Englishman in seconds. Of course, her image of the bandit was just that: imagination—with an annoying dash of Christor thrown in—but she had faith.

"Rubbish to you, Mister Lyndhurst," she said derisively, waving a pair of sewing shears aloft with a cavalier flourish. "I'll back An Cú against you any day with both hands tied behind his back and a blindfold over his eyes!"

"As much as I admire the mythic tales of your dashing bandit, even I might cede the advantage to Lyndhurst under those circumstances."

Ailís ignored the mutinous shiver of her pulse and scowled at the door. Christor was leaning against the frame, face smudged and eyes alight with a wicked spark that would have quite melted a woman with less than Ailís's fortitude. He looked perfectly comfortable and she wondered if he had witnessed her little tirade in its entirety.

"Haven't you anything better to do than following me about like some plaisham hound?" she muttered, returning the shears to the table with more noise than grace.

"Plaisham. I must say you have me with that one. I shudder to imagine what the word means."

"I'll leave it to your imagination, then."

He compounded his various sins by grinning at her tone. "I have a very good imagination, Ailís, but we'll leave that for another time." He strolled into the room, carefully avoiding the cheerful clutter of fabric, half-wound bobbins, and pincushions. "So, I put you in mind of a hound, do I?"

Aye. Oh, aye, he did. Or rather, whenever she thought of An Cú she was put in mind of Christor Moore. Now, as he moved closer, all dangerous grace and wicked eyes, she was thinking far more of a wolf. In very expensive clothing.

"You'll stop there," she announced not quite firmly, "before . . . before you go treading on my mother's new dress."

He did stop, thankfully, not three feet away, and surveyed the spread yards of lightweight mauve wool. In order to conserve funds, simpler dresses were made at home rather than by a modiste. Ailís could well imagine what Christor was thinking as he surveyed the wool: plain, rustic, altogether suitable for the widow of a simple country gentleman. She stiffened against the unspoken insult to her beloved parent.

"Your mother is a remarkable woman," she heard instead. Christor's voice was a bit distant, musing. "I find myself wondering if there is something in the Irish air that produces . . ." He blinked, shook his head. "It was very kind of her to include me on her guest list tonight."

Ailís, well on her way to being charmed yet once again, gave a deliberate snort. "And so very accommodating of you to attend tonight. I daresay the company is honored. In fact, I should think your presence has been missed. Perhaps you ought to go back and mingle a bit more."

For the first time since meeting him, Ailís saw a flash of anger. It was gone in an instant and really had amounted to nothing more than a fleeting tightening of his mouth and glimmer of ice in his eyes. But she had seen it. For her own brief moment she was cowed— and contrite. He'd been nothing but pleasant and she had been . . . only herself, as a matter of fact, she reminded herself sharply. She'd never asked for his attention or his company. In fact, she had done everything short of telling him to leave her be. He hadn't.

The moment of weakness passed, she lifted her chin and met his gaze as squarely as she could. It didn't help her state of mind or dubious upper hand that, standing as he was, she had to crane her neck to see past his knife-sharp collar points and sculpted jaw.

"I'll apologize for those last words, my lord. They were unnecessarily—"

"Shrewish, perhaps? Rude?"

"No more rude than your barging in on me here!" Ailís snapped. She certainly did not need him rubbing her nose in her churlishness. She had apologized, hadn't she? And he had deserved the blast, impolite or not. "I'll thank you to give me my privacy now."

He merely propped a hip against a table and regarded her from his great height. "Shrewish. Yes, that suits. You have some remarkably shrewish moments." Before she could let loose a stinging retort, he continued, "God only knows why, Ailís O'Neill, but I seem to want to be near you, sharp tongue and all."

"Oh." Ailís struggled for a riposte. Nothing came, save for a sinking feeling in her stomach that was not altogether unpleasant. "Oh."

"Yes, I find myself speechless on the matter, too. I am ordinarily much more adept at choosing friends who are in equal desire of the acquaintance. You are an exception to rather a great deal of familiar qualities." He shrugged. "Ah, well. We are becoming friends, are we not?"

"Friends?" Ailís found something mildly unsatisfactory in the word. Or rather in the concept, she decided. Of course she did not want to be friends with the Earl of Clane. She did not even like him—much. The fact remained, however, that he was standing next to her, and to refuse would be more impolite than even she could manage. "I suppose we are."

"Splendid."

Christor had watched the play of emotions across her lovely face. She wanted to snipe at him, he could tell, wanted, too, to toss his invitation of friendship back in his face. But shrewish moments notwithstanding, she would not be so rude.

He was beginning to have high hopes for his relationship with Ailís O'Neill. He had every confidence that he could vanquish her disfavor, even make her like him. Beyond that, he wasn't certain—of either what he could have from her or what he wanted. Oh, he was very clear on the fact that he would enjoy nothing more than to taste the passion evident in nearly everything she did. The problem, of course, was that she was a gentlewoman, albeit a very lively one, and she was Eamonn's sister. A jolly tumble, one full of flame and empty of obligation, seemed very much beyond his reach.

Still, there were a great many steps between friendship and matrimony. He thought he might be able to tread a few with Ailís, and with her complete willingness. She was a fiery creature, this scion of Donegal Gaels, with an adventurous spirit that was hardly satisfied by what entertainments crossed her daily path.

If only she hadn't gone so starry-eyed over the mention of An Cú, Christor thought, somewhat grumpily now. It was going to be damnably inconvenient if he was forced to compete—with himself, as it happened—every step of the way.

He'd never intended for his endeavors to be regarded as heroic or romantic; simply boredom-eradicating and helpful. And now not only did he have half of Ireland's military after him, but the woman he was after seemed determined to go moonish over the wrong him.

It was enough to give a saint a headache.

This impostor was on the verge of becoming a serious thorn in Christor's side. He had not minded at the beginning, when word had reached him in London that someone was riding the night roads outside Dublin, divesting Anglo gentry of their purses and jewels. As best Christor's source could tell, the funds were anonymously finding their way into the hands of the Irish poor, just as Christor had originally arranged.

As far as he had been concerned, the unknown person could rob at will. As long as the money went to the right places, the fellow was welcome to the name and notoriety. The problem was that whoever was behind the highway robberies was sloppy, had been from the beginning. More than one too-important personage had been robbed; there had been too much gunfire. To date, no one had been injured, but the Marquess of Carricknock had had a head-sized hole blown out of his carriage—a mere foot or so from where Lady Carricknock had been slumped in a dramatic swoon. Distressed complaints had begun flooding London; high-ranking military ears had been bent.

Now it appeared the wealthy English physician Peter Bertram had nearly been sent into the next realm. The Lord-Lieutenant, whom Mr. Bertram regularly attended, would not be pleased. It was only a matter of time before catastrophe struck, endangering not only quarries' lives, but also those of Christor's old band of light-fingered cronies and the people they had aided. Not every tongue would remain silent if the threat or reward were great enough.

Christor had had no choice but to come home. There was a reasonable need for An Cú's work. He would be damned if he would let a bumbling impostor ruin the careful scheme he had created all those years ago, no matter how good the fellow's intentions.

A rustle drew his attention back to the immediate situation. Ailís was twitching in her seat. He had already learned that she seldom sat still for long unless she was being well entertained. He imagined his prolonged reverie had been something less than diverting for her.

"Shall we return to the others?" he asked, with some regret. As much as he enjoyed her company in public, he greatly preferred having her to himself. Unrealized or not, the salacious possibilities were endless and delightful.

"Aye. I expect we should," was her slow reply. Christor nearly grinned at the reluctance in her voice until she added, "My mother will be wanting me to play at socializing and I'm wanting nothing more than to be done with the whole dismal affair. I've a hare waiting for my attention."

She had more than a blasted rabbit waiting for her attention, Christor wanted to tell her. And a great deal more to gain than an evening with paper and paint. Instead, he said, "Yes, your paintings. You did promise to let me see your work."

"You promised to bring your *bodhrán*," she shot back. "Not that I'm often in the mood for dilettantish thumping and rattling, but we did have a bargain."

So the shrew was back. And now Christor thought perhaps he knew why Ailís's tongue had been especially sharp that evening.

"Ah, I see. I apologize, Ailís. I fully intended to attend your mother's dinner, was very much looking forward to it, as a matter of fact. Had circumstances not made it completely impossible, I would have been here as planned, bells on my toes and *bodhrán* hanging from my neck."

Ailís smiled, just as he'd intended her to do. It was a fleeting smile, to be sure, but it brightened her remarkable eyes and did splendid things to his body. He rather expected she enjoyed the image of him as jester, drum bouncing against his chest as he danced a jig. For a moment, he wondered if he might encourage her to imagine him wearing only the bells and *bodhrán,* and quickly quashed the wholly scandalous thought before it could evolve into too many imaginings of her wearing nothing but a dab of paint here and there.

Half amused, half annoyed, and quite aroused, he decided it might be a very good idea for him to sit down before Ailís saw more than she ought. He reached for a muslin-draped chair. Ailís promptly rose to her feet.

"The arrangement stands, my lord. You'll see the pictures when I see the drum."

"Should that not be 'hear' the drum?" he corrected her vaguely, willing his blood to cool. He could just smell her perfume now: subtle, a bit tart, rather like . . . turpentine. He nearly laughed aloud. Only Ailís O'Neill could stir a man's blood with the scent of her paintbrush cleaner.

"That remains to be seen. Or heard," was her retort. "I'll see you with stick in hand first, if you please. Should you manage that well enough, I'll hear you play."

"I am honored by your favor," he murmured dryly as she swept past him and headed for the door.

"As well you should be," she announced over her shoulder. "The truth of the matter is, I'm not so very enamored of the *bodhrán*. But I suppose it's worth showing a sketch or two. Now, for a tune on the *uillean* pipes . . ."

"Minx," he muttered after her graceful back. And wondered if he were too old to take up the pipes. He had a long list of what he would like to see in exchange for a slow air or lilting jig.

Ailís stopped abruptly in the doorway. Christor, having hurried to follow her, once again found himself in close proximity to her impressive breasts, shown to full advantage that evening by a simple, very nearly fashionable, marvelously low-cut bodice. For her own part, she seemed wholly unaware of the view she gave any man of moderate height. Either that or she just didn't care. Ailís, Christor was learning, never bothered to either push or restrict her abundant charms, physical or otherwise. He expected that were a man to tell her that her utter nonchalance was more alluring than any provocation or demureness, she would laugh heartily, then dismiss the unfortunate fellow with one sharp lash of her clever tongue.

"By the by," she was inquiring now, "what happened to your arm?"

"My arm?"

"Aye, and your face, too. You've an interesting collection of bruises, Lord Clane. I'm curious as to how you came by them."

Christor's hand instinctively went to the other arm. He could feel the bandage beneath his coat. For an instant, he found himself wondering what would happen should he tell Ailís precisely how he came by the injury. The result would certainly be interesting. But he wasn't ready to shuck his mild-mannered, very convenient shell for her just yet. In fact, he was not sure he ever could.

"I had a battle of wills with my horse, as it happens. He won."

Ailís tilted her head, humming quietly. "Just as Eamonn said, then. I didn't believe him."

"Well, now you've heard it from the horse's mouth, so to speak."

"Aye, and I am not certain I believe the horse, either." She gave him a bright, brief, hard smile. "Just so you know, sir, plaisham . . ."

"Yes?"

"It means 'idiot.' " Then Ailís spun on her heel, ready to sweep through the door.

Christor reached out, captured her arm in a flash—and felt a now familiar flare of heat as his skin touched hers. She froze, her eyes snapping up to his. He thought he saw temper there, and behind it, confusion.

"Dangerous games, my dear. Do you honestly believe I will continue to accept your little snipings without any retribution, Ailís? Do you truly believe that is the sort of man I am?"

For a moment she just stood, wide-eyed. Then her chin went up. "It was you who wished to be friends, my lord. Where I come from, one takes friends as they are, by the cover, so to speak. If you want me to be different, I suggest you reevaluate your desires."

Christor had no need to evaluate them at all. They were all but smacking him in the face. And propriety bedamned, he'd had enough of allowing her the upper hand for one evening. "By the cover, is it? What if I were to tell you that it is what's beneath your covering that interests me most?"

He had only meant the comment to be half crude. Oh, he would like to see Ailís in all her unclothed splendor, but he wanted, too, more glimpses into the very center of her where her fierce heart and equally fierce intelligence burned.

Ailís, apparently, heard only the crude meaning. It took a moment, but a blush began to spread from her jaw and over her cheeks, deepening from the palest pink to rich rose. Her mouth opened and closed soundlessly. And a silent Ailís, while not Christor's only ideal, suited him perfectly just then.

"You might do well to look beneath my cover as well, Ailís O'Neill. I daresay you would be surprised at what you find."

He tugged gently at her arm, drawing her toward him. She offered some resistance, but not enough. Slowly, firmly, he pulled until they were nearly chest-to-chest again, giving her every opportunity to protest, to snap at him or clip him soundly with her free arm. She didn't. He could hear her breathing, quickened and shallow. It could be anger, he knew, but he hoped there was something else making her pulse race beneath his fingers.

"Ah, Ailís," he murmured, his gaze fixed on her lush mouth, "I have been waiting . . ."

The sound of footsteps in the corridor had him glancing up sharply, had Ailís stumbling backward like a sleepwalker suddenly awakened. He released her, cursing under his breath, just as Fergus appeared around the bend in the hall.

"My lord"—the footman sketched a quick bow, showing no reaction whatsoever to the scene into which he had barged—"I have a message for you."

Resisting the urge to send the fellow bumping back down the corridor on his posterior, Christor accepted the proffered note. He scanned the lines quickly, crumpled the paper, and thrust it into his waistcoat pocket. "Is the gentleman still present?"

"He informed me he will be waiting outside, my lord."

Christor nodded. Then he turned to Ailís. She was standing stiffly upright, hands clasped at her waist. Only her eyes, sharp beneath her dark brows, belied the serene pose. He knew there would be hell to pay at their next meeting. He looked forward to it.

"My apologies, Miss O'Neill. I am afraid my presence is required elsewhere. We shall have to postpone our . . . dance until next we meet." He debated reaching for her hand and thought better of it. It might come swinging at his chin. He bowed instead. "Good night."

"Good-bye, sir," was her clipped reply. Nothing more.

Suppressing a grin, Christor strode down the hallway.

Ailís watched him go, her indignation rising with each vigorous step he took. How dare he, she fumed silently, take such liberties with his speech—and with her person. This was the second time he had manhandled her so, the second time he had made her feel quite . . . agitated.

Blast him, he had a way of bringing out the very worst in her, then somehow turning her into a mass of overwarmed porridge. He alternately made her furious, flustered, then helplessly curious. Beyond that, now, as she stood listening to his receding footsteps, she felt somehow disappointed. And in moments of clear self-examination, she had often decided that she took disappointment very poorly indeed.

"Ploid on him!" she snapped, finding rustic vocabulary much easier to grasp at the moment with her muddled brain. Fergus, hovering nearby, coughed. "The devil take him!"

With that, she gathered her skirts and stomped off in the earl's complacent wake.

He was gone when she reached the drawing room. Her mother, looking altogether too placid and content for Ailís's state of mind, beckoned her to the side of the room. "Lord Clane has left, dearest, and wished me to—"

"Aye, I know he's gone, and good riddance!"

Anne's brows went up in mild surprise. Then she sighed. "What did you do now, Ailís? And why do I have the sneaking suspicion that his lordship's request that I bid you his farewell was more politeness than inclination?"

For a brief moment, Ailís was tempted to haul her little mother into a quiet room, plunk her onto a chair, and tell her the entire, dismal tale. She was certain that Anne, in her fierce motherly way, would be appropriately dismayed at the earl's conduct, and would ban him from the house. And then she would be quite free of the man, with next to no effort on her own part.

The problem, however, was that she couldn't possibly discuss her own part in the scenario—her elevated pulse or strong, stunning wish that those firm lips of Clane's would hurry themselves and reach hers—without looking very foolish and not a little guilty. Guilt was yet another emotion she handled poorly—not at all, if she could help it.

She made her decision. "I did nothing to Lord Clane, *Máthair,* save treat him as I always do."

"Oh, Ailís."

"Please, no scolding. His lordship and I are north and south, opposite sides of very different coins, and that is that. I did nothing to make him hare off, but I'll not say I'm sorry to see him go."

"Now, Ailís—"

"And I've a hare of my own awaiting me upstairs. Make excuses for me, will you, *Máthair.* Please. I'm in no mood to face the slavering masses at the moment."

Anne sniffed. "Do you think perhaps you are overestimating your importance in this soiree, dearest? But yes, I will explain your disappearance. Should anyone ask."

"Ah, a mother after my own heart. Tell them I've a fierce headache. It's true enough." Ailís gave her mother a smacking kiss on the cheek. "You will be canonized, you know."

"I've had the trials, certainly," Anne replied dryly. "Now if I could just instill some manners in my adult offspring, I'd have the miracle, too. Tell me, darling, if you would, where I went so awry. Eamonn flitted off, too, not ten minutes past."

"Did he?" Ailís's mind whirled. "Did he say where he was going?"

"He did not. He merely bade me make his excuses and ran."

"Curious," Ailís murmured. "Ah, well, off to Ursula."

"Ursula?" Anne's eyes narrowed. "I assume you are not speaking of my sister."

"I'm not, nay. It's my hare. Her nose twitches and her little nostrils pinch in just such a way that I couldn't help but see Auntie Ursula."

"Ursula's nose does not twitch."

"It does, I tell you, each and every time I visit her."

"Well, if it does," Anne said wearily, "it is only because you have a habit of entering her house with all the grace of a whirlwind."

"And is it my fault she has filled the place with useless little china objects?" Ailís kissed her mother again. "I'm off, then. Don't you be letting Philly Lorcan anywhere near the pianoforte after he's been drinking. We'll have Purcell ringing from the rafters half a key off."

"No fear of that, actually. Both Philip and Gerald have departed."

"Already?" Ailís was surprised. She had never known either of the pair to depart before draining the last glass.

"Already. And most disappointed to have missed you." Anne eyed her daughter cannily. "I don't suppose you would care to tell me where you have been."

"Nowhere nearly so important as where I am going now," was Ailís's deft reply. She knew her mother would not press.

She slipped out of the room and up the stairs. On a whim, she paused on the first landing and peered out the window. She could just see a carriage at the end of the street. A booted foot which might have belonged to anyone disappeared into it, followed by Christor himself.

Ailís wondered if it had been Eamonn's boot. And why, as the vehicle rolled out of sight, she had a very odd feeling in the pit of her stomach.

Chapter 7

Christor crouched beside his horse, mud up to his ankles and gorse briars pricking at his rump, and waited for something—anything—to happen. He'd been concealed in the copse for nearly an hour now, watching this section of the road that ran between Dublin and fashionable Blackrock. His source had informed him that not only was Sir John Alderton, a man whose wealth and girth were surpassed only by his foul temper, to be attending a supper party held by the local squire, but that there might very well be a surprise visitor to the post-supper roadside fete.

An hour's wait in dismal conditions had done little more than assure him that every sensible person was staying in that evening.

Alderton was the perfect prey: obscenely wealthy, Unionist, and no friend to his Irish tenants. Even so, Christor would not have removed himself from the comfort of the O'Neill home had he not had a better reason than money alone. If he knew of Sir John's expected travels, chances were likely that the impostor An Cú did, too, and would make an appearance. So here he was, hunched over in the rain, cursing everything from Irish weather to his well-meaning informant who, to his credit, was hunched in a similar gorsey spot some ten yards away.

Another quarter hour passed. Christor's borrowed hat, like all of the dark clothing that had been waiting for him in the carriage, suited the occasion, but not the weather. Rain had started finding its way under the brim a good twenty minutes earlier and had, he was convinced, soaked the entire back of his homespun shirt and rough coat. He was wet, cold, and ready to toss it all in for a nice life among the Hottentots.

A low whistle reached his ears at last from his companion's hiding place. He listened carefully and, moments later, heard the faint sound of hooves. Someone was coming and, from the sound of it, that someone was in a large carriage. Fully alert now, the familiar thrill his nighttime exploits had always given him rising in his gut, he reached behind him for his horse's reins.

A second whistle came just as the coach appeared. A gaudy crest, depicting something that resembled a flying cow but was, Christor knew, meant to be Pegasus, was just visible on the near door. Apparently it was their lucky night. Alderton had arrived. In a single lithe motion, Christor swung into the saddle and rode down the slick embankment. To his right, Séamus Cleary followed.

Despite the substantial length of his absence and the relative brevity of his return to the business at hand, Christor had not lost his touch. He guided his horse from the shadows just as the carriage's team was passing, and had his long-barreled pistol pointed at the startled driver before the fellow could so much as fumble for his own weapon. No words at all were exchanged as the driver hauled the team to a shuddering halt. In an instant, Séamus had taken his place, gun trained on the box so Christor could turn his attention to the passengers.

As it happened, the pistols might very well have been unnecessary. Christor didn't think he imagined the smirk on the driver's face or the faintly tipped hat as he passed. Apparently Sir John's servants did not like him any better than most of Dublin.

At that moment, the man himself thrust his head from the window. "Why in the devil have we stopped?" he demanded. "Damn and blast it all! I'll have your head, MacGonnigle—"

Christor's gun barrel in his nose put a quick end to the tirade. In the light from the carriage lamp, the jowly face flushed a furious purple. He wheezed for several seconds, looking very much as if he were about to burst apart at the seams. Then, "The Dog, I presume."

" 'Tis the Hound, if it's all the same to you," Christor replied in his best Wicklow brogue. "A grand evening to you, sir. I'll be seeing your hands, please."

Sir John looked ready to refuse. A slight wave of the gun had him lifting pudgy fingers to the lowered window, however, showing several impressive rings but no weapon of his own. Christor rode closer, peered through his black cloth half-mask into the lamplit carriage. Lady Alderton, blindingly peacock-garbed and turbaned, thin and pinched as her husband was overblown, scowled from her seat. No swooner, this. The lady appeared fully capable of skewering them all with a butter knife, without batting an eyelash.

"I'll be making good use of you, m'lovely," Christor announced. She hissed. Christor doubted she would speak breathlessly of him later—as a few ladies in the past, despite losing their jewels—had done. He tossed a large, empty leather pouch through the window and into her lap. "You'll fill that now, beginning with what hangs 'round your own sweet neck."

"I'll see you with a noose about your neck," Alderton spat, some bravado recovered. "Filthy son of a—"

"Ah, now, are you after hurting me feelings, then, sir, insulting m'sainted Ma?" Christor shoved the gun forward until it pressed against Alderton's nose. "I'd bide a wee moment before doing that." The man subsided, even whimpered once, a circle from the gun barrel imprinted in the middle of his bulbous nose. When another hiss and no movement at all came from the lady, Christor advised, "See to your beauteous wife's neck, there, and quick. Much as I love the rain, I'd not like to see much more of it flooding your fine conveyance."

Sir John managed a strangled command, but it wasn't until Christor flicked his pistol to the side that Lady Alderton obeyed, hurrying to unfasten the clasp of her necklace. Christor hadn't pointed the gun at her, would never have, but clearly the Aldertons expected nothing so noble from a notorious bandit. In seconds, a tangle of gold and sapphires clinked into the bag, followed by matching ear bobs and bracelet. It was a hideous set, but taken apart should bring a decent price. There would be new livestock on a few rural plots come the sennight.

Alderton's rings, watch, and stickpin followed, then the contents of his pockets. A tidy take, but Christor wasn't finished. "Now the box, if you please."

"Box? What in the devil do you mean, box?"

"Ah, now you're after insulting me. Do I look like a stupid man?"

Christor could see Sir John squinting into his masked and shadowed face, trying to get a good enough look to report to the local lawkeepers. No doubt the report would be eloquent and dramatic, and would include absolutely nothing whatsoever of use to the authorities.

"You look—" Another twitch of the pistol had Alderton swallowing his words audibly. "No, not a stupid man."

"And he a wise one himself," Christor cheerfully informed the glowering Lady Alderton. "Now, sir, the box, and I believe we'll have the lady retrieve it."

He wasn't taking any chances on Alderton's going for a weapon and haplessly shooting himself or his wife in the process. Christor had never much cared for the sight of blood.

True to expectation, Lady Alderton soon held out a cherrywood coffer. It held, Christor knew, the monthly tithes from the district. The coins, he thought with pleasure, would soon be back in many of the hands from which they had been squeezed.

" 'Tis grand, that," he announced, sliding the box into the waiting maw of his saddle bag. "You've been most accommodating. And now if you would—"

A shout from Séamus, who had remained silent through the proceedings, had him jerking his head up. He heard the hoofbeats just before a lone rider appeared ahead in the road. In the darkness, Christor could see no more than a flapping cloak and wide-brimmed hat. He thought there might be the shadow of a mask, too. It hardly mattered. There was no doubt in his mind that he was having his first face-to-face encounter with his erstwhile replacement.

"After him!" he shouted to Séamus, who was already wheeling his mount about.

Seeing an opportunity, empty as it was now, Alderton bellowed "Drive!" out the window.

"I wouldn't advise it," Christor countered. As expected, MacGonnigle did not budge. Instead, Christor saw the man calmly remove a bottle from the folds of his coat and take a long swallow.

Ahead, the scene took on an almost comical air. The counterfeit Hound, having comprehended what was happening, was hauling back on his horse's reins with all his might. The beast, a massive gray, was churning at the wet ground with all four feet, trying to get purchase. Mud was flying in every direction, spattering Séamus. As Christor watched, Cleary spat, scrubbed at his face, then spent a long moment trying to steady his own mount. In that time, An Cú the Wrong had wheeled about and was thundering off down the road.

Christor prepared to follow. He was done with the Aldertons. The Aldertons, however, were not done with him. A wise bandit never took his eyes from his prey. For all the silent self-congratulating he had done of late, lauding the fact that he had not lost his touch, Christor committed that very basic, very serious lapse.

Later he would acknowledge how fortunate he'd been that the object which came hurtling out the carriage window was neither bullet nor blade. As it smacked solidly into his chin, however, his only thought was that Ailís O'Neill's feet had nothing on Lady Alderton's. The peacock-blue, hard-heeled shoe was bloody enormous.

"Take that, you foul behemoth!" the lady bellowed, then, in tones that could probably be heard all the way to County Waterford, "Drive on!"

It seemed ignoring Sir John was one matter; disobeying his wife quite another. With a convulsive leap, the pitiable Mac-Gonnigle went into action. His arms flailed, his bottle went flying, and the team lurched forward. Before Christor could do more than pull his own mount out of the way, the Aldertons' coach was bouncing down the road, spitting mud and her ladyship's strident invectives in its wake.

Christor sat very still in the saddle for a minute, one hand gripping the reins, the other pressed to his aching jaw. Then, sighing once, just loudly enough to satisfy his beleaguered soul, he set off after the other two mounted figures.

He met one not fifty yards down the road. Séamus's hat was gone, his mask dangled from one ear, and it appeared one sleeve had separated from the shoulder of his coat.

"Good Lord, man," Christor demanded, concerned, "what happened to you?"

Cleary shoved one hand through his wild red hair, sending his mask fluttering to the ground. "He vanished, m'lord, right into thin air. I was right behind him, gaining—he rides like a blind hunchback—then suddenly he wasn't there. I could hear him, blundering off, but couldn't see a blasted thing."

Christor refrained from commenting that had Seamus tied his mask properly, he might have seen a good deal more. The younger man was clever, tough, and trustworthy, however, and didn't need to have his nose rubbed, so to speak, in a piece of black cloth.

"Come along, then, we'll see what we can find."

It took some time, but they did locate Cleary's thin air, which turned out to be a narrow space between more gorse bushes. Either the second Hound had had enough time to carefully plan his routes or he had been extremely lucky. He certainly had not been smooth in his escape. His hat rested on one bush, a large patch of rather fine black cloth in another. And tangled in a third spiny clutch was a stirrup, complete with leather strap. Whoever he was, the man would have an interesting ride home.

The trail vanished in a small stream. In one direction lay Dublin, in the other, Blackrock and Kingstown port. "Don't suppose we'll find him tonight," Séamus muttered, straining to see up the stream toward Kingstown.

Christor gazed thoughtfully toward Dublin. "No, I don't suppose we will." But he knew where to begin looking.

There was something very familiar about that monstrous gray. Like the carriage which had nearly run him down the week before, he had seen the horse before. It had to have been in Dublin. Unfortunately, for his life, he couldn't recall specifically where or when. Still, one couldn't very well conceal a beast of that size for long, especially not in the city. Unless the impostor swapped mounts, his identity was not long for secrecy. An Cú the Wrong could only hope An Cú the Right found him before the authorities.

Plans rolling through his mind, Christor turned his horse back toward the road. The carriage, along with his clothing from earlier in the evening, was waiting in the shed of an abandoned farmhouse. No matter how unlikely the chance of being stopped, he did not want to ride to his doorstep as he was. Earl or not, a man garbed in ill-fitting black from head to toe might raise a few eyebrows and some suspicions.

Cleary, following close behind, pulled his mount to a sudden stop in the road where the Alderton coach had stopped. He dismounted for a brief moment, then rejoined Christor, bright blue shoe in his fist.

"Didn't I see this very color on the banshee?"

Christor winced at the memory. "You did. She heaved it out the window at my head."

"Missed, did she?"

"Not precisely."

Séamus let out a low whistle. "This would fit a few strapping lads I know. Did she nearly knock the block off you?" He chuckled at Christor's growl, uncowed. "I think I'll be keeping this for the time being."

"I wouldn't advise it. Toss it back where it was."

The younger man ignored him and tucked the shoe into his saddle pouch. Then, whistling a cheerful tune, he trotted ahead into the darkness.

Christor arrived home several hours later. He was cold, exhausted, his head ached, and he was convinced there were a few elusive gorse thorns in his breeches. Grumbling all the way, he mounted the stairs to his bedchamber, the Aldertons' possessions clinking in a pouch at his side. He'd sent the money off with Cleary for distribution, but kept the jewels himself. Coins and notes were easily enough explained; he didn't want Séamus caught with anything that could be identified.

He tucked the pouch into a drawer in his writing desk. There was a sizeable parcel on the surface. From his friend Lord Lucas Gower in London, he noted. It would wait. He needed a basin of hot water.

His valet arrived several minutes later in response to his ring. Christor never demanded the fellow wait up for him, and felt a tug of remorse at having dragged him from his bed. Figgis was struggling to get his shirt tucked into his waistband with one hand and fumbling with his spectacles with the other. Never the most efficient creature, the man was definitely slowing as he exited middle age. But he had served Christor's father well for years, the son loyally after, and Christor knew retirement would be far more of a slap than a gift. The valet had been wounded enough by Christor's decision to leave him in Dublin when he left.

"Sorry to wake you, Figgis, but I am in need of some hot water."

The valet drew himself up stiffly. "There is no need to apologize, my lord. It is my duty to attend you at whatever time you should require my services." With that, he stalked with slightly creaky ceremony across the room and tugged at a secondary bell-pull, dragging another hapless soul from bed.

Christor sat in somewhat guilty patience as a small parade of footmen arrived with his hot water, Figgis providing them with unnecessary directions all the while. "No spilling, Donal." "Pour that into the bath, if you please, Daniel." "*Hot* water, young man. Hot." With his wild gray hair, rolling eyes, and waving arms, the valet rather resembled a mad conductor deep in the throes of a Haydn symphony.

When at last Christor was able to sink into the hip bath, he did so with a grateful sigh and a wince. The steaming water felt wonderful to all but those parts of him which stung from countless gorse prickles. He dismissed Figgis for the night, resolutely ignoring the valet's wounded glance as he departed. There were certain things a man was meant to do alone, he believed, and while bathing was not necessarily one of them— damp female company having its great merits—pondering a night of illegal activity was.

No doubt Alderton had wakened half the county by now. There would be heavy-eyed meetings, a good deal of port consumed, and more sentries on the roads come the following night. That did not bother Christor insofar as lost monies were concerned; that night's take would last a while. But he was concerned about his miserable imitator. The fellow would either disappear for a time, making finding him more of a challenge, or he would stumble right into the clutches of the law, making him most likely dead. Neither was an appealing concept.

They would have to locate the horse. And soon. Christor knew Séamus and his hot-blooded colleagues would groan a bit at the task of searching Dublin's countless stables yet again. They would groan more loudly at the prospect of touring any number of farms in the area. The realities of an adventurous life, Christor knew too well, rarely lived up to the expectations.

That was just too bloody bad. He would join in as much of the search as he could. And he would be damned cheerful about it. After all, slogging through stable muck or not, he could be in London instead.

That thought, and the fast cooling water, had him climbing from the bath. Several minutes later, he was seated at his writing desk, the Alderton jewels to one side of the blotter, Gower's parcel to the other. He imagined it contained a sheaf of political rot. Lord Lucas, a younger son with little chance of becoming the Duke of Conovar, took his position in Common's quite seriously, and had hounded Christor mercilessly during past sessions. During Parliamentary session, Christor did not mind at all. But the Season was over, those resolute Tory dragons who forever needed slaying were safely tucked up in their country estates, and politics was the last thing on his mind.

It really was time for Lucas to find something else to occupy his time. A wife and nest of little Gowers would do, but the man refused to recover from a nasty jilting—literally at the altar–keeping rule and regulation his most frequent bedmates. Instead of a pretty face at the breakfast table, Gower faced any number of dull-as-dirt, ill-written discourses. It was hell on any man who should happen to be the first friend Lucas encountered each day.

Christor unwrapped the parcel with no small amount of resignation and just a smidgen of hope. The thing was unusually flat for a Lucasian communiqué.

As it happened, there was not a Parliamentary note or treatise to be seen. *I thought perhaps you might find these amus-*

ing, read Gower's brief note. *They are to be seen all over Town these days. Ireland, apparently, is in vogue.*

Christor lifted the first print from the small pile. The drawing was quite good, the coloring mediocre, and the image had him blinking—then chuckling heartily. Castlereagh was depicted as a goose, skinny-legged and beak-nosed, his swelled chest and flapping bird tongue leaving no doubt as to the volume of his honking.

Personages of Ireland, the caption read. *No. 6. An Unpleasant Noise.*

The next caricature was even better, if less caustic. Grinning, Christor studied the fox who wore Wellington's hat and boots—and the general's massive nose. The darker hairs on the creature's face expertly depicted Wellington's proudly lifted brows, the white curve at the ears the definite recession of Wellington's hair. And lurking in the background, small but exquisite, was Bonaparte in chicken feathers.

All in all, it was exceedingly clever. *No. 1,* was the caption, *Wile Stalking.* No doubt the duke would not be overly pleased at being depicted as a diminutive fox rather than, say, a looming wolf, but Wellington was not a large man and any who knew him knew well that his brilliant success was due far more to wile than brawn.

There were four more prints: the elderly Lady Louisa Conolly, *née* Lennox, as a wrinkled butterfly, Grattan as a stoat; Lord Cloncurry as a majestic fallow buck; and Lady Morgan as a rather lovely song thrush.

The artist obviously knew Irish wildlife as well as he knew Irish personages. Christor traced the sweeping lines of the Cloncurry antlers. A nationalist, he mused, comparing that image to Grattan-as-weasel. He found himself picturing a middle-aged man, comfortable in expensive wools, a gentleman who had perhaps supported Emmett and Wolfe Tone in the '98 Rebellion, but whose position in life and artistic bent had made him a man of pen and paintbrush rather than saber.

Interesting. Christor wondered if the fellow were in Dublin, perhaps frequenting the same entertainments as he himself. But no, the print at the bottom of the pictures read *G. Humphrey 27 St. James St.* Humphrey was one of the premier printers of London; Cruikshank was one of his caricaturists. So this satirist of Irish figures might well be Dublin-, Cork-, or Kerry-born, but was probably now living in England.

Christor chuckled once more over the Castlereagh, then set the prints aside. He would show them to Ailís, he decided. No doubt she would appreciate the animals and the nationalistic leanings. And perhaps she would flash that glorious smile, give that silvery, set-a-man's-blood-pumping laugh—and let one hot-blooded man steal a kiss or two.

Ah, Ailís. Christor propped his elbows on the desk and wearily ran both hands through his hair. She was rather like the gorse, he thought: prickly, inclined to get under a man's skin, and difficult to remove. In fact, he mused as he shifted carefully in his seat, testing to see if he was still sporting any briars, the more time he spent thrashing around clumsily in the woman's presence, the more little barbs he received, the more stuck he became.

He wanted Ailís O'Neill rather desperately. Thorns and all. And he had no idea precisely what he was going to have to do to have her.

Those tactics he had used on other women in the past would not work. She would probably laugh at poetry, not that he had ever been a particularly adept poet. She clearly liked music, as long as it was of the traditionally Irish variety, but she had been quite right, albeit unwittingly, when she had implied his skill at the *bodhrán* would lack finesse. It often did. And jewels would only offend her unique but adamantine sense of propriety.

His eyes drifted to the pouch nearby. He reached over and tipped the contents onto the blotter. With his chin propped on one hand, he had a very close view of the tangle of gems. Much closer, not to mention better lit, than earlier.

Before his incarnation as An Cú he had possessed little interest in jewels and less knowledge. He had learned quickly, however, and had become rather good at valuing the pieces he and his cronies gathered. It was a skill he had not lost.

He reached into the pile and withdrew the earring that had caught his attention. Then he withdrew a small, gold-rimmed jeweler's glass from the hollow back of a desk drawer. The large sapphire he examined was suspended from an intricate swirl of diamonds and gold. It was a gaudy piece, a gaudy stone.

It was also as fake as a unicorn horn.

An untrained eye might have missed it. The thing was certainly sparkly enough. Flaws, too, did not dismiss the value of many stones. Nature was imperfect. But it didn't take much expertise at all to know real gems did not have perfectly spherical air bubbles inside.

Lady Alderton's very large, very glittery parure was glass. Well-made glass, to be sure, but glass nonetheless.

Disgusted, muttering, Christor dragged the lady's other pieces from the tangle. One after another proved to be imitations, worth less than the instrument with which he viewed them, and not worth a fraction of the risk he and Cleary had taken in procuring them. Cursing aloud, he rapped the large ruby pinky ring he had taken from Sir John against the desk top. He fell silent mid-epithet when he gave the thing a cursory glance through the glass.

The single stone was pigeon's-blood red, the size of his thumbnail, and in a London jeweler's establishment would cost a good five hundred pounds. Christor hurriedly replaced it with the diamond stickpin, then another ring—also diamond—and the sapphire-encrusted watch fob.

All totaled, the set was worth at least two thousand pounds. Sir John had been wearing a small fortune in the finest quality jewels on his pitiful person. His wife had been sporting paste. And she probably hadn't a clue.

Whistling cheerfully now, Christor returned the lot to the pouch and tucked it, with his glass, into the hidden drawer. He would remove the stones from Sir John's pieces later and hand them off to his jeweler crony in Westmoreland Street. He had no idea what he would do with the glass pieces just yet.

What a shame he couldn't tell Ailís about Sir John's deception. He thought she would get a great deal of pleasure from the tale. But it was out of the question. *Ah, Ailís.* He caught himself wondering if, tucked warmly into her bed those mere blocks away in Fitzwilliam Lane, she might be dreaming of him. Unlikely as the possibility was, it delighted him. As he took to his own bed, he willed his own thoughts toward such things as gargoyles and Lady Alderton. Thinking of Ailís, he knew, would not be conducive to a relaxed slide into slumber.

He gave up an hour later and headed for the cold water in the wash basin. Whatever Ailís O'Neill was doing in her own bed, she was an altogether too lively presence in his.

Chapter 8

"You are intent on making me the laughingstock of Dublin, are you not?" Ailís demanded sourly. "Be honest now. 'Tis all some ill-begotten plot for your amusement."

"Now, Ailís—"

"Nay, I'll hear none of your excuses. I have been patient. I have been obliging. As a matter of fact, I've been an utter delight, and this is what I get for my saintly behavior?"

"If you would just—"

"I think not, thank you kindly." Ailís gave an airy wave. "Now, I believe I will be on my way."

"You will stay right where you are, miss." Anne brandished her lacy parasol with a *Fian* warrior's fierceness, preventing her daughter from taking so much as a step from the modiste's fitting stool. "You look the angel in that dress, Ailís, quite lovely enough to cause adoring, motherly tears, and if you so much as twitch before Mrs. Farrell gets those pins in, I'll be after you with an oak shillelagh. *An bhfuil tuigeann tú?*"

"Aye," Ailís grumbled. "I understand." Her mother lapsed into Gaelic only under extreme provocation. And when she did, woe to the next person who spoke a contrary word.

Ailís had been perched atop the stool for nearly half an hour, enduring the poking and prodding which went with being fitted for a dress. A dress she did not need, she thought in exasperation. And one they could ill afford. The silver tissue over white silk, when completed, would cling altogether too tightly in what little there was of the bodice, and Ailís was certain she would send the tiny, gossamer sleeves flying off with one good gesticulation. She told her mother so.

"Well, dearest, you have two options," was Anne's reply. "You can refrain from gesticulating, or we can have Mrs. Farrell sew your gloves to the skirt."

The harried dressmaker looked up from fiddling with the hem and snorted around a mouthful of pins. There was little doubt she would be delighted to sew Ailís right into a chair to keep her still and add a nice little silk gag as an accent.

"Truly, Mama"—Ailís stilled her restless foot tapping—"it's an extravagance. I've the white and the blue, and the godawful pink from Auntie Ursula. And we could use the funds for Eamonn—"

"I have two children," Anne said firmly. "I'll not slight one for the other."

"Oh, *Máthair,* I hardly feel sl—"

"The pink is not godawful, but, much as I hate to dismiss my sister's generosity, it is close. The white, if I understand correctly, suddenly developed brown spots which, while both you and Sweeney insist they are spilled tea, look suspiciously like mud to me. And at last sight the blue had a new and interesting criss-cross pattern across the skirts."

Ailís sighed. The white had indeed been ruined by her near encounter with the runaway coach. And she had been so intent on getting back to work after Clane's exit from the party three days earlier that she had neglected to change her dress. She could not possibly have foreseen that Tilly the maid's entrance would so startle Ursula the Hare that the creature would go scuttling first through her paints and then across her lap. And back again when the maid made her own convulsive leap onto the bed.

"Fine, so perhaps I can make use of a new dress. But we could do up something at home. . . ." She gave the modiste an apologetic shrug. Mrs. Farrell merely rolled her eyes and continued poking away. "What of you? You're well past due your own new evening dress."

"I do not paint in my evening garb, dearest," Anne replied blandly. "Besides, how I look at the Lord-Lieutenant's ball does not matter in the least."

The affair promised to be as extravagant as any such entertainment in Dublin and just as tedious. "Must I go? Eamonn hardly needs me at his side to troll for support."

"True. In fact, if you insist on behaving as if you are on the way to the scaffold at every party, he might do far better without your company."

"Precisely!" Ailís agreed, delighted her mother was finally grasping the concept.

"So, you will simply have to behave yourself," Anne went on, ignoring Ailís entirely, "and in that dress. You really are beautiful, you know."

Anne's eyes indeed went misty. Disarmed, Ailís was silent—just long enough for an idea to form. She narrowed her eyes and regarded her mother sharply. "Would you happen to be knowing if Lord Clane will be in attendance, *Máthair*?"

"Of course he will. I heard . . . Now, Ailís . . ."

"You are at it again, the matchmaking!" Ailís darted a quick glance at the dressmaker, who had scuffled off in search of more pins, no doubt, with which to torture her. The woman did not appear to be listening, but Ailís lowered her voice nonetheless. Dublin was not London, to be sure, with London's gossip mill. Ailís knew it was not even close. In little Dublin, she thought grimly, gossip traveled twice as fast. "Is it Clane, Mama, or do you simply want me gone from the house?"

Three days. Three whole days and not a peep from the arrogant sod. She had a hefty piece of her mind to give him for his behavior in the sewing room, was more than half inclined to tell him she had no wish to see him again. But she couldn't very well do it, could she, if he refused to pay a visit.

Her mother wanted them matched. *Hah.* Her beloved if misguided parent, Ailís thought grimly, was in for something of a disappointment.

"Actually, dearest," Anne declared, straight-faced, "my one true, heartfelt hope, the one on which I base my very happiness and well-being, is that you shall remain forever unwed and *in* the house. Will that not be jolly? Me in my dotage, you there to fetch my embroidery silks and camphor wraps, and let me win at endless games of cassino. What more could a mother possibly desire?"

"You do not play cassino, *Máthair*."

"I will learn. As for the earl, I find him delightful. I expect I would find him a delightful son-in-law. I am certain I will like him just as well when he marries Maria Farnham, provided he leaves her at home when he comes to pay visits to Eamonn."

Ailís's smart reply was stalled by the dressmaker's reappearance. The woman did not need to hear her opinion on either Maria Farnham or the Earl of Clane.

"Maria Farnham," Mrs. Farrell announced tartly as she untangled herself from a length of wide, fluffy-looking white lace, her West County roots in grand evidence as the prim Dublin accents vanished, "is no better than she ought to be. Looked at this very fabric, she did, whispering all the while about wedding dresses."

"But she did not buy it?" Anne inquired with deceptive nonchalance.

"Nay. She took the white voile to be made into that dress. Not for a wedding, I'm thinking, but as the first step toward it."

The woman pointed to an open pattern book on a nearby table. Anne gave it a casual glance over her shoulder. Ailís nearly fell from the stool trying to get a good look.

The next moment, both were looking wide-eyed back to Mrs. Farrell. She nodded sagely. The dress made the one planned for Ailís resemble a nun's habit. One good breath, let alone a sweeping gesture, would have a good part of Maria Farnham displayed for all to see. And no doubt she would be breathing down Christor's neck at every opportunity.

"As good a way as any to snare a man, I suppose." Mrs. Farrell eyed the silk-draped Ailís cannily. "Of course, elegance works wonders, too. Perhaps a little tuck here . . ."

"And a bit more of a sweep in back," was Anne's quick addition.

"Ah, grand." The pins were back again. "The sleeves a bit farther out on the shoulder?" the dressmaker suggested. "I daresay he'd appreciate that."

"Of course. You'll wear my pearls, Ailís," Anne announced. "They are a lovely touch."

"Oh, she'll outshine them all!" Mrs. Farrell, clearly into the spirit of earl-enticing now, twitched a fold of fabric here, tugged there. "Now"—she waved the length of lace excitedly—"what shall we do with this?"

"Here." Ailís, who had remained silent through the little *pas-de-deux* the other ladies had danced, took the stuff from the woman's hand, deftly fashioned it into a makeshift noose, and dropped it over her own head. Holding the free end aloft, she demanded, "How is this?"

"Oh, Ailís," her mother moaned. Then, wearily, *"Tá uisce beatha uaim."*

Ailís had no idea where her mother was going to find that whiskey she so emphatically said she needed, but wished her the very best of luck nonetheless.

An hour later—laceless, fuller-trained, and smaller-sleeved dress expected within the sennight—they continued their shopping along Dame Street. Anne, without her whiskey, had recovered her calm and good spirits as quickly as she always did. In fact, she apparently felt strong enough to haul her disappointing daughter into several shops. Ailís, feeling slightly and uncomfortably guilty for her behavior at the dressmaker's, went along docilely. They inspected shoes, gloves, and perfume. "Turpentine as scent," Anne announced, "sadly went out of vogue with the Renaissance."

Ailís sniffed at her hands. She never noticed the smell any more and Eamonn had stopped teasing her for smelling like an apothecary's shop a good year ago. Not that she had ever paid him any mind. But now, nose to wrist, she had a flashing recollection of herself and Christor with his nose and her wrist in much the same position.

She and her mother quitted the shop ten minutes later, one bottle of subtle violet perfume tucked securely into Ailís's reticule.

She balked somewhat at the milliner's. She had several perfectly serviceable bonnets and even one fashionable military style hat, designed to resemble those worn by the beloved 88th Division Connaught Ranger corps with whom Eamonn and so many other Dublin lads had fought. She had bought it on a whim with the part of her meager first payment from London that she had not slipped silently into the family's "pin" money coffer. The hat only came out of its box late at night when she was alone in her chamber, a folly she could not bring herself to show anyone else.

Now, as her mother browsed happily through the straw and silk, she idly twirled a puce silk cap *à la russe* and waited. Her disinterest lasted only until Anne girlishly removed her own plain brown bonnet and lace cap and settled a massive, green yeoman's hat complete with sweeping yellow ostrich feather atop her dark curls. Surveying herself in the mirror, she laughed softly. "I look like a character from that wretched production of *Alcina* that Thaddeus praised so lavishly."

"The contralto was . . . er . . . well-favored."

"So she was." Anne studied her daughter's reflection critically in the glass. "You need . . ."

Moments later, Ailís was sporting a truly ridiculous, broad-brimmed confection of pink sarcenet, towering silver feathers, and a spray of silk bluebells added just for good measure. Her mother, with the cheerful participation of the shop assistant, was sorting among the bright, beaded Mary Stuart caps for a replacement for the abandoned yeoman's hat.

"I," Ailís announced in her best English drawing room tones, "am Lady Dandiprat, Patroness of Almack's, and scourge of all things unpretentious. That"—she pointed one finger imperiously at the pretty cap her mother was examining—"is altogether too unostentatious for my impeccable tastes. No voucher for you, madam!"

"Now where is sweet Emily Cowper when one needs her?"

Ailís slowly lowered her 'nose and her pointing finger and turned to face the door. With the warm little leap her pulse did at the sight of Christor lounging there, she only had a moment to be embarrassed that he had caught her at such dismal play-acting, and to recall how peeved she was with him in general.

"I was passing by and spied you through the window, Mrs. O'Neill. I hope I do not intrude."

"Lord Clane. What a pleasure to see you." Ever gracious, and unencumbered by gaudy headwear, Anne greeted him warmly. "Should I ever require a voucher to Almack's, may I count upon you to intervene with Lady Cowper?"

"Indeed, madam, it would be my pleasure." He had removed his own tall hat and, when he sketched a bow, Ailís noticed a curious whorl in the thick hair at his crown. Odd, she thought, that she hadn't noticed it before. Then she realized she had never seen the top of his head. For some reason, she felt the warm shivers again. When he turned to face her, grinning, she nearly grinned back. "That hat, Miss O'Neill, is a horror."

She shrugged as she hurriedly untied the ribbons. "I'll not be suggesting you wear it to your Almack's, then."

She watched, surprised, as he suddenly started toward her, narrow-eyed. She'd seen that look before, intent and predatory. Usually before he touched her. Her first thought was that this time her wrists reeked to high heaven from the different perfumes she had tried. Her second was that if he were thinking to grab her again, he could have chosen a thousand better places than a Dame Street shop with her mother standing not ten feet away.

But he did not actually touch her at all. Instead, he grasped her hat by the edge of the brim on either side and deftly plucked it from her head. "All you need, Ailís O'Neill," he said, setting the hat aside, "is a pearl or two at your ears and stars in your eyes."

Ailís couldn't help but catch her breath, then release it in a wistful, silent sigh.

"How lovely," was Anne's approving response. "How very gallant. And just right for your new dress."

"A new dress?" Christor had seen Ailís's eyes go soft at his words. This was a lady very much in need of some honest wooing. That charmed him. But he had also seen her mouth thin, and knew this was one weakness she would hate to have known, a need she could probably not acknowledge even to herself. Best, he thought, to turn her attention to something else. But what a pity . . ."Allow me to hazard a guess. Bright orange satin with shoes to match, for Mrs. Tomlinson's literary salon."

He was rewarded with a quick smile from Ailís as she shot back, "That would be bright *blue* satin with *stockings* to match, if you please, sir. One cannot spend an afternoon with *Childe Harold* in any other color."

"No, I suppose not. But isn't *Childe Harold's Pilgrimage* rather old news? Last year, and from what I've heard, Mrs. Tomlinson is a stickler for being *au courant*."

"Apparently *La Giaour* received a mild review from Edinburgh," Ailís replied, "and La Tomlinson allows only the foremost and finest to be read in her circle."

Amused by her contemptuous tone, desirous of learning anything about the sustenance she took for her sharp little mind, Christor queried, "And you? What do you say?"

"*Childe Harold* was splendid, Byron is quite probably brilliant, and *La Giaour* was a crashing bore."

"*Childe Harold* was overrated, Byron's best work comes when he is blind drunk and is altogether unfit for genteel eyes, and should I ever learn the correct pronunciation for *La Giaour,* I might actually read it."

This time, Ailís laughed aloud. For once, he thought, restraining himself from crowing in victory, he had made her laugh, and not at his expense. When she leaned forward, eyes starry, he felt his chest swell. Until she asked, "You know Byron? Truly? You've been in his company to hear him compose poetry?"

Damned if she wasn't melting over yet one more notorious man who was the *wrong* man. Christor ignored the fact that she had deflated his pride more efficiently than Sadler had ever released the air from his monstrous balloon. "I have heard him compose," he muttered, "but I would not call it poetry precisely, even if it does have rhyme and meter."

"Well, what is it, then?" she demanded.

"Songs to various parts of various women," he replied bluntly, "and the man cannot sing."

Neither had seen Ailís's mother making her stealthy way toward the door; both spun to face her at the sound of her not so delicately cleared throat. Christor winced, expecting her—quite rightly—to take him to task for crudeness.

She did not. "Do forgive my abrupt departure, my lord. I have promised to call on my sister and have just realized how terribly late I am. Are you coming, Ailís?" Scarcely giving Ailís time to respond, she nodded. "Very well, then. My lord, might I impose on you to escort Ailís home? I shall take a sedan chair to Great Denmark Street."

"I would be honored, madam." Christor turned to Ailís. "You do not attend your aunt?"

"I did not know we intended to," was her terse reply.

Already on her way out the door, Anne called back, "How quickly you forget things I say, dearest." Then, "Good day, Lord Clane." And she was gone.

"Well." Christor blinked, suddenly at a loss. "I suppose . . ."

"I suppose I ought to be going." Ailís dropped her head as she donned what was most certainly her own bonnet: straw with only the ribbon tie to decorate it.

He held the door open for her, did not move nearly as quickly as he might have when she brushed against his arm. In fact, he followed her a deliberate breath too soon, allowing himself the pleasure of feeling her soft form fully against him for a moment. When she reached the street, the sunlight reflected off her little spectacles, hiding her eyes.

"I . . . Good day, my lord."

"Good day? We are not parting, are we? I was under the impression that I was to walk you home."

This time, it was the brim of her bonnet that hid her expression as she studied one of her gloves with apparent interest. "You were thrust into that responsibility. I will certainly not hold you to it. I am more than capable of seeing myself home."

Christor sighed inwardly. He recalled such games as an adolescent when boys and girls were brought together at the occasional party and expected to behave like adults. He would suggest some activity, the girl would demur, leaving him with the burning question of whether she liked him but did not wish to be a trial, or whether she would far rather be walking, riding, whatever, with Jonathan Lyndhurst or William Wellesley.

It had been then and was now nearly enough to send him running to a monastery.

"It would be my pleasure to see you home," he said wearily, then bared his teeth in what was probably a very poor smile but might serve to show some of the enthusiasm he did feel.

"Oh, really. It isn't necessary . . ."

His patience snapped. Enough. "Ailís. Do you find the concept of my company unpleasant?"

"I . . ." There was a formidable pause. "Nay, I do not."

Christor hadn't realized he had been holding his breath until he released it in a quiet whoosh. "Good. Then, shall we be on our way?"

He offered his arm; she took it. And he nearly stumbled over his own feet with his first step. Damn but he never expected the force of that instant flare when she touched him.

Dame Street, wide and elegant, lined with Dublin's finest shops, was bustling with activity. Footmen and pages rushed by, laden with parcels to be hurried home. Gentlemen bent from the waist to peer into bootmakers' and haberdasheries, prevented from simply lowering their chins by absurdly high collars. Ladies, in pairs and gaggles, drifted by in their fashionably flimsy dresses and the heavier covering necessitated by the typical Irish summer weather.

The previous year had indeed brought a return of Society to Dublin, Christor mused. So many of the aristocrats and gentry had left after the Union with England, choosing London for the Season that Dublin no longer had since its Parliament had been dissolved. Now it appeared some of those same persons had come home, for the city's quiet elegance and far lower costs of living.

He had gone, too, to war. He had abandoned his home, his tenants, the very country he loved, to fight. He hadn't had a choice, really. Through his youth, he had seen the stone watch-towers rising along the coast, had watched gentry and farmer alike doing drills with whatever was to hand: muskets, sabers, pitchforks, all in case the Little Corsican should try to land on Ireland's shores.

He had been a good soldier and a good leader, he thought. He had certainly believed in the cause. What he had not been during those years was a good Irishman. He'd seen to it that his lands were tended, his tenants' needs addressed: the better sort of absentee landlord, certainly, but an absentee nonetheless. It had taken someone else shouldering the responsibilities of An Cú to bring him home again.

And at the moment he was heartily thanking the fellow, whoever he was, ineptitude and all. Had the impostor Hound not been so prolific—and so clumsy—Christor would not be here now, walking along a familiar Dublin street with a beautiful, feisty Irish girl on his arm.

A quick glance down revealed that Ailís's face, what he could see of it beneath the rim of her bonnet, was set in thoughtful lines. He couldn't resist saying, "Dreaming of your work, I assume."

She blinked, then shook her head, sending a dark curl sliding out from its restraints. He resisted the urge to tuck it back along her smooth cheek. "Nay. As a matter of fact I was thinking of heroes."

"Were you?" He had several rather ostentatious medals stowed away at home. He supposed he could easily dust them off and . . .

"I worry for An Cú and his men. Word has it watch patrols have been doubled. I don't think I could bear to see the Hound fall. It would break m—a great many hearts."

For once, Christor allowed himself to sigh aloud. "Do you think perhaps you are making an overly romantic figure of this fellow? He is a thief, after all."

It was a novel experience, indeed, debating against the figure he had created. When Ailís lifted her little chin and glared at him, snapping, "He is a friend to the poor and hence a friend to all who care for their fellow man!", he found himself wishing with all his heart that he had never taken that first midnight ride.

Feeling a familiar Gordian knot forming in his temples, he decided to let the matter drop. He wanted a nice walk with Ailís, and refused to let it be marred by argument. Her mention of An Cú had, as it happened, reminded him of just why he had been strolling down Dame Street in the first place. The sight through the shop window of mother and daughter playing with hats had so charmed him that he had forgotten his errand.

He remembered now, and had a new reason to complete the task. If he could persuade Ailís to accompany him to Westmoreland Street, he would have those extra minutes in her company. Perhaps by the end of them, he would have come up with a better plan than simply sticking to her like a limpet in the hope that she might come to desire him as he did her.

"Would you object terribly to a stroll up toward Carlisle Bridge? I know it is out of the way and you might have far better—"

"Aye. I'd like that."

Simple as that.

They walked in silence to the end of Dame Street, past the imposing stone front of Trinity College, then up Westmoreland Street. Edmund Ross's shop was perhaps not as large as many of its neighbors, but Christor knew that behind the glossily painted door was a haven of craftsmanship and elegance fit to rival any jeweler the isles had to offer.

Ailís eyed him suspiciously when he announced his intention to enter. "You'd not be buying today, would you?" she demanded.

"And if I were?"

"Then I'd be bidding you yet another good day and heading on my way."

"I am not buying." Christor smiled to himself as he escorted her inside. He had no idea what she had been suspecting— whether an inappropriate gift for herself, or perhaps one for another woman. The possibility that it was the latter, and that the concept might bother her a bit, cheered him. There was nothing like a twinge of jealousy, he believed, to accelerate an acquaintance.

Ross himself greeted them from behind the mahogany counter. Christor had always thought the man would look well in the robes of a university don. With his piercing blue eyes, wild brows, and seamed professorial face, he appeared for the lectern made.

But circumstance and talent had made the man a master jeweler. His heart had made him an invaluable asset to An Cú.

He was studying Ailís, who had been distracted by a case of small glittery objects, with ill-suppressed curiosity. He looked back to Christor, hoary brows first raised, then waggled in question. Christor had always believed in the adage that business and friendship ought to be kept separate; they had not in this case. He expected he would have to explain Ailís's presence to Ross another time. But it would have to be another time.

"Repair," he said brusquely, and handed over the pouch containing the dismembered pieces he had taken from Alderton.

The jeweler peered inside. "Of course, my lord." Then, "Will there be anything else? Perhaps the lady would like to see—"

"No," said Christor.

"Aye," said Ailís at the same moment. Ross strode across the rich carpet to where she stood. "This watch chain, is it your work?"

"It is." The jeweler proudly drew the thing from its velvet tray. "It is a unique design. You'll not find another anywhere."

Ailís drew one fingertip over the chain. "Lovely. And the fob. I'm not wrong, am I? It's Cuchulainn."

"Ah, you know of the Hound of Culann?"

Christor coughed loudly. The other two glanced at him briefly, then turned back to each other.

"It's a grand legend," Ailís murmured.

"With modern application, no less, my dear."

"You mean . . ."

Christor cleared his throat. He coughed again. And finally got Ailís's attention by taking a firm grip on her arm and steering her toward the door. "Good day, Ross," he said through clenched teeth.

"But I was—" Ailís protested.

"Off to visit Carlisle Bridge before I so rudely halted our walk."

"But Eamonn would so like—"

"Eamonn has a watch chain. We the officers of the 88th presented it to him not a year ago."

"Some men of fashion have been known to sport more than one," came the helpful suggestion from Ross. Christor merely glared at him and hustled Ailís back into the street.

She looked ready to give him a thorough tongue-lashing. He steeled himself and wondered if she could scold and walk at the same time. As it happened, whatever vitriol she might have been planning to loose on him never came.

Had Ailís been able to will the earth to open up and swallow her, she would gladly have done so in that instant. Ahead, approaching them at a brisk, henlike clip, was her Aunt Ursula.

And the woman at Ursula's side was not her mother. Ailís had known very well that Anne's sudden disappearance had nothing to do with a promised visit anywhere. She was simply mortified that Christor was about to learn it as well.

There was no way to avoid the encounter. Ursula had spied them and was approaching, her best friend and worst enemy Mrs. Harcourt in tow. "Well, hell," Ailís muttered.

"What was that?" Christor asked.

"Well, how lovely. Aunt Ursula. And Mrs. Harcourt, too. What a pleasure to meet you here." The words stuck like dry oats in her throat. "Are you acquainted with Lord Clane?"

Ursula, small and dark as her sister, but too pinched-looking for beauty, ignored her niece and announced, "I do not believe we have met, sir—"

"We have!" Mrs. Harcourt pushed in front of her companion with her formidable bulk, squeezed today into a dress of the signature purple she favored and which Ailís believed made her resemble an overgrown aubergine. "How delightful to meet again, Clane!"

It was clear to Ailís that Christor could not recall ever meeting the woman, an insult which would no doubt send Mrs. Harcourt to bed for a sennight and Ursula into alternating spasms of commiseration and glee. But neither woman seemed aware of the fact.

"How do you happen to know my niece?" Ursula demanded. "She is hardly—"

"You were with that nasty little Italian count, or so he claims to be, at the Fitzgerald fete. Blasto? Blister?"

"Conté Bellistono?" Christor supplied coolly. "My cousin Katherine's husband."

"Is he really?" Mrs. Harcourt pursed her lips. "Amazing the persons who descend upon Dublin these days. All foreigners, it seems."

The lady, if Ailís remembered correctly, had met her husband when his coach had broken down outside her father's colliery in Wales.

Ursula, in rare diplomatic form, turned the topic from descending foreigners. Badly. "Where is your mother, girl?" she demanded. Ailís flinched. "I have been awaiting a visit from her this past fortnight. Inconsiderate, I say, especially as I promised her the gray cloak I never wear. Moths, you know, but only at the hem."

"Well, she is so busy, ma'am. I am certain she meant to call—"

"Always gadding about, your mother," came Mrs. Harcourt's pronouncement, "seeing to matters meant to be left to the servants. Shameful." She shook her purple-turbaned head sadly, then, brightening, "Will I have the pleasure of seeing you at the Unsworth fete tomorrow eve, Lord Clane? Howth is such an ungodly trek from town, of course, but I could not possibly miss it. Why, every single invitation was accepted, and by only Dublin's finest citizens."

From Ursula's more-pinched-than-usual expression, Ailís assumed she had not been invited.

"Actually, madam," Christor replied, "I declined. But I wish you the enjoyment of the evening."

Mrs. Harbourt blinked, no doubt wondering if she had just been somehow insulted. Apparently deciding to the negative, she gushed, "What a shame you cannot attend. I daresay it will quite be the event of the summer. Ah, well . . ." She nodded toward Ross's shop. "As a matter of fact, I was just on my way to collect the Harcourt emeralds. That . . . person was cleaning them."

"Person?" Christor's voice was perfectly even—and slightly deadly. "Do you mean Mr. Ross, by chance?"

"Is that his name? No, it cannot be. I call him Mr. Gold. Are not all Jews Golds and Goldmans? I daresay they believe it lends them consequence. As long as he gave the proper attention to my emeralds—they belonged to my husband's mother, you know, quite priceless—I don't much care what he's called."

Clearly concerned with the fate of her precious emeralds now, she made her vague farewells and toddled off. Ursula was not quite so rude—to Christor, at least. "Good day, my lord. I do hope we meet again. Now, Ailís, you will come with me. I'm sure you haven't anything better to do, and you can make use of yourself by carrying my parcels."

Ailís promptly looked to Christor, expecting him to explain that Miss O'Neill certainly had something better to do. She was on her way to stand above the Liffey with him. But he was not even aware of her presence. Instead, he was staring after Mrs. Harcourt, eyes cold and considering.

"Come *along,* girl!" Ursula demanded. "I haven't all day to wait on you."

"My lord," Ailís began, waiting for Christor to turn, to look at her.

After a long moment, he did. "Hmm? Ah, yes, of course. Quite. Good day, madam. Miss O'Neill." Expressionless now, he tipped his hat, sketched a brief bow, and strode away down Westmoreland Street, leaving Ailís to blink at his departing back.

Chapter 9

Bored with pacing his library floor from door to window, Christor swiveled in the middle and changed his tack from fireplace to south wall. This altered the scenery somewhat, but only lasted until he did half of the first loop and was forced to maneuver around the desk. He checked the mantel clock. Ten past ten.

He spun at the sound of a scratch at the door. "Enter!" he snapped. It was bloody well about time. Séamus Cleary was ten minutes late.

Instead of the butler, it was Figgis who appeared in the doorway. "Begging your pardon, my lord, but you rushed out incompletely attired. I am very pleased to have caught you before you departed."

Christor gave himself a cursory chest-to-toe glance. Everything seemed to be there: waistcoat, coat, breeches, shoes. True, he had not waited for the valet to complete his fussing, but the clock had been approaching ten and he had not wanted to make Cleary wait.

"I see nothing amiss."

Figgis's nostrils flared. "Surely, my lord, you would not wish to appear at Daly's without this."

For an instant, Christor thought the man had gone around the bend and was imagining he held some item of clothing in his outstretched hand. Then he spied the emerald tie tack in the center of Figgis's palm and sighed. Even if he were going to Daly's club, he could easily have done so without risking the state of either his cravat or his status as a reasonably well-dressed man without a cravat pin.

Of course, he wasn't planning on going anywhere near Daly's. It had simply been convenient to pretend he was. "Thank you, Figgis," he said wearily, and reached for the pin.

The valet, however, true to form, would not be satisfied until he himself arranged the emerald.

"Much better, my lord, if you will allow me to say so."

"I am glad you approve."

He was done with the little conference. Figgis apparently was not. "I could not help but notice you chose the black cape, my lord."

"And?"

"And it is rather windy outside tonight, sir. As you are not attending the opera or such, but merely your club, perhaps it might be wise to substitute your greatcoat."

Christor closed his eyes for a moment, counted five. "Tell me something, Figgis, if you would."

"Of course, my lord."

"Do you have a hobby?"

The valet paused in the act of removing invisible lint from Christor's sleeve with his omnipresent brush. "A hobby, my lord?"

"Angling. Whist. Reading. Button-collecting, for God's sake."

"Of course I do not collect buttons, my lord. Or . . . angle. I could not possibly . . ."

"Learn," Christor suggested grimly. "Tonight."

The valet's eyes widened and his mouth opened and closed soundlessly, giving him the appearance of a sandy-headed carp. Finally, he managed, "Are you suggesting I am no longer able to perform my duties, my lord? That you wish to . . . *re-tire* me?"

"You make it sound like such a violent act, Figgis." Compassion overcame pique quickly, however, and Christor reassured the trembling manservant, "No, I do not intend to *retire* you. I simply thought you might occupy some time—"

"Oh, I couldn't possibly, my lord!" Figgis was back to work with his brush. "Not with all I have to do. But it is most generous of your lordship to suggest it."

"Think nothing of it," Christor muttered, and willed Cleary to get the bloody lead out of his boots.

*   *   *

Ailís yawned hugely, then again. It had been a trial, swallowing urge after urge for the past two hours, but she had been convinced that had she so much as allowed herself a tiny yawn, her aunt would have smacked her soundly with the massive fan she carried. Now that the lights from the Unsworth house were receding behind the carriage, she indulged herself freely.

Beside her, Aunt Ursula was nattering away with Mrs. Harcourt. Once the sting of having been one-upped had faded, that lady had graciously offered to transport the other two to the fete in her carriage. Ailís suspected she was still slightly miffed that Ursula had attended at all, but it had given her a companion in gossip during the course of the evening.

Ailís had given them both added enjoyment as the recipient, albeit unwilling, of their sage advice regarding her posture, her speech, and even her dress. Ironic, that, she thought, as she was wearing the ghastly pink dress that Ursula herself had chosen.

Ironic, too, though hardly out of character, had been her aunt's participation in the constant needling. A bit of gratitude would not have been amiss. It was Ailís, after all, who had given Ursula an entree into the Unsworths' hallowed halls. The invitation for herself, her mother, and Eamonn had arrived a fortnight earlier and, against her wishes, had been accepted. Anne had then had the very poor and unmotherly manners to catch a cold the day before. A note to Lady Unsworth, requesting that Ursula act as Ailís's chaperone in her stead had been answered with a gracious affirmative.

Ailís's insistence that she hardly needed a chaperone if Eamonn were to be there had fallen on deaf ears. But apparently Eamonn would not be attending. Their mother had either known or, with her familiar Gael instinct, guessed. Neither had bothered to pass the information on to Ailís. And of course her announcement that in that case she was not going either had been useless. How devastated Ursula would be, Anne said sadly, to be deprived of the opportunity to attend such an anticipated event.

As little loyalty as Ailís felt for her aunt, she felt an even greater dislike for Mrs. Harcourt. So go they would. Little had she known that spite would get her several interminable hours in the lady's carriage on top of her constant company at the interminably dull ball.

"I cannot help but think, Ailís," Mrs. Harcourt was saying now, "that you were unforgivably rude to Mr. Fitzjohn."

"Was I?" As far as she was concerned, she had tolerated Gerry's roving feet and blathering tongue with far more patience than usual. In fact, she had been desperate enough for respite from the old harridans' presence that she had danced with him twice. A banner evening for Gerry.

"He offered to escort you home, girl. Your refusal was terribly uncivil."

Ailís's refusal had been polite and necessary. She had been in a carriage with Gerry before. When seated, apparently, with his feet out of commission, he could not keep control of his hands.

"The boy seems to fancy you for some reason," came Ursula's contribution. "I daresay he could even be convinced to marry you. There is so little choice for an elegant young man here. You could be an Honorable, if you play your cards right."

Ailís rolled her eyes but held her tongue. Mrs. Harcourt had no such compunctions. "You are a perverse creature to turn up your nose at such a catch. You could not hope to do better. But then, I suppose you think you might have a chance with Clane."

"With Lord Clane?" Ursula demanded. In an instant, both women were squawking in delight at the very absurdity of the thought.

"Oh, wouldn't London Society just welcome that," Mrs. Harcourt gasped, wiping at her eyes. "The Earl of Clane suddenly appearing with an Irish Nobody in tow."

"A paint-smeared Nobody," Ursula added helpfully, "with a tendency to lapse into *Gaelic,* of all things."

"With mice in her pockets! Poor Clane would be laughed out of White's."

Ailís sighed. "Brooks's."

"What was that?"

"The club," she said wearily. "He would be laughed out of Brooks's, not White's. He does not frequent White's."

"Of course he frequents White's. All earls frequent White's when in London." Mrs. Harcourt gave Ailís a sympathetic smile, showing very pointy teeth. "Poor girl. Best snap up Gerry Fitzjohn and thank God each and every day for the honor."

Ailís had been too well beaten into bored submission that evening to argue. Instead, she rested her forehead against the window, blocked the sharp chattering from her ears, and stared into the night.

Why shouldn't she have the Earl of Clane if she wanted him? Of course she didn't want him, but there was nothing preventing the match. Her forebears might not be aristocratic, but judging from his tales, neither were all of his.

My mother's name was Maeve Katherine Ryan and she gave me my first bodhrán when I was three.

Maeve Katherine Ryan wasn't so very different from Ailís Mary O'Neill. And the Earls of Clane, according to the current edition, had a propensity for marrying Irish girls . . .

Ailís shook her head in disgust. As if she would accept Clane. Not if he were the last man on earth and could play a Kerry jig on four instruments at once. Of course, he could be so very charming when he wished. But then, he had shoved her into her aunt's company the day before without so much as a by-your-leave. Inconsiderate, arrogant clod. Ah, but those Irish blue eyes of his, that poet's mouth . . .

"Halt!"

Startled from her thoughts, jolted by the sudden stop of the carriage, Ailís blinked in disbelief at the moonlit sight outside the carriage. There were two horses in the road, one at the head of the team, the other near the driver. As she watched, jaw slowly going slack, the second slowly rode until he was next to the window. He was clothed in black from hat to boot, his face obscured by shadow . . . and a black mask.

An Cú.

She knew without a doubt. This was An Cú, out of her dreams, in the flesh. And he was about to rob the very carriage in which she sat.

It was easily the most thrilling moment of her life.

"Down with the window!" The voice was deep, rough, filled with the magic of the wild Wicklow hills. "Now, if you please."

"Don't do it," Mrs. Harcourt hissed. "He cannot reach us through the glass."

Ailís very nearly giggled. A man with a gun, just visible in his gloved hand, could do anything he pleased. Not that she would have defied him in any case. She stretched out a hand and deftly lowered the window.

"Oh, we are lost!" Ursula moaned, and promptly slid right off her seat and onto the floor.

The bandit did not so much as glance her way. His eyes, a flash of white behind the mask, were fixed on Mrs. Harcourt. "Remove your cloak," he commanded.

"My . . . my cloak?"

"Aye, and quick."

"Oh, God, he means to ravish me!" Mrs. Harcourt wailed to no one in particular.

Ailís might have been mistaken, but she thought she heard the man chuckle. Of course, it might merely have been the pounding of her own heart, loud enough to echo in her own ears. *Look at me,* she begged silently, willing him to even notice she was there. *Féach, mo Cú!*

He leaned forward in the saddle, rested his hand on the lowered window. Ailís was certain her heart was going to burst right through her chest. "I've not decided as yet about the ravishment, madam, but you'll be the first t'know. Now, off with the cloak."

"Do it!" came a frantic squeak from the lump on the floor. Apparently Ursula had not fainted at all. "For God's sake, Claudia, do it or he'll kill us all!"

Mrs. Harcourt undid the ties with trembling fingers, revealing a heavily powdered bosom. And her massive emerald necklace.

"Ah, grand. I'll be having the sparklers for a start."

For all her customary bluster, Mrs. Harcourt was a gibbering wreck now. There was a protest or two among the whimpering and absolutely no movement toward the emeralds.

"Now!" the Hound snapped.

One of Ursula's bony hands came up in a flash, grasping the chain and tugging. Mrs. Harcourt's own hands lifted to cover the piece and there was a brief, pitiful tussle before the clasp gave with a snap. Ursula, still huddled on the floor, thrust the necklace toward the window. It promptly vanished into a large, gloved fist.

"Now . . ." Ailís's pulse leapt as he leaned into the window for a few precious seconds, not two feet from her own flushed cheeks, and gave her a slightly hazy view of a square jaw and wide mouth. She silently cursed first Mrs. Harcourt for refusing to have the lamp lit and then herself for not having donned her spectacles the moment she climbed into the carriage. "The rest of the lot. You on the floor, too."

Mrs. Harcourt managed to hand over the bracelet and earrings without any assistance. In an instant, the topaz parure that Ursula was forever threatening to leave to Ailís should she behave as a dutiful niece ought, joined the Harcourt emeralds in the bandit's saddle bag. Ailís very nearly gave them a delighted wave farewell. Instead, she reached for her reticule. Enough was enough. She was not going to waste another thrilling moment without her spectacles.

The movement got the Hound's attention at last. He peered into her corner, eyes first on her hands. When he saw the reticule, he began, "You'll empty that . . ." and looked up. "Well, I'll be damned."

Ailís swallowed audibly, struggled to find her voice. He was so close, too shadowed for a decent view, but near enough to touch. All she had to do was reach through the open window. "I . . . I have little of value to give, but I'll give it gladly."

"For your life?" he demanded.

"For your work," she replied softly.

"I take it you know who I am, m'lady."

"Of course I know who you are, what you do. And I am no one's lady."

"Are you not?" He smiled faintly, or at least so Ailís thought. "You should be." Then, "Step out of the carriage."

"What?"

He slid from his mount and hauled the door open. "Step down. Now."

"Ailís, *no!*" Ursula gasped. But Ailís was already clambering from her seat, clumsy in her haste. She thought she felt a feeble push as she grasped the frame and wondered if Mrs. Harcourt had just employed a plump foot.

He was so tall, she thought breathlessly as she looked up into the man's masked face. With shoulders broad as the Liffey. And . . . dear God, he was reaching for her. The pistol had vanished and both of his huge hands were reaching for her.

They closed around her shoulders with enough force to make her gasp, yet gently enough that she felt only warm pressure. When his thumbs slid inward to hook in the edge of her worn cloak at her collarbone, she stopped breathing entirely.

He drew the fabric back, over her shoulders. The ghastly pink dress hardly counted as fashionable; the neckline was a good three inches higher than any others she had seen that night. Ailís gave a fleeting thought to the amount of pale skin she was not exposing to the Hound's eyes. Then she thought of the fully visible necklace she was wearing.

Her mother's pearls. For the first night in eons, she had removed her simple jade pendant and worn the pearls. They were the only piece of true value Anne possessed, and they were about to be lost.

All for a worthy cause, she tried to convince herself, knowing her mother would agree, and shakily reached up to undo the clasp.

His fingers were over hers in a second, sliding upward along her neck to meet at her nape. Ailís's hands went limp, along with much of the rest of her, dropping helplessly to her sides. She waited, silent and weak-kneed.

He did not remove the pearls. She felt his thumbs slide along her jaw this time. Gently, firmly, he tilted her face toward his, dark and still blurred at the edges by her unspectacled eyes.

"Will you have a bit of advice from the likes of me, my lady?"

Again with the address. But this time, Ailís thought she had heard an emphasis on the *my.* She swallowed audibly. "I will."

There was a nerve-wrackingly long moment before he said, "I'd see you out of this dress."

"Wh-what?"

"Aye. Out of it entirely." Only the quick drop of his hands back to her shoulders kept her from sliding into a jellied heap at his boots. "Pink doesn't suit you. When next we meet I'd have you in silver, *cailín,* like the moonlight."

"Oh," Ailís whispered. "*Ó Naomh . . .*"

He chuckled, drew her up until she stood on her toes. "And what saint would you be calling there, my lady? Let's choose one together, shall we? St. Augustine? Grant us chastity, but not yet . . ."

Ailís heard the hoofbeats ahead on the road, echoing the pattern of her heart, growing louder.

"Patrols!" the Hound's companion shouted from his place at the front of the team. "In force, too."

The bandit's gaze slewed from Ailís to the road ahead and back again. "Go," Ailís urged him, some sense returning to her head. She pushed at his chest, tensed and granite-hard beneath her palms, to shove him away.

"Dammit, man, now!" the second bandit snapped.

Instead of feeling An Cú move, Ailís suddenly found herself flat up against his chest. "Help yourself to your saints," he muttered. "I'd sooner have you."

His mouth covered hers. Hard, hot, demanding, and gone before she could gather her thoughts around the incredible sensation. Then his hands were gone, too, and she staggered, almost going down onto her bottom.

"*Déan deifir!*" His companion was almost bellowing now. "Move your bloody legs!"

The Hound swung onto his horse in a flare of black cloak and hauled the beast into a tight circle. For a moment, he gazed down at Ailís from that height. Then, with a curse, he bent low along the horse's side, wrapped Ailís in an iron arm and lifted her completely from the ground. "Ah, the hell with it."

This time, the kiss lasted just long enough for Ailís to revel in it, and to kiss him back. She threw her arms around his neck, making him grunt and sway dangerously toward the ground. Still his grasp did not falter, nor did his lips leave hers for an instant. They slanted again and yet again, finally coaxing hers to part. In that moment, when his tongue tangled hotly with hers, Ailís felt the lightning strike, felt the sizzle all the way to her toes.

When he let her go this time, releasing her and righting himself in the saddle in one fluid motion, her knees failed her. Her posterior hit the earth with a solid thump. Not that she minded, or even really noticed. Her full attention was on An Cú. His teeth glinted in the dark, a flashing grin she could have seen in utter blackness, spectacles or no. Then he lifted his hand in a sharp salute.

" 'Tis a fair mouth you've got on you, *cailín*. I'll be having my share of it again, I know."

Then he was gone, thundering off into the night, his comrade not a beat behind. Mere seconds later, a uniformed quartet hauled their mounts to a skidding halt beside the carriage. One jumped down and grasped Ailís's arm.

"Are you hurt, miss?" He pulled her to her feet, not waiting for an answer before demanding, "Was it the Hound?"

Slightly more clear-headed than moments earlier, Ailís answered as slowly as she could. "I am fine, thank you. I do not know, not really, who . . . what . . ."

"Of course it was the Hound, you idiot!" Mrs. Harcourt bellowed through the carriage window. "He stole my emeralds—"

"And my topazes," came a plaintive squeak.

"Oh, do hush, Ursula! No one cares a whit for your baubles. But my emeralds . . . He stole the Harcourt emeralds, the knave. Now"—Mrs. Harcourt's emerald-less arm shot through the window, finger pointing up the road—"go retrieve my jewels!"

Ailís doubted the men were thinking of the lady's jewels as they galloped after the bandits. Nay, they'd be thinking of bringing down An Cú, of the handsome reward they'd collect once he'd been sent swinging from the gibbet. Her heart thudded painfully and she offered a fervent prayer to Bríd, Patrick, and Augustine himself to see the Hound safely away.

"Get in the carriage, girl!" Mrs. Harcourt snapped. With nothing to do but obey, Ailís did, settling herself once again next to her aunt, who had either recovered enough to retake her seat, or had been hauled up. "Did that creature hurt you?"

Surprised that the woman would even ask, Ailís replied, "Nay, not in the l—"

"Might have been better if he had. There's naught like an injured maiden to spur the troops into action."

"I assure you, madam," Ailís muttered through clenched teeth, "I am quite well."

"More's the pity." Mrs. Harcourt rapped against the roof trap. "Drive on!"

As they rolled toward town, Mrs. Harcourt's outraged hissings melding with the sound of the wheels, Ailís kept her face pressed to the window. At each turn in the road she half expected to see the patrol halted, to see a long, black-clothed form stretched over the earth. But her heart told her the Hound could outrun the best His Majesty and Dublin could offer. And, as the lights of the city finally appeared, with no sign of either the bandits or their pursuers, she believed he had.

Christor listened intently for one more full minute. "I'd say it's safe."

"About time, too." Nearby, Séamus shifted carefully and grunted. "We could have been on our way a good half-hour past, after they went by."

"And taken the chance that they might double back? I think not. Stop grumbling. We've only a mile to walk."

"Easy enough for you to say," Cleary retorted. "You had the wider branch. I haven't felt my arse for the past quarter hour."

As they slowly extricated themselves from the higher reaches of the roadside oak, Christor privately sympathized with the younger man. If the branch on which he had been perched had been any wider, it wasn't by much. He wasn't feeling much in his rump, either.

"And you owe me a new horse," Cleary continued as they reached the ground. "I'd only had that one three days."

"You know that was the plan," Christor said wearily, "why we've switched mounts. They won't be recognized and won't find their own way back to the stable."

"Aye, I remember, but I thought you were daft at the time." Séamus rubbed intently at his stiff muscles. "I still think you're daft, letting loose two perfectly good beasts and with the saddles still on them, no less. We could have outrun those muggins in a blink."

"Perhaps." Christor was in too placid a mood to argue. Horses and saddles were easily enough replaced. With luck, the two they'd lost would find their way to a deserving home. The jewels were safe in his pocket, the night was mild and prime for walking, and he'd kissed Ailís O'Neill.

He hadn't meant to do it, of course. Even now, as he contemplated the muddle he'd no doubt caused by allowing An Cú to do the kissing rather than himself . . . as himself, he cursed the timing. But he had no regrets. He'd kissed Ailís O'Neill and now he had her well in his blood. There would be plenty more meetings of their lips ahead.

He had been genuinely surprised to see her. She had made no mention of attending the Unsworth party. The Harcourt woman had. And she had insulted Ailís, his cousin's Italian husband, and Edmund Ross in nearly the same breath. He'd already planned to be on the Howth road that night, watching for An Cú the Wrong. The prospect of depriving Mrs. Harcourt of the precious emeralds Ross had so carefully cleaned had been an added bonus.

As it turned out, An Cú the Wrong had not made an appearance. Harcourt's carriage—easily identified by Cleary, who had snuck in to have a look at it the night before—had. And Ailís, for whatever reason, had been inside it.

He really had not meant to kiss her. He probably should not have done it, most certainly not *twice*. But she had looked so damned bewitching, there in the corner of the carriage with her eyes bright, then again in the moonlight with her eyes aglow.

It would have taken a far stronger man than Christor ever professed to be to have resisted her. Not when she had faced him bravely, proudly acknowledged his cause, and then been fully prepared to give him her pearls.

That simple act, reaching up to undo the clasp for him, had been his undoing. He had seen the pearls on Anne O'Neill enough times to know they were her only good piece. He knew, too, that their loss would have been mourned, even as both O'Neill women would have gladly contributed them to a cause such as An Cú's.

He had taken a different prize, and if it didn't do much of anything for the country's poor, it had certainly done amazing things to him. Things he would remember, dream of, and struggle not to repeat the very next time he saw Ailís in public.

"Clane. For God's sake, man!"

He blinked. "Hmm?"

Cleary shook his head, then gave a low chuckle. "I've been talking to you for a full minute. Now I know where your mind was. I daresay I'd be deaf to the world, too, had I been locking lips with Ailís O'Neill." At Christor's responding growl, the younger man raised his hands in mock defense. "Not as you're thinking, man."

"No?"

"Nay. She'd have boxed my ears smartly had I ever tried. And I haven't," Cleary added solemnly. "Many's the man who has and has gone away with his ears ringing."

The knowledge that Ailís did not welcome kisses from other quarters pleased Christor mightily. Then he remembered that the man whose kisses she had accepted and returned had not been he—not precisely, anyway—and he cursed under his breath. Ailís had taken a kiss, then another from the Hound. Should the Earl of Clane try to repeat the experience, he might very well find himself with boxed ears.

"Now, if you're thinking to have another go at her . . ." Cleary's voice took on a stern tone, "I'll tell you now you'd best be serious about it. We're all mightily fond of our Ailís here in Dublin, and won't tolerate a fellow charging and stealing kisses without marriage on his mind."

Christor did not know whether to be amused or annoyed by the young man's interference. He opted for a tired sigh. "Lower your hackles, Séamus. I would say the chances of my stealing anything at all from Ailís O'Neill are about equal to La Harcourt getting her jewels back."

He recalled his words with ironic detachment as, half a mile from home, he and Cleary were forced to spend another dismal hour up a chestnut tree while a squadron of the Lord-Lieutenant's soldiers scoured the acres around them. Fame, Christor decided as the incompetent troops plodded in blind circles below, was a damned nuisance.

Chapter 10

Fame, Ailís decided, was a brightly wrapped gift from the devil. Less than a full day after her encounter with An Cú, the news had spread through Dublin. The speed with which word traveled did not surprise her, although she did wonder if either Aunt Ursula or Mrs. Harcourt had slept a wink the night before. What baffled her was the sheer number of people who had flocked to the house.

Never in memory had Fitzwilliam Lane seen such traffic. Carriages vied for space, a contest made nearly comical by the fact that there was no outlet at the end of the little street. Had Ailís not felt rather sorry for her neighbors and even more sorry for herself, she would have been amused by the sight of Lady Carricknock's drivers and grooms haplessly trying to back up the elaborate, crested town coach through the hordes trying to move forward.

The admiring, the disbelieving, the luridly curious, and the simply bored were filling the O'Neill house. Anne, ordinarily delighted to have visitors at any hour, had lost much of her good hostess's cheer upon being forced to send Fergus out for more refreshments before the clock had even struck noon. Dublin, once famous for its epicurean excesses, seemed to have regained its taste for large amounts of drink and small cakelike objects overnight.

"Again?" Sweeney demanded when the maid deposited yet another empty tray on the kitchen table. Ailís, having fled the parlor for a desperately needed reprieve, shrugged sympathetically. "What've you got in there, Miss? Ravening wolves?"

"Very nearly." Ailís ticked the current visitors off on her fingers. "Mrs. Farnham and Maria Farnham, Lady Alderton, the Miss Butlers, and Philly Lorcan and Gerry Fitzjohn, who have both been here almost since daybreak and have consumed a week's worth of pastry."

"What on earth do they want?"

"Details," Ailís replied wearily, refraining from mentioning that both Sweeney and Fergus had mercilessly badgered her for the same the night before. "And to gawk at the girl who was pawed by the Dread Hound."

"Ah, but he didn't paw you now, did he?"

Ailís had left out as much of the pawing bit as she could. Aunt Ursula had seen almost nothing from her seat on the carriage floor, Mrs. Harcourt had apparently been too distressed over the loss of her jewels to notice that Ailís had been kissing the bandit—twice—with utter gusto. Ailís, in telling and retelling the tale, had mentioned facing the Hound outside the carriage, had mentioned that he had briefly had his hands on her shoulders. She had kept the fact that she had pawed quite happily at the man to herself.

And each time she silently recalled those moments, little sparks shot through her from head to toe. The memory was delicious; the sensations indescribable.

"Nay, Sweeney, he did not paw me." Knowing the cook wanted to hear the right words yet again, Ailís repeated, "He was a perfect gentleman."

No doubt few would classify a thief as a perfect gentleman in any case, but this noble bandit had been just that. He had been terse but not cruel, fearsome but not threatening. He had never raised his gun above the edge of the window. Ailís was having a very hard time indeed reconciling her experience with that of others who had been stopped by the Hound. He had not shot out any part of *her* carriage and, to the best of her knowledge, he had not kissed any of *them*.

He had kissed her. Twice. He had thrilled and melted and charmed her. Her. And he had implied he would do it again.

How? she wondered eagerly. *Where?* And most importantly, *When?*

"Here, now." She was dragged back into the unromantic reality of the kitchen when Sweeney shoved a newly filled cake tray into her hands. "Kitty's busy enough as it is. Take this in to your wolves."

It was, Ailís knew, the least she could do considering the fact that the overabundance of visitors was her fault, so to speak. Her steps dragged somewhat as she headed back to the parlor. One more hour of enduring the gawking, of answering the endless and imbecilic questions—altered and repeated when she did not give the desired response—was one more than she thought she could bear.

"Ah, there she is!" Lady Alderton, a shrill scarecrow in blinding chartreuse, peered at Ailís through her lorgnette. "Now, you were most unclear before you scurried off, Miss O'Neill. You say the man threatened to strike you rather than shoot you?"

Ailís caught her mother's sympathetic smile as she deposited the tray on a side table. Gerry was there in a second, ears flopping, to refill his plate. She resisted the urge to swat at his hand with a rolled-up *Journal.*

"Nay, madam. I said he did not threaten me—us—at all."

"Well, he most certainly threatened me! Thrust his bayonet right beneath my nose. You must have swooned and been unconscious through the worst of it."

"I did not swoon."

"Struck your head, then."

"I assure you, Lady Alderton, I did not. I was quite lucid during the entire encounter." *Except, perhaps,* Ailís amended silently, *when he was kissing me witless.* "Nor did I so much as spy any bayonet."

"Hmph." Temporarily routed, Lady Alderton lapsed into a miffed silence.

"Did he stink like the devil?" Philly demanded, grinning. "Old Carricknock insists he reeked like a cesspit."

The Marquess of Carricknock was known to compensate for his own infrequency of bathing by liberally applying cologne. He was also known for his appreciation of port. Lots of it.

"He smelled of leather and horse," Ailís replied, stopping herself before elaborating on just how nice that combination of scents had been on this man. "Nothing excessive and certainly nothing in the least foul."

"Tell me, dear"—the elder of the Miss Butlers, aged spinsters with little money, impeccable breeding, and a generally

disregarded abundance of charm, leaned forward in her seat—
"did he look as one might imagine Robin Hood would?"

Philly guffawed, Lady Alderton snorted, and Maria Farnham took on the appearance of a cranky mole suddenly caught
in bright light. Miss Butler, clearly stung, began to shrink back
in her seat. Ailís promptly dropped to her knees by the
woman's chair and gently grasped one frail hand.

"He was Robin Hood, Cúchulainn, and Lancelot in one,
Miss Dorothy. Eyes bright and sharp enough to rival a *Fian*
sword and a jaw like the cliffs of County Clare."

"Oh." The older woman's faded blue eyes glowed. "Oh,
Ailís."

"A queue?" the second Miss Butler queried. "Did he have a
queue? And lace at his throat?"

Ailís knew the lady was imaging the gentlemen of her
youth, when she was young and pretty and they would come to
call on her and her sister. Before the Butler money ran out,
leaving the sisters with each other, their slowly crumbling
house in Merrion Square, and their memories.

"I saw no queue, Miss Imelda, but there might have been
one, black as night. And 'twas but a simple cravat, pure white,
but I believe I might have seen the glint of a diamond in it."

As the elderly pair giggled and sighed, imagining a man
who walked in their dreams, Ailís found herself thinking hard
on just what she had seen. True, she had not been wearing her
spectacles, but she did recall a glint within the folds of the
Hound's neck cloth, the feel of a stone against her own breast
when he had held her.

A trinket he had stolen? That did not fit, somehow. From
what she knew of An Cú, he kept none of his spoils. Pounds to
pence, they went into other people's pockets, their paddocks.
Ailís sat back on her heels. Could it be that the Hound was a
gentleman? Perhaps even someone she knew, someone who attended the same parties, had perhaps partnered her at
dinner . . .

"You make the fellow sound positively dashing, Miss
O'Neill," Gerry Fitzjohn announced jovially, startling her,
startling the dreamy Miss Imelda into bobbling her china cup

and saucer. "Why, one would think him a splendid fellow indeed."

Ailís blinked. She tried to imagine him, to imagine floppy, puppylike Gerry in cape and mask. Gerry with his beloved dogs . . . The Hound? Nay, she thought, it couldn't be. It was simply beyond even her imagination.

"Puts us ordinary, law-abiding fellows quite to shame," was Philly's contribution. "Why, if half of Dublin spoke of him half as well as Miss O'Neill here, we would all be donning masks and traipsing through the dark in search of carriages with ladies in them to stop."

Philly was even more of a stretch than Gerry. But he had always loved a drama, had been devastated when his doting Mama's abrupt turn into noteworthy if short-lived ill health had prevented him from enlisting with the 88th. As if the corps would have had him. And both he and Gerry had departed the Unsworth ball before her, had quitted her mother's party early on the same night that the Aldertons had been stopped on the Kingstown Road. . . .

Impossible as it was, as firmly as Ailís felt against the possibility that she had been kissed by either man, she still had the urge to rush upstairs and rinse out her mouth.

"One would almost think Miss O'Neill has some intimate knowledge of the beast."

All eyes swung to Maria Farnham. She batted golden lashes, smiled prettily, and took a large bite from a gooseberry tart. Anne snorted; the Misses Butlers shook their mobcapped heads in disapproving unison. Everyone else in the room turned back to Ailís, six pairs of fascinated eyes above six twitching noses.

"Oh, aye," she snapped. "Over a tea he'd laid out atop his saddle, we discussed the weather, the current value of topaz, and his sad childhood in the mean Wicklow hills. Then we took a stroll in the woods, hand in—"

"Why, Lord Clane!" Anne clapped her hands in loud delight and sprang to her feet, making Philly and Gerry fumble to set aside their plates and rise, putting a quick end to Ailís's outburst. "What a pleasure to see you."

The earl, in what seemed his favored mode of appearing in a room, had propped one shoulder against the doorframe. He straightened now. "I beg your pardon for simply walking in, Mrs. O'Neill, but the front door was open and your staff obviously occupied."

Fergus staggered into view, hair and eyes wild, a lemon sticking out of one pocket and a layer of flour dusting his coat. Anne shook her head with a smile and gently waved him off. "Consider our door always open to you, my lord."

She gestured him toward the room's only empty chair: a singularly ugly and uncomfortable creation of hard walnut and minimal green-and-brown embroidered upholstery. He waited until she had taken her own seat before gingerly lowering himself into his. Ailís thought she saw him wince and understood. Throughout childhood, that was the chair in which she and Eamonn had been placed when they misbehaved. What little stuffing the thing had ever possessed had long since been plucked out through an invisible hole by their bored fingers.

"Tea, my lord?" Anne inquired, casting a distressed glance at the once-again empty cake plate.

"Thank you, madam, no." Clane offered the room a thin smile. "Now, it appears I have intruded upon an interesting discussion."

"Miss O'Neill was just describing her midnight meeting with the Hound," Maria announced smugly.

If she expected the earl to look scandalized, she was bound for disappointment. He turned to Ailís, who was still seated awkwardly on the floor next to Miss Butler's chair. This time, his smile was slow and easy, displaying the deep crease beside his mouth and causing Ailís's heart to do a sudden little thump.

"I have heard you had an encounter with An Cú, Miss O'Neill. Was it very thrilling?"

He understood. Ailís knew, somehow, that he was not mocking her with the question. Confused, she merely blinked at him. Then, opting for uncharacteristic restraint, she thought carefully for a moment before replying, "It was certainly unlike anything else I have experienced, my lord."

"Is that so? How . . . intriguing." *Unlike anything else I have experienced.* Christor very much liked the sound of that.

He had no idea why he was so obsessed with the concept of Ailís being inexperienced in the marvelous world of kisses, but there it was. "Actually, Miss O'Neill, I arrived hoping you might honor me with your company on a stroll in Stephen's Green and tell me all about your evening."

He saw her lovely eyes go sharp behind the glass of her spectacles, saw her glance quickly around the room. "I . . . thank you, my lord, but as you can see, we have guests. I could not be so rude . . ."

"Of course you could." She wanted to come, he knew, reading the desperation in her voice easily. Yes, he was beginning to understand Ailís quite well. Now it was time for him to behave as Society oftimes expected of its aristocracy: with assurance, arrogance, and basic disregard for its own manners. He was positive none of the other guests would gainsay him. "I am certain your mother will be more than happy to entertain *her* guests without your presence."

Mrs. O'Neill, splendid woman that she was, stifled a smile before responding, "To be sure. You have entertained us quite long enough, my dear. Go."

And she did. In less than two minutes, Ailís was bonneted, spencered, and skipping ahead of him out the door. She took his arm almost before he'd offered it, and guided him toward Merrion Street, toward the Green. He gently turned her in the opposite direction.

She gave him a familiar, suspicious look. "I know better than to think you have mistaken the location of Stephen's Green."

"Wise girl. No, I thought we might have our stroll to Carlisle Bridge, to replace the one I so abruptly and rudely aborted at our last meeting."

He would never know if she had planned to snipe at him about that lapse. She merely nodded and matched his pace. Then she startled him by saying, "Thank you."

"For . . . ?"

"For the rescue. It was very gallant and very much appreciated."

This was *not* a familiar Ailís. Christor stared down at what he could see of her face and was reminded of just why he disliked women's hats so much. They hid most of the interesting bits and tended to display any number of useless feathery objects and fake flowers. To be fair, Ailís's bonnet was a simple affair of straw and ribbon, but it covered altogether too much of a face into which he very much enjoyed gazing.

He contemplated a polite response and immediately decided upon candor. "Maria Farnham is a harpy."

"And I am a shrew. What little good you have seen of the Dublin lady, my lord. We must all seem dismal creatures."

"Ah, Ailís. When I invoked the shrew, I did not mean—"

He was further startled to hear her laugh. "You mistake me. I'm not taking you to task, though perhaps I should."

"What is this, Ailís?" he demanded, pulling her to a halt. He never cared for being off balance and, considering it was his customary state around this woman, doubly disliked the added disequilibrium. "Why do I have the feeling a custard is going to come flying out of the sky and into my face?"

"I have no idea. Do you often contemplate imaginary flying sweets?"

"Ailís."

"Oh, very well. But let's walk, please. I wish to put as much distance as possible between myself and the home I once loved." As they continued along Merrion Square, she explained, "I find myself feeling inclined to be more pleasant, my lord. I am tired of sniping at you."

"Ah. Because you have discovered I am not such a bad fellow?"

"Because I have discovered more pleasure in my acquaintance with other persons in general. Anyway, don't you be needling at me, or I might revert to form."

"Fair enough." For all his equable response, Christor was silently cursing. Other persons, no doubt, meant the blasted An Cú, whose pleasurable performance had made Ailís feel mellower toward the lesser creatures of her sphere. As a lesser creature, the Earl of Clane felt something less than grateful. "So, tell me of your encounter with the notorious Hound."

She hummed thoughtfully for a moment. Then, "It was very brief with very little said, as it happens."

"Sources say otherwise."

"Oh, what nonsense!" She blew out an exasperated breath, sending one dark curl briefly into view beyond the brim of her bonnet. "By this afternoon the tale will involve a horde of dancing bandits, a king's ransom in jewels, and a soliloquy *à la* Richard Brinsley Sheridan from the Hound's lips. By tomorrow it will all be forgotten."

"Forgotten? By a few perhaps. But by you . . . ?" He wasn't certain what he wanted her to say, but he soon discovered that her words were far less important than her tone.

"Nay," she said softly, a wealth of emotion in each following syllable, "I'll not be forgetting a bit of it, ever."

Specially tailored hairshirts had never been his chosen style, nor did they go well with chest-thumping. Reminding himself of that, Christor quashed the urge to ask more questions, to coax her into sharing just what she had felt in the presence of An Cú. It would be far easier and less headache-inducing to simply try to enjoy a nice stroll.

And it might have worked out just splendidly had he chosen the road to the north of the College rather than the south.

A sizeable crowd was gathered on College Green, more arriving as Christor and Ailís approached. The steps of the Bank of Ireland building, once the hallowed seat of Parliament, were crowded; streams of young men jostled their way through Trinity's portals. Several aged dons, black-garbed and flapping like distressed crows, were shouting useless commands to disperse. A few stiff-necked, pinch-lipped gentlemen, bank lackeys no doubt, added their ineffective tongue clucking and shooing. For the most part, the rest of the multitude was laughing, some even singing, buoyed with bonhomie, whiskey, or the view.

It was not uncommon to see a crowd gathered around the statue of King William, or "King Billy" as he was better known. Pompous and overblown, the mounted figure was the recipient of endless pranks. It had been painted, coated in egg, and even dressed in facsimiles of women's clothing on more than one occasion.

Antics surrounding King Billy had sent countless college and government officials into fits of apoplexy and entertained generations of Trinity lads and passing Dubliners. Christor himself had once anointed the statue with the results of too much cheap whiskey. He had been terribly proud of himself at the time and was benevolently amused by the incident now. Stopping to have a peek at the latest decoration seemed a harmless enough thing to do.

He really should have known better.

Tucking a willing Ailís behind him for safety, he pushed his way through the throng. He felt the first twinge of unease at a brief glimpse of black cloth. The sensation rose as they got closer to the statue.

"What is it?" Ailís demanded. Christor felt her bouncing up and down against him, clearly trying to get a look over his shoulder. "What have they done this time?"

He debated turning on his heel and hustling her out of the area before she saw anything. That, he knew, would be an act of futility. Assuming the decorating had been done in the early hours of morning, the story would be all over Town by now. He had no idea why it had not reached the O'Neill household. It would.

Sighing, muttering under his breath, he slipped an arm around Ailís and moved her to stand in front of him, her delightfully soft posterior nestled against decidedly harder parts of his own anatomy. Then, against better judgment, he grasped her by the waist and lifted her until she could see above the crowd. In other circumstances, he never would have done so— or at least not in public and never unless she were facing him. But he was convinced that Dublin had gone generally mad as it was. A cross-eyed earl hefting a respectable young lady around College Green would not cause a single batted eye. And it did not.

"Oh." Above him, Ailís threw back her head and laughed. "Oh, how marvelous! Get closer."

Christor was doing no such thing. Ignoring Ailís's protest, he turned with her still aloft and pushed his way to a clear spot near the bank. Then, slowly, he turned her and lowered her until they were eye to eye.

"Clane, really. I do not understand why you would not . . ." Something she saw in his eyes widened hers. "I . . . perhaps you ought to put me down. I am not the lightest . . ."

He held her there, her mouth, that soft mouth that had tasted of blackberries and champagne the night before, mere inches from his. "You might be surprised by how long I could hold you, Ailís."

Then he set her on her feet.

The small sound of disappointment escaped her throat before she could stop it. Ailís scanned his stunning face, searching for any sign of . . . something, of an emotion she could read. All she saw was vague annoyance as Christor gazed off toward hapless King Billy.

For that moment, she was not interested in the unmistakable costume of black cloak, hat, and mask someone had fashioned for the statue. She did not have a heart-thumping recollection of the night before. Instead, she stood, waist tingling where this man had held her, and wondered at the simple fact that he had done so. He had lifted her as if she weighed nothing, held her aloft, then with what was almost certainly a clever play of words, implied . . .

"Well, I'll be damned. Two of my favorite persons in all the Isles and beyond."

Blinking, trying to clear the tumbled thoughts from her head, Ailís turned to face her brother. He looked hale and handsome as ever, and was sporting a grin which, as it always did, brought an answering smile to her lips. "Unless you've been maintaining a correspondence with some fair creature on the Peninsula," she teased, "you know no one beyond the Isles."

"A piddling matter of semantics, *mo cál bheag*," Eamonn retorted. "Credit me with the sentiment."

"Sentiment, indeed." Ailís had never much cared for his calling her a little cabbage, an affectation he had picked up at school from some silly French novel. It sounded worse in Gaelic. She poked him in the middle of his silk waistcoat. "Where have you been, you great turnip? I've seen neither hide nor tail of you in aeons."

"She exaggerates," Eamonn explained affably to Clane, who had stopped scowling at King Billy the Hound to greet him. "A terrible flaw, but one we've managed to keep hidden till now. I saw you but last night, Ailís."

"Aye, through the eyes in the back of your head as you skulked out of the house. I was forced to spend the evening with Aunt Ursula and Mrs. Harcourt and ended up in the midst of a highway robbery."

"So Mother said." Eamonn chucked her under the chin. "Met your Hound, did you? I suppose I must be the good brother and ask if I ought to call him out."

"Aye, sure and I'd let you even if there were a reason, which there is not. With your aim, you'd be lucky to fire close enough for him to even *hear* the shot." She did not mention his leg; she would never be so cruel, but she did glance down to see if he were leaning heavily on his cane or if it were one of his blessedly pain-free days.

"You must be a favored son, Clane," Eamonn was saying, "for God to have spared you sisters."

"Sometimes I wonder."

"Ah, Éamonnán." Ailís tapped again at his chest.

"Hmm?"

"Where did you get the new stick?"

"Hmm?" he repeated, glancing down. Gone was the sturdy ash, replaced by glossy ebony, gold-topped and obviously expensive. "Oh, merely a gift. Now, Clane, where were the two of you off to?"

"He was helping me to run away from home. Eamonn—"

"Pity, that, as I've got to take you right back. Uncle Taddy is expecting one of us to accompany him to the afternoon concert at the Park, and as I cannot go, you'll have to." With that, he looped his free arm through hers and steered her in exactly the direction from which she'd fled. "Are you coming, Clane? Hurry up, man. Move your feet, if you please."

"I . . . ah . . ." Christor gazed at them thoughtfully for a moment. "No. I think perhaps I'll give you two time alone. Miss O'Neill." He bowed, his eyes not leaving Ailís's. "We shall reach our goal eventually. Soon, I hope. O'Neill." He saluted smartly, then stepped back into the crowd.

Torn between gratitude that he would give her time with her brother, and pique that yet one more of their walks had ended so abruptly, Ailís watched him go. In fact, she might have stared after him indefinitely had not Eamonn tugged her into motion.

"And home we go."

"Oh, Eamonn, must we? There has been a crowd in our parlor since morning and I cannot bear it."

He gave her a lopsided grin. "Fame," he announced, "is the very devil. But then, infamy is worse. Don't fret. We'll sneak in through the back."

As they made their way toward home, Ailís refrained from asking again about the new stick, no matter how badly she wished to know. She did, however, demand, "Where have you been of a night? I was beginning to think you had taken up with a theater troupe."

"Business, *cailín,* and sport. Nothing you would not find boring and silly to discuss. Now Mother said you've been wishing to speak to me . . ."

Deciding to take advantage of what she could, Ailís managed to get out the story of Séamus Cleary and the ear bob that had so distressed his grandmother. Eamonn listened patiently, only smiling at the mention of the thing's size. "Sounds like Billy's new footwear," he mused.

"What was that?"

"Ah, you must not have seen the far side. Someone attached a perfectly monstrous blue shoe to King Billy's foot and placed a sign above it. It reads *Alderton.*"

Ailís felt her jaw dropping. "Good heavens. I was fending off Lady Alderton's foolish barbs only an hour past."

"I daresay she doesn't know, then. Not yet, anyway." Eamonn tapped his stick in a quick pattern against the cobblestones. "Can't say I've ever had a look at her feet."

"Monstrous," Ailís announced, and laughed with him. "About Séamus . . ."

"Aye. Séamus. Well, perhaps you'd best leave him to his big-eared doxy. If she graced him with a souvenir of their . . . er . . . friendship, who are any of us to comment?" He stopped then, hauling Ailís to an unsteady halt. "I don't suppose it has occurred to you that Séamus Cleary and An Cú might be one and the same."

"*What?* Have you gone daft?"

Eamonn shrugged. And in truth, Ailís was less serious than appalled. Could it, could it possibly have been Séamus who had . . . Nay. Impossible. But he did have the hot blood, the dislike of the Anglo gentry, the ties to the country . . .

"If the bauble is half so gaudy as you describe, it sounds as if it could well suit Lady Carricknock. She favors such things and did have a run-in with the Hound, after all."

"Nonsense," Ailís snapped, but without much force.

"Ah, well . . . I'll have a word with Séamus if it will make you happy."

"Aye. Aye, if you would. Nay, do not . . ."

Eamonn snorted. "You'll let me know when you decide. Now pick up your not-so-tiny feet, *cailín*. You're late home."

As her brother hustled her back toward the madhouse they inhabited, she was reminded of the words he had said to Clane. *Hurry up, man. Move your feet* . . . And the words the second man had spoken to An Cú the night before. *Déan deifir!* Hurry up. *Move your bloody legs* . . .

"Eamonn."

"Hmm?"

Ailís shook her head, tried to make sense of things. She couldn't. "Oh, I think I might be getting a wretched headache!"

"Aye, well, wait till you and Uncle Taddy have sat through half the concert," her brother said cheerfully. "You'll be certain of it then."

Chapter 11

She was dazzling. Christor watched Ailís promenade down the line of dancers at Philip Lorcan's side and was, quite literally, dazzled. In her silver dress, pearls at her throat, she looked as she had in moonlight—like moonlight itself.

The Lady-Lieutenant had gone all-out with this fete. Everything not moving in Dublin Castle was draped in garlands of silk and flowers. There were enough candles stuck into every available receptacle to give a very good simulation of daylight. It was blinding, but not nearly so much so as the guests themselves.

There were brilliant blues, glistening greens, vivid whites, silks and satins, all offset by sparkling gems. And that was just the men. The women far surpassed their escorts. Neither expense nor taste had been spared. As Christor watched, Lady Ferrisett glided past, resembling nothing so much as a walking garden. She had a garland of multicolored flowers draped up and around the hem of her skirts, an abundant floral crescent at her bosom, a towering collection of matching circlets atop her head. And of course, not a piece of it was real. Christor had his questions about the heavy string of glossily pink pearls at her throat as well, and wondered if Dublin were by chance developing a *tendre* for the gaudy and the fake.

He was forced to admit that the lady did have a knack for completing an ensemble. All but trotting at her side, eyes fixed on the flower arrangement at her bodice, was a bee. In truth, it was merely Thaddeus O'Neill, garbed in his usual and unique antiquated resplendence: black silk and yellow brocade, alternating coat to shoes. The effect was impressive, to say the least.

"Interesting family, the O'Neills." Lyndhurst took a thoughtful sip of his champagne. "One really would never know they are a mere two steps from the farm."

Christor watched Thaddeus buzz off with Lady Ferrisett and twirled the stem of his own glass. "What is the correct number?"

"I beg your pardon?"

"Steps. What is the number of steps from the farm which removes them from comment?"

"A total absence is ideal," Lyndhurst answered, sarcasm lost on him. He seemed conveniently to be forgetting that his own ancestors had been Wexford sheep farmers before one had had the clever idea of betraying one of his Catholic, madeira-smuggling neighbors to Queen Elizabeth's troops. "You are in a strange mood tonight, Clane. Am I to take it that your inquiries into the O'Neills' situation have not gone well?"

"My inquiries," Christor replied mildly, "have gone perfectly well. O'Neill is not your man."

"You sound very certain."

"I am certain. Leave him alone to stand for Parliament."

In truth, he wasn't so very certain after all. He, too, had noticed Eamonn's expensive walking stick, had recognized the man's waistcoat as coming from one of Dublin's finest tailors. And there was no doubt that the pearl fob adorning his watch chain came from a far more reliable source than Lady Ferrisett's pink marvels. Tip to tail, Eamonn O'Neill had been sporting a more expensive get-up than Christor himself.

He was presently propping up a wall off to the side of the Lord-Lieutenant's ballroom, the gold head of his cane glinting in the light of the countless candles, a sapphire stickpin flashing against the stark white of his cravat. Around him, several young ladies were simpering and preening, tapping and plucking away at his coatsleeves. Apparently Dublin Society was finally beginning to take notice of the handsome young war hero with his elegant appearance and bright future.

The question of the moment was how O'Neill was funding his rise to public notice.

"I will trust your judgment on the matter, Clane. I cannot say I like the idea of another Irish Whig in Parliament, but you have never caused me undue concern, so I suppose I cannot cavil too greatly at O'Neill's stand."

"Gracious of you."

"Mmm. We do what we can. I will say, however, that this barrister O'Connell makes me uneasy."

"As well he should."

Lyndhurst blinked, clearly having expected reassurance. "Well, he is Catholic. I daresay his political reach will be limited."

Christor gave a noncommittal grunt. He had a very good feeling that Daniel O'Connell, nominal Tory though he might well be, would prove to be a mighty thorn in the sides of those who hoped to keep Irish Catholics impotent. But only time would tell.

"I am thinking of perhaps giving my patronage to young Fitzjohn."

Christor snapped back to attention. "Gerald Fitzjohn? For Parliament? Good God, man, you must be jesting!"

"Not in the least." Lyndhurst drained his glass and casually deposited it in the nearby plant that happened to be closer than any of the scuttling footmen. "I dined with him before the Unsworth bash. He expressed an interest in politics and I believe he might be a viable possibility."

"You mean you believe he will be a malleable one."

"Isn't it all the same in the end? As it happens, I do have one rather serious concern about his suitability."

"Fancy that," Christor drawled, his mind filled with images of Gerry Fitzjohn flopping about the floors of Parliament, goggle-eyed and slack-jawed as a landed salmon.

"Yes, he is speaking of taking a bride, a wholly unsuitable girl."

"You don't say."

"Miss O'Neill, as a matter of fact."

Christor felt his own jaw dropping. "Now you do jest."

"I do not. As attractive as she might be, and as acceptable as her family appears to have become, we simply cannot have it. An MP's wife who spouts Gaelic and has the audacious ignorance to publicly defend common criminals . . . Appalling."

"*Ailís* O'Neill? You are certain?"

"Quite. He seems quite determined to have her, and I daresay she will accept him. God's teeth, Clane, can you imagine it? Country jigs at her soirees, Gaelic at Gunter's, oratory in defense of pickpockets at Vauxhall . . ."

"Excuse me, Lyndhurst." Thrusting his glass at the other man, not caring where it would ultimately be stuck, Christor stalked toward the center of the room.

The dance was just ending. He intercepted Ailís as Lorcan was leading her from the floor. "Evening, Clane," Philly offered genially.

"Good evening, my l—"

"I believe the next dance is mine, Miss O'Neill."

One of her dark brows arched upward. "Actually, it is not. I have promised Mr. Fitzjohn—"

"Tell him you were already engaged." All but elbowing young Lorcan out of the way, Christor got a grip on Ailís's arm and steered her back toward the dance floor. He did not stop there, but hustled her right past the forming set, across the room, and out onto a balcony.

"Well." The minute he released her, Ailís took a step away and crossed her arms over her well-exposed—he noted—chest. "Have you an explanation for that little act of Dark Age brute behavior, or do you simply enjoy slinging me about?"

He was in no mood to banter. "Ailís—"

"It's a serious question, sir. I do not expect Gerry Fitzjohn to keep his limbs to himself, he is incapable. You, however, should be better at controlling who and where you touch."

The image of Gerry Fitzjohn with his hands on Ailís, her ready acceptance of such, had red flashing in front of Christor's eyes. "I might have precious little control over the urges to touch you, but I'm damned well capable of deciding where I do so."

Where, as it turned out, was chest to thigh. He hauled her against him, barely giving her time to get her crossed arms out of the way, and lifted until she was standing on her toes. "You see?"

"I . . . I . . ."

"Well answered," he announced, and covered her mouth with his.

His temper drained away with that first touch. He waited a beat, then gently parted his lips, coaxed hers to follow. She tasted again of champagne, tinged with ginger and sugar this time, and smelled of . . . violets. He would ponder the appeal of that against turpentine later. For now, he had more important matters to attend.

Ailís had gone very still the moment he grabbed her. Now, so softly that he barely heard it, she moaned deep in her throat and opened herself to him. He would have shouted in triumph, but that would have involved lifting his mouth from hers and he did not plan to do that for some time, if at all.

She squeaked at the first sweep of his tongue against hers, her eyes going wide. Christor, a firm believer in seeing what he was enjoying, silently reveled in the fact that Ailís went into a kiss in the same way she did everything: open-eyed and unshrinkingly. A moment later, she was returning the caress, beginning a slow, sensual duel that nearly had his coat buttons melting.

Not so far away, the sounds of the ball reached his ears. He did not care. He was kissing Ailís O'Neill and Ailís O'Neill, dammit, was kissing him back. *Him.*

Gentle still, resisting the urge to devour her in a single bite, he dragged his mouth away. She whimpered a soft protest that quickly turned into a purr as he nipped his way lightly along her jaw, down the long column of her neck.

"Oh, *Ó Día*," she whispered. "*Ó Naomh Pádraig. Fóir orm!*"

Calling to God for assistance was one thing, Christor decided, but she wasn't going to get much aid from Saint Patrick. The man had had his one chance at banishing all serpents from Ireland. If he'd missed those of the aboveground, temptational variety, he couldn't be faulted, but he certainly wouldn't be coming back to finish the job.

Christor skimmed his teeth along Ailís's collarbone, then back to the place at the base of her throat where her pulse beat, strong and rapid. "Oh, *Críostóir!*" she gasped, and let her head drop back weakly.

He grinned, unable to help himself, at the sight of all that glory, inch after inch of pale skin glowing above the few silver inches of fabric that displayed far more than they concealed.

"Ah, Ailís," he growled, and buried his lips between her breasts.

She had not meant to yell. Even as the primitive cry left her lips, Ailís knew she hadn't meant to do it. As if she could have helped herself. Certain sensations could not possibly go unacknowledged and this one, the feeling of Christor's mouth in that sensitive hollow, was high among them.

She cried out; he jumped, jerking upright. Ailís's heels hit the stone floor with a jarring thump. In an instant, the doorway was filled with curious faces. Despite the fact that she was very nearly cross-eyed with the effects of what Christor had been doing to her and not wearing her spectacles, Ailís thought she saw the Lord-Lieutenant among them.

She had spent enough years commending herself on a quick mind. Now, as images of just what could result from being caught on a balcony all but in Lord Clane's arms flashed though her head, she snapped into some semblance of sense.

"Nay, my lord," she cried, quickly flattening her palms, which had been curled in Christor's lapels, against his chest. In what she hoped was a convincing show of attempting to prevent him from charging forward, she continued, "I will not allow you to be so gallantly foolish! There were too many."

Then, to the jostling crowd in the doorway, she announced, "Down there, in the gardens! I spied at least a dozen men, all in black . . ."

Nothing more was needed. A stream of gabbling gentlemen poured onto the balcony and flowed toward the steps to the garden. Among cries of "It's the Hound with his men!" and "After the blackguards!", nearly every male guest thundered over Dublin Castle's carefully tended flowerbeds and through the hedges. Ailís saw Eamonn go by, stick skittering against the stones, Uncle Thaddeus behind him, his cane waving in the air like a lance.

Christor gave her one wry, fleeting smile before he, too, was borne away by the flood.

Ailís offered up one silent prayer, more of an apology, really, for any couple who had thought to attain some amorous privacy in the gardens, then allowed herself to be guided back inside by a gaggle of chattering women. She would much rather have watched the men in their futile search for An Cú and his comrades, but prudently decided to put some distance, visible and not, between herself and the Earl of Clane.

The consensus among the younger women who were soon flocked around her, wide-eyed and breathless, was that everything interesting of late seemed to happen to Miss O'Neill. How very vexing, several were heard to lament, that they could not be in the center of such chaos more often. The older generation, wise or foolish, was far more concerned with the fact that they might be surrounded by ruthless bandits on the one night when each and every last one of them had worn only their best jewels.

Restless, growing more so by the minute as the chattering around her competed with the thrashing noises and shouts from outside, Ailís gnawed at her thumbnail and wondered just what she had done to deserve the current chaos that was her life.

"You know, dearest," her mother murmured, appearing suddenly at her elbow, "I really must have done something clever as a parent. Life with my children is never boring."

"God grant me boredom," was Ailís's fervent response.

"Be careful for what you wish. You might—"

"Attain it. Aye, I know. I know."

"Actually," Anne said, tucking her arm through her daughter's and guiding her away from the crush, "I was going to say 'you might find yourself passing your life with a Gerry Fitzjohn,' but your version suits, even if it is a bit nonspecific."

"Thank you, Mama."

"You are most welcome, dearest. Now, shall we discuss Lord Clane?"

"Nay," Ailís replied bluntly.

"He fancies you, Ailís. Any fool can see that. And you—"

"He does not and I do not, and there's an end to it."

Anne shook her head, gently cupped her daughter's face in her gloved hands. "What scares you so? I did not raise my children to be frightened by love."

"I am not frightened by . . ." Ailís rolled her eyes. "Don't you be looking at me like that, *Máthair*! I am not . . . Oh, fine.

I will not, positively will not give my heart to a man whose mind—and heart—are so different from my own."

"You truly believe Clane is such a man?"

"Of course he is. His life is in England, among the rest of his sort, free of obligation and care for aught but amusement. I need a faithful heart in my lover, Mama, one that won't leave me behind when the next pretty candle shines in the distance. And I need a man with an unselfish heart. Lord Clane possesses neither."

"So very certain, are you? I am sorry you think so." Anne gave a delicate shrug and straightened her gloves. "Now, since the gentlemen have vacated the card tables in favor of tromping through the gardens, Lady Morgan is organizing a few tables of commerce. I believe she knows all the rules."

"Fiddling while Rome burns?" Ailís muttered.

"Sydney Morgan always was a clever woman. I sincerely doubt the gentlemen will catch anything save perhaps an unfortunate rabbit or a cold. And I've a inclination for a bit of brandy and some gambling. Are you coming, or would you prefer to glower into the plants?"

By the time the gentlemen began to filter back in, Anne was twenty pounds richer and had taught the Lady-Lieutenant, Lady Carricknock, and two dowager viscountesses the words and tune to *"Cailleach an Airgid"*—"The Hag with the Money."

It was not until much later, when the gardens were empty, the excitement had died down considerably, and the guests were beginning to leave for home that Ailís realized there had been a handful of gentlemen who had not returned from the gardens at all. Among the missing, and she scanned the remaining revelers carefully, were Philly Lorcan, Gerry Fitzjohn, her own brother, and Christor.

He was still chuckling over her playacted histrionics several hours later, despite being up yet one more tree on yet another rainy Irish night. Soft weather, the country folk called it. Wet was his more concise description.

This time, however, he didn't mind overmuch. He was cheerfully distracted by the memory of Ailís sending every male fool at the ball—as well as a few ordinarily sharp minds—into the garden in search of skulking bandits. No man with a whit of sense in his head would be able to resist her, could keep from falling a little in love with her.

In love with her. Christor felt a cool chill skitter down his spine. He was not in love with Ailís O'Neill. He could not be. Inconvenience aside, it would just be a bad choice. Not that he'd ever planned to fall in love in any case, but it certainly would not be with a young woman whose very character was so different from his own. Irreverent, impetuous, single-minded. That was Ailís O'Neill. That those traits suited her from the tips of her not-small feet to the top of her lovely head hardly mattered . . .

"Oh, hell," he muttered. "Damn and blast and saints preserve us!"

Below him, branches parted. "What is it?" Séamus Cleary hissed. "Are there patrols coming? I can't see a bloody thing through these leaves!"

"No patrols."

"No carriages, either, I suppose."

"Not at the moment."

"We could have taken the last one," the younger man grumbled, letting the branches above him slap back into place. "Dark or not, I'm telling you I saw plenty of glitter."

Christor did not respond. There was no sense in it. He'd already made their mission perfectly clear. If Cleary chose to whine and groan about it into the wee hours, so be it.

Robbery was not Christor's motive this time. True, countless fortunes were criss-crossing their way across Dublin as the last of the Lord-Lieutenant's guests made their way home, but he would not be taking any of them. Ross was already overburdened; he could handle only so many gems at a time. And there had been no pleas or requests from the country.

No, the right An Cú was not plying his trade that night. He was lying in wait for the wrong one to make an appearance.

He had the Scannal brothers and several other trustworthy accomplices watching other roads. His gut feeling that his quarry would choose the Ranelagh Road had determined where he and Cleary would be waiting—in a tree, as it happened, their horses safely concealed some twenty yards away. If his instincts were correct, the impostor would not be able to resist the temptation of the Lord-Lieutenant's guest list, and would choose the road least likely to be ridden by patrols and most likely to be driven by wealthy residents of those areas just south of Town.

Christor and Séamus had been waiting only a quarter-hour. Several carriages had gone by, but no masked figures. Plenty could go awry, Christor knew: he could have chosen the wrong road, his prey might have opted not to ride, or worse, been apprehended. Still, he had nowhere else to be, he'd managed to grab a not-terribly-uncomfortable seat, and the rain was really more of a dense mist.

Such rosy-eyed optimism, he decided immediately, was a heap of manure.

"Tell me something, Cleary," he demanded quietly. "Why are you not married?"

"Me? God forbid, man! I'm but four-and-twenty. Ask me again in ten years and I might be starting to consider the possibility, but I'll tell you now, it'll take a good five years beyond *that* to see me taking up the shackles."

"Shackles, is it? What of the joys of marriage?"

Cleary snorted. "What did they give you to drink at that fancy ball of yours? There's plenty of fair ladies willing and ready to give the joys without having a ring, and I'd hardly think begetting an heir with some horse-faced English girl would be much pleasure for you."

Christor plucked a green acorn and chucked it down in Cleary's direction. There was neither force nor much aim in the act, but he felt the vague need to defend such English beauties as Aurelie Tarrant and Grace Avemar. "Has it ever occurred to you that I might choose an Irish girl?"

"Sure and your London cronies would love that. Nay, you leave ours to us and we'll not come reiving over the Irish Sea." Cleary ceased his scuffling among the branches, no doubt in search of an acorn of his own, and hissed, "There. Hoofbeats."

Christor heard them, too. Stretching to his full length along the branch, he scanned the road. It was difficult to tell in the darkness, but he had a very good idea that the approaching horse was indeed a massive gray.

"Go!" he snapped, and followed Cleary as the other man shimmied to the ground.

The impostor An Cú had had plenty of time to spy two men on horseback at their first meeting. This time, however, his mount was nearly atop the standing pair before it skidded to a jolting halt. The man bounced several times in the saddle, black cape flapping. At the same time, he was hauling back at the reins, urging his animal into a tight turn.

Christor raised his gun and cocked it, the sound cracking above scrambling hooves. "I'd halt right there, if I were you."

An Cú the Wrong glanced quickly about, but the sight of Séamus, now standing to his side, gun raised, relaxed his hands. "What do you want?" he demanded, voice muffled by the full mask.

"Your money or your life, perhaps?" Christor quipped. He took a step closer, then held up at the sight of the gray's rolling eyes. An ill-tempered beast—and one he *knew*. Damned if he could put his finger on how or where. "Dismount."

"No, my lord."

Startled, Christor peered intently into the covered face through his own half-mask, for all the good it did. "You know me."

"All of Dublin knows you, Lord Clane."

"Not as An—" Christor snapped, cutting himself off with a hiss.

"You are no longer An Cú, sir. You abdicated that post when you went off to war. But some among us know who you once were."

"Dismount," Christor repeated, his ire increasing.

"I will not."

Christor could see Séamus lifting his gun barrel another notch and waved it down. He was not going to tolerate much more disobedience from the mounted sod, but he wasn't going to allow Cleary to shoot him, either.

"I will ask you once more . . ."

"You may ask me all night if you wish. I prefer to stay where I am."

Male vanity and basic aggravation had Christor lifting his empty hand, ready to haul the fellow down by his booted ankle. But something in the man's muffled voice stopped him. There was something he recognized there, not in the voice itself, perhaps, but in the tone behind it. Pride, tinged with a fear the man would not give in to. Steadfastness. All those elements which had created and sustained An Cú in the first days of his rides.

"I know why you are doing this," Christor said gruffly.

"Do you?"

"I also know that you will stop. You will hang up your mask and your saddlebags and go back to wherever you came from, to whatever you did before."

"And you believe your command will make it so, do you?"

This time, Christor did grab the man, but by the cloak rather than boot. Only the restless shifting of the gray's massive hooves kept him from pulling until they were face-to-face. "It had best do just that. No matter how noble your goals are, if in fact they are so noble, I will not allow you to flail about Dublin's roads, risking lives and limbs that do not belong to you. Are you hearing me?"

The horse wheeled about, forcing Christor to release the rider and turn his attention to avoiding equine teeth. Above him, his sorry imitator adjusted his cloak with a stiff jerk.

"I hear you, my lord. Beyond that, I'll say no more. Now, may I go, or do you plan to dispose of me after all?"

Christor pocketed his gun. "Begone."

The man's departure was graceless, his seat more than a bit unstable, but it was swift. Christor watched horse and rider vanish into the mist and shadows, his mind whirling. "I've met him before," he mused, "and not so very long ago."

"Well," came Cleary's tart retort from behind him, " 'tis a good thing I didn't shoot him, then. I was all set to do it. 'Twould have pained me sorely to know I'd put a bullet in someone you once met."

"Sarcasm," Christor muttered, "does not suit you any better than that hat." He heard the younger man scuffling, no doubt feeling the dramatic black monstrosity he wore atop his head. "Never fear. Should I recall that I did not *like* the fellow once I identify him, I'll let you shoot him."

Chapter 12

Ailís bid farewell to Mrs. Cleary and, groaning quietly, made her slow way toward the carriage. Fergus rolled off the box with a grunt to assist her in. From all appearances, and his coat appeared to be straining just a bit across his gut, the Sunday dinner he had shared with his sister and her family had been much along the same lines as the one Ailís had taken with the Clearys.

She had not meant to stay quite so long, certainly not after dark. But the welcome had been sincere, the food delicious, the company warm and cheerful, and she'd had neither the desire nor reason to decline.

"You'll come again Sunday next?" Mrs. Cleary called from the doorway, dishcloth waving. "When your English lessons are finished—you'll come again for supper!"

"Thank you, ma'am. If I am able. . . ." Ailís ignored Séamus's knowing grin as he made his own way past her and toward the sheds where the Clearys kept their animals. His step, curse him, was springy as could be, despite the fact that he'd easily eaten as much as the rest of the party put together. "Good night, Mrs. Cleary."

"Safe home to you, Ailís. You're a godsend, you are."

Apparently the glittery earring had disappeared, and had not been replaced by any other baubles beneath Séamus's bed, putting the old woman's heart and mind at ease. She seemed convinced that Ailís was singlehandedly responsible for her grandson's return to grace. For her own part, Ailís had no idea if Eamonn had spoken to Séamus, if Séamus had simply grown tired of his amour, or if there were another issue at hand.

For the present moment, it hardly mattered. She was too busy trying to decide just how she was going to haul her overstuffed self into the carriage to think of much else.

Fergus offered a hand, then belched. "Sorry, miss," he murmured, ears reddening.

Ailís waved off his apology. "Your sister's famous beef stew, was it?"

"Nay. Tonight Dymphna served rabbit pie. With all the trimmings." He managed to look both agonized and euphoric at the same time. "And you, miss?"

Ailís tried not to contemplate the possible fates of Ursula the Blue Hare, who she herself had loosed behind the church before beginning her lesson. "Coddle," she sighed. "Buttermilk bread. Pear tart with a crust thick as the soles of your shoes. Oh, Fergus."

"I know, Miss. I know."

"Sweeney was baking a ginger cake when we left."

"Aye, so she was."

"I cannot resist her ginger cake."

Fergus belched again, then gave Ailís a solemn salute. "Who can? Tell you what, miss. I'll drive slow, and watch for holes in the road. We'll be fit as rain by the time we reach home."

"Good man yourself, Fergus." Satisfied, oversated, Ailís allowed him to assist her into the carriage, where she settled with a stifled grunt onto the worn leather squabs. As the vehicle rattled and rolled slowly from the Cleary's yard, she closed her eyes and recalled every aspect of the rich coddle: the savory farm sausages and bacon cooked slowly in meat stock with potatoes and onions.

No wonder Tommy and Séamus possessed such an air of genial contentment, she thought as the latter galloped past the carriage with a debonair wave. Their grandmother fed them as if there were no tomorrow.

True to promise, Fergus drove slowly, and by the time they reached the thick copse of chestnut trees which signaled the halfway point back to town an hour later, Ailís was feeling very nearly human again, if still a bit pear-shaped. Sweeney's cake would pose a challenge, but not an insurmountable one. If the alternative were facing the cook's disappointment and displeasure, Ailís would find a way to eat a tree.

A sudden crack outside the carriage, followed by a jerky halt had Ailís thinking in a fanciful moment that one of the faeries who kept the chestnuts had heard her thoughts and had thrown a branch into the road, ready to make her eat her words. The two figures she spied when she peered through the window were rather large to be *na síogaí*. They were also black-clad and familiar.

Her heart gave a thump at the sight of the moonlit An Cú as he approached Fergus. It wasn't much of a thump, really, but she felt it, felt her lips curving into a smile. She could see neither a second rider nor a gun, but she imagined both were present.

"Who are you?" she heard Fergus demand.

The voice came, deep and rough, wild-Wicklow-tinged. "Some call me the Hound."

"Ah, well then, I'll not put a lead ball in you, sir. I'd advise you to be announcing yourself earlier, though. I might have shot first and learned your name later."

There was a long pause and Ailís thought she saw the rider reach up to adjust his hat, or perhaps scratch his head, before offering, "I'll be sure to have that in my mind next time."

"Always pleased to help." Fergus doffed his own floppy hat; Ailís just saw it sweep down beside the box. "May I say 'tis an honor—and that the lady in the carriage agrees. She has naught to give you but her commendations. I've a few pence—"

"Keep your money, man. All I want is a word with the lady."

Heart beating a merry rhythm now, palms damp, Ailís lowered the glass. The Hound guided his mount to stand beside the carriage door. He seemed to fill the window opening, to fill the very night.

She was wearing her spectacles this time. They did not help much. As before, An Cú was garbed from head to toe in black, with a wide-brimmed hat and a mask that covered all but his mouth and chin. Even those features were hard to distinguish in the moonlight. Ailís reached for the lamp, intending to increase the light, but was halted when one black-gloved hand shot through the window to cover hers.

"Good evening, Miss O'Neill. You've kept me waiting a fair time this eve. Forgive me, but I think it best if we leave the light low."

"You know my name," Ailís breathed, then, suddenly recalling the large amount of onions she had consumed with supper, hurriedly passed a hand in front of her face. Testing one's breath without appearing to do so was a difficult task ordinarily, all the more so when one was feeling breathless. "How?"

"I have my ways, *cailín*?"

"And . . . you have been . . . waiting for me? How did you know . . ."

He grinned, teeth flashing white in the faint light. "I know a great deal about you." In a single, lithe movement, he swung down from the saddle to stand by the carriage. He propped himself comfortably against the door, forearms resting on the window ledge. "Been out teaching my people about the taxes they're to expect, have you?"

"It was Parliament, actually, today. I thought it might be useful for them to comprehend just how the government works."

"All in one session?" He let out a low whistle. "Most impressive."

"Not so very." Still awed that the great An Cú knew so much of her activities, Ailís tried to think of something more impressive to say. "I've just come from Sunday dinner."

"Have you now?" She was beyond adorable when she was flustered, Christor thought. It was such a rare state for her. "And did you enjoy it?"

"I did. It was coddle, and I . . ." Even in the limited light, he could see her toying with her skirts, twisting pleats into the worn fabric. Brown, he thought, and ready to come apart should she tug too hard. "Why were you waiting for me?"

"As it happens, I've been thinking long and hard about those pearls of yours and thought I'd collect them after all."

Her fingers released her dress and fluttered to her throat. "I am not wearing them! It's Sunday and I'd not thought—"

Christor hid a smile. "I jest with you, *mo muirnín*. I waited because I wanted to see you."

"Oh . . . Oh."

He waited for her to say more. When she did not, he reached down and opened the carriage door. He had his speech all planned, and thought it best to deliver it from inside, seated.

"Don't kiss me!"

Christor paused, half in and half out of the carriage. Ailís had shrunk away from him and was now pressed all the way back against her seat as if she wanted the thing to split open and swallow her. Surprised, pride already beginning to smart from what could only be her poor opinion of their last kiss—or rather the first, the one they had shared on the road—he grumbled, "I hadn't planned on it, as it happens, but you might as well tell me why I shouldn't."

Too late, he realized his Wicklow brogue had slipped. Fortunately, Ailís didn't seem to notice. She was still trying to mash her way through the leather squabs.

"I've had dinner, sir . . . Hound . . . Cú . . . Well, bother. I haven't the slightest idea what to call you!"

"And I bloody well don't care. . . ." Christor snapped, then, taking a calming breath, "Cú will do."

"Aye. Cú. Well, as I said . . . dinner. Mrs. Cleary's coddle. I had that for my meal. And you have not . . ."

Christor levered himself into the carriage and took the seat opposite Ailís. He crossed his arms over his chest and studied her, wondering if perhaps Séamus had shared some of the ale he liked to sneak to his grandmother's Sunday table. "You've eaten; I've not. Is that why you don't wish to be kissed?"

"I never said I didn't wish . . ." Ailís broke off, scowled, and wriggled once more in her seat. "Do I need a reason?"

"Ah, perhaps not," he conceded, forgetting for the moment that he really had not planned to kiss her at all during the encounter. "But I do."

She sighed, a small, forlorn sound. "The coddle isn't enough?"

He blinked, confused, thought of the traditional Irish dish with its simple ingredients. Potatoes, cured bacon, onions . . . Suddenly he laughed, loudly enough to make her jump. "Oh, Ailís. You are a wonder."

"And why is that?"

"As if I would balk at a bit of onion . . . Marvelous."

He realized he would have done better to keep his delighted amusement to himself when she snapped, "It's not a laughing matter, sir. I prefer not to smell of onions, bacon, or—"

"Turpentine? Sweet as your new violet scent is, the turpentine suited you. As does coddle. And paint smudges, blue hare hairs, bats . . ."

"How did you know about the paint? About my animals?"

Cursing himself for once again letting his guise slip, Christor announced, "I know a great many things, Ailís O'Neill."

This time, she snorted. "None of that mystic, all-powerful rubbish, if you please. It is not appealing." Then, eyes narrowed, she gave his shadowed face one more long perusal. "Séamus?" she demanded. Sharply.

"Aye?"

Both turned toward the open window. A horse's face appeared first, followed by Cleary's as he bent down to peer inside.

"Bloody marvelous," Christor muttered.

"Oh," was Ailís's comment.

"I . . . er . . ." Séamus cleared his throat once, then again, "You said . . . 'shea' . . . er . . . 'say Mass,' did you? 'Tis Sunday, after all . . ."

"Oh, Séamus," Ailís sighed, then giggled.

"Enough!" Christor snapped at the same time. Then, to Ailís, "I fear this interview is at an end, Miss O'Neill." He shoved the door wide, making Cleary pull back in a hurry.

"Wait." Ailís's grab at his cloak as he reached the ground stopped him. He turned to face her. "You know I won't tell anyone," she insisted ardently, grip tightening, tugging. "You must know that."

Of course he did. "I do."

"Good." He heard her release a soft breath. "Then you can tell me . . . please. Who *are* you?"

For a moment, Christor was ready to do it, to pull off the hat and mask. To give her only a heartbeat to absorb the knowledge before he hauled her out of the carriage and into his arms. For a moment.

"I am An Cú," he said gruffly. "The first and only true Hound. And this will be the last time we meet, Miss O'Neill. *Dia dhuit.*"

Before she could respond, before she could get a better grip on his cloak and hold him there, he slipped from her grasp. In a flash he was mounted again and, without a backward glance, cantering toward the dark copse. Séamus—there was no doubt now in Ailís's mind that it was Séamus Cleary—followed close behind.

"God bless you, too," she whispered as they disappeared into the night.

Seconds later, Fergus's face appeared in the window. He was grinning broadly, one hand thrust into the sparse hair at his crown, making it stand up in comical spikes.

" 'Twas An Cú, Miss!" he crowed, a moot but clearly pleasure-giving announcement. "The very one. And he spoke to me, he did! Thought I was going t'fall off the box. An Cú . . ."

"Mmm. An Cú indeed." Ailís forced a smile, not wanting to spoil the man's joy with her distraction.

"And young Séamus Cleary at his side, bold as brass and twice as bright."

She snapped to full attention. Her present opinion of Séamus's brains, aside. "Now, Fergus, you must not—"

"Don't you even be saying it, Miss. You know me better than that. My lips are sealed."

He pinched his lips together with his fingers to illustrate, eyes dancing all the while. Ailís smiled; she couldn't help it. "I know. It will be our secret."

Fergus's hand returned to his head. "Aye. Our secret." He rubbed a quick circle, sending his hair into further disarray. "Do you think we'll ever know who the Hound is really?"

"I don't know," was Ailís's soft reply. "I don't know."

But as they turned into Fitzwilliam Lane less than an hour later, Ailís was beginning to think An Cú's true identity might not evade her for very long. She had played and replayed their encounter in her head during the drive, and while she couldn't quite put a finger on just what should fill the blank spots in her memory, she felt sure she eventually would.

There was something just out of her reach, something clear and important and somehow welcome. Something that would illuminate her like a flash of lightning. She was sure of it.

Her mother was waiting just inside the door when she got inside. "I've been worried sick, Ailís Mary O'Neill!" she announced before her daughter had even begun to untie her bonnet. "Just look at the time!"

Ailís's eyes swung guiltily to the hall clock. It was past ten. "Oh, Mama, forgive me. I . . ." She decided in a blink not to mention An Cú. Not yet, anyway. "I supped with the Clearys and lost track of the time."

"I assumed as much, hoped as much." Quick, as always, to calm, Anne gave her a fierce embrace. Then a quick, light smack on the top of her head. "Honestly, Ailís, you will be the death of me. Now, come sit. Sweeney just brought in a tray of tea and ginger cake and I'm past weary of my own company."

"The men are out, then?" Ailís queried as she followed her mother into the parlor.

"Thaddeus is dining with Lady Ferrisett; God only knows when he'll totter home. Eamonn, I believe, is at Daly's with Lord Clane."

"Oh, there's a heartening thought." Ailís dropped onto the settee beside her mother, rattling china, and tried to ignore the ominous twitch of her stomach at the sight of Sweeney's massive, sugar-iced cake. "One roll of the dice and we'll all be a'begging in the streets. Eamonn has all the sense of a bean goose at games, and even less innate instinct."

"Ailís, really. Eamonn's good sense aside, you ought to find more apt comparisons."

"Fine. A widgeon, then."

Anne rolled her eyes and sighed. Then, waving toward the gilt console table, "Speaking of wildlife, a letter arrived for you today. From London. It must be important; it's marked as money." She winced as Ailís sprang to her feet and loped across the room. "I assume it involves your illustrations."

"Aye." Ailís tore eagerly at the seal. "Aye. I'm sure it does."

Moments later, with a squeal that brought the servants rushing from the back of the house, she hauled her little mother from her seat one-handed, and pulled her into a merry jig around the parlor. All the while, she kept her other hand aloft, waving the bank draft like a miniature standard.

"I am," she sang to the tune of "The Ha'penny Jig," quoting from the publisher's letter, " 'to be found all over London Town and quickly sweeping Bath! Soon to be found in every city of any size within the Isles'."

Wide-eyed, laughing, her mother gave herself up to the moment just long enough to execute a set of Donegal quick-steps that would defeat the best dancing master in all of Europe, then pulled Ailís to a bouncing stop. "Enough. Tell me, has the first book been printed, then? Is it to be a series?"

Ailís grinned, fanned her hot cheeks with the draft. "Hang the book, *Máthair*! I've found the path to a pot of gold here. God bless George Humphrey! God bless the silly Londoners who will buy anything if they think it fashionable!"

"Ailís . . ." Anne reached out, her own smile turning to a concerned frown when Ailís's shoulders suddenly slumped. "What is it, dearest?"

"Oh. Oh, Mama." Ailís dropped heavily into the nearest chair, eyes lifting bleakly to her mother's worried face. "I've just thought . . . realized . . . God help me when they arrive in Dublin!"

Christor shoved aside the plate containing the remains of his thrice-heated supper. He had not been able to eat on arriving home; he'd required a full, appetite-spoiling hour in the library, giving Séamus Cleary a dressing-down that would have made his own draconian, ever-pontificating father proud were he alive to witness it. Once Cleary had slunk off, having sworn on the souls of his own departed parents to watch his tongue doubly well in the future, Christor had indulged in a large whiskey and small self-congratulation for handling the situation with Ailís as well as he had considering the circumstances. She would never expose what she knew, was still ignorant as to the identity of An Cú himself, and would not be expecting to encounter the man ever again.

Now, halfway through the after-dinner port which had become mid-dinner port and most of his dinner, done with his overcooked beefsteak; he turned his attention to the parcel beside his plate. He had carried it with him into the dining room and was ready to open it now.

It was from Lucas Gower, and this time he did not expect political rot. In fact, he was very much looking forward to whatever waited inside the heavy wrapping.

More of the same, Gower wrote in his brief letter. *These are my favorites yet, though you might disagree with one or two. Prinny himself was overheard to say that No. 7 was "a damned brilliant piece of work," while Clare, as you can well imagine, is* not *pleased. Of course, No. 12 will reign forever in my esteem. Do try not to burst anything in viewing . . .*

Christor set the letter aside and viewed the first of the caricatures. The same hand as the previous set had taken wicked glee in designing this one. *Personages of Ireland,* read the caption. *No. 7. Clarity of Vision in Absentia.*

It was young Lord Clare, school chum of Byron and intimate of the Lorcan family. He was depicted in all his sartorial absurdity as a drab, pudgy caterpillar, furtively attempting to slip into a garishly colored, overly decorated butterfly suit. The bulk of the caterpillar's myriad legs were fashioned into multiple fob-laden watch chains, the faux wings decorated with several gaudy patterns that were more than familiar to anyone viewing the day waistcoats belonging to male members of the *ton.*

Delighted, Christor propped the image against his glass for later perusal, and flipped through the other prints. There was the Marquess of Carricknock as a vividly red-nosed vole, then his wife as an old bat, complete with ostentatious baubles hanging from the large ears. *No. 10* depicted the Earl of Drogheda as a coot, followed by Colonel Ellsworth as a pigeon.

At first, Gower's favorite—*No. 12. A Persistent Annoyance*—did not stand out as anything but a clever drawing. The blackfly, well known for its habit of flying around people's heads and easily avoiding swatting hands, was drawn in bold detail. The black body, shown in profile, was a perfect replica of the typical gentleman's evening suit, down to white stockings and shiny, black-bowed shoes. The creature's wings were fashioned into the shape of coattails, its forearms ending in hands holding an exaggerated glass of amber liquid and a quizzing glass. The latter was pictured over the one visible eye, magnifying it to the appropriate size for a fly.

The head, that huge orb aside—and Christor noted the feature was colored an ocean blue—was completely human. The hair was dramatically dark and swept back from the brow; the nose drawn straight and bold. The creature even had a man's chin, jutting like a coastal cliff.

All in all, it was a delightful drawing, and an amusing one. Some typical dandy, Christor mused, ever-present and pesty. Leinster, perhaps? Charlemont? He could not tell. Clearly the artist had, for some reason, erred on the side of subtlety with this caricature. The identity of all the other subjects had been patently obvious. Or perhaps, unlikely as it was, the fly was meant to be a personage Christor did not know. Gower seemed to know who it was. Perhaps an Irishman elevated to some noteworthy status with the *ton* while Christor had been on the Peninsula, then away from both London and Dublin upon his return . . .

Then he spied what appeared to be a design hidden within the pale, lacy pattern of the near wing. Yes, he decided, taking a closer look, it was almost certainly a deliberate image, rendered in an upside-down, shield-shaped area. Beyond that, he could not recognize it.

Curious, mellowed by the port and the earlier whiskey, he seized his glass in one hand, the caricature in the other, and headed for his library. Once there, he settled himself comfortably in his desk chair. Laying drink and paper on the blotter, he dug his jeweler's glass from its compartment and peered through it at the print.

It took him far longer than it should have, but he eventually realized it was the design that was upside-down, rather than the image within the image. He rotated the paper. Not merely a shield, he saw, but an escutcheon, complete with coat of arms. A pair of lions . . . no, wolves, facing each other below a bush . . . no, a flame . . .

Slowly, almost reluctantly, his eyes rose to the wall above the crackling fire, to the massive escutcheon mounted there. Ancient, famous, it had belonged to the Moore family even before the earldom. Two wolves, facing each other below a burgeoning flame. The same image was painted onto several sets of dinner china, engraved on the gates of the various Clane estates, emblazoned on the doors of the brand-new, glossy black barouche Christor had ordered ready for his return to Dublin.

"No," he growled, beginning to see flames himself. "Bloody well not possible."

But there it was, in black and white and muted colors on the paper in front of him. Now he could see the line of his brow, his nose, his distinguishably Moore-family chin. Of course he had not seen it at first. What man was familiar with his own profile? Or apt to identify himself in such a caricature? Only one who was parodied often. In profile.

The last time Christor had seen his image from the side had been a month past. Anne O'Neill, at one of her small dinners, had brought out a silhouette screen. He had sat for her while she fashioned his portrait out of paper with scissors, his acquiescence a matter of indulgence rather than true interest. And he had completely forgotten to take the finished product with him at the end of the evening.

Muttering vague invectives now, he stalked back to the dining room and the prints he had left there. He shoved aside the vole, the coot, the caterpillar, the pigeon.

The bat. He knew that bat, had made its acquaintance nearly nose-to-nose, in broad daylight in the middle of a Dublin townhouse.

Chapter 13

For the first time in recent memory, Ailís arrived downstairs for breakfast the following morning to find her entire family at the table. Her mother was at the sideboard, spooning baked mushrooms onto her plate, Uncle Taddy was smiling at the far wall, conducting an imaginary orchestra with his coffee spoon, and Eamonn had his nose buried in the *Freeman's Journal*.

"Good morning, dearest," Anne greeted Ailís cheerfully. "Did you sleep well?"

"Very well, thank you, Mama."

In truth, she had not. She'd tossed and turned her way through the night, going from dreams of An Cú riding a small dragon back and forth over the Carlisle Bridge, to Christor sweeping first the Marchioness of Carricknock and then Lady Alderton across a darkened dance floor. All in all a most restless night.

"Would you care for some mushrooms, Ailís?"

For some reason, the thought of food did not sit well. "Nay, thank you, Mama. Not yet. Tea, I think . . ." She padded across the carpet to her chair, pausing to kiss her brother and great-uncle on the tops of their heads as she went. Uncle Taddy, she noted, smelled of roses. As curious as she was about his occasional evening with Lady Ferrisett, she knew better than to ask.

She was not so forbearing regarding Eamonn's night out, however. "Did you enjoy yourself at Daly's, Éamonnán?"

He peered over the paper for a second, blinked, then disappeared again. "I did, thank you very much."

"How much did you lose?"

"Less than you might think."

"And Lord Clane? Was he blessed with good fortune at the tables?"

Eamonn shook the *Journal* so the top folded outward and quirked a now-visible brow at her. "I'm sure Clane would be most gratified by your interest. I'll be sure to mention it when next I see him. As it happens, we did not go together and if he did happen to be there, I was not aware of the fact. I was . . . preoccupied."

"Goodness, is Daly's truly so large that you might miss someone there?"

The paper dropped a few more inches. "What is this, Ailís? An inquisition?"

She shrugged, then, deciding against tea, poured herself some chocolate. She was not feeling particularly sweet so far that morning and thought she might as well get her sugar where she could. "I am merely curious. I daresay I shall never see the inside of the club."

"It's dark," Eamonn grunted, "sometimes even in the day."

Ailís had heard that the famed Dame Street gambling club sometimes blocked the windows and reduced the light in the middle of the day to increase the atmosphere for deep play, but she had never quite believed it. Nor did it really matter. She was sure as stone that Eamonn had not been there the night before, or the night before that, and so on. He was up to something, and it was not accompanying An Cú on his midnight rides. That, she now knew beyond a doubt, was Séamus Cleary's province. And there was only one An Cú, after all. Whatever it was keeping her brother out till all hours, she was determined to uncover the secret.

Before she could begin her next question, however, he'd vanished back behind the *Journal*. "I say, Uncle Taddy, don't you know a David Scott of Mary Street? *Uncle Taddy?*"

Thaddeus's spoon baton stopped mid-sweep. "Did you say something, lad?"

"David Scott," Eamonn repeated loudly. "Did you not once exchange shots with him?"

"I did. 'Twas in Phoenix Park in '79."

"Good heavens." Momentarily forgetting her quest for the truth of her brother's activities, Ailís gaped at the older man. "What on earth drove the pair of you to that?"

"Necessity, my dear. We both wanted into MacNally's Duelling Club, y'see. All the rage back then, duelling. But no club would have us unless we'd blazed. So off we went to the park with our pistols."

"Uncle Taddy, you might have been shot!"

"Not by David. Always a poor shot, was Scott. Besides, we aimed wide. Now walking *to* the spot was another matter. Damned dangerous in those days, with all those stray balls whizzing about. Old Clonmell once had his hat knocked off him on his way to fight Tyrawly, and again on his way home. . . . Ah, what grand days those were!" He slapped his bony knee in delighted reminiscence, then asked, "What was it you were saying about Scott, Eamonn? The man's been dead these twenty years and more."

"Shot?" Anne asked dryly.

"Squashed, by a falling port barrel," was Thaddeus's phlegmatic reply.

"Must be his son, then, listed as a bankrupt. Selling everything." Eamonn read from the paper: *"The entire household furniture, including Northumberland and Dining Tables, Waggon Roof and other Bedsteads, Feather Beds and Bedding, Mahogany Parlor and Drawing-room Chairs, Cane and Rush ditto, Pier and Chimney Glasses, Plate and Plated Ware, with several Dozen of Choice Old Port Wine, and excellent Jaunting Car Horse, and Jaunting Car, &c, &c."*

"Oh, how sad," Anne announced, shaking her head sadly over her napkin before setting it in her lap. "I do so hate hearing of bankruptcies."

"I wonder about that port," was Eamonn's cheerful comment.

Thaddeus grunted. "Never could hold onto money, the Scotts."

"Still . . ." Anne murmured. "Well. Is Davison's advertising today?"

Eamonn scanned the page. "It is. What do you need?"

"Tilly was coughing a bit again this morning as she helped me dress. The American Soothing Syrup worked wonders last time."

"American Soothing . . . two shillings threepence."

"That's rather dear, isn't it? But I suppose I cannot pinch pence everywhere. Ailís, will you trot up to Parliament Street later to fetch the syrup? Tilly will go with you."

"Oh, Mama, I meant to paint . . ." And do a bit of deductive reasoning, Ailís thought, but as her mother would not be cheap over the syrup, she would not make the little maid wait for it. "Aye. Of course."

"And some Fisher's Golden Snuff, if they have it," Uncle Taddy added.

"One and three," Eamonn read the price.

"Robbery," Thaddeus grunted. "I recall when it was but six-pence."

"All the more reason to give it up," was Anne's mild comment. "It's terrible stuff, Uncle."

"Aye," the old man replied, grinning, "terribly grand."

"Here's something for you, Ailís," Eamonn announced. "The Celebrated Abstergent Lotion."

"And what, pray, is that?" she asked, already assuming she did not truly wish to know.

"For removing all Kinds of Pimples, Tetters, Ring-worms, Carbuncles, &c, from the Face and Skin."

"Eamonn!" their mother chided.

He continued, *"When the All-powerful Charms of our Fair Country-Women are capable of attaining the breadth of Youth to noble Enterprise and laudable Pursuits, who in turn expect to be rewarded with the enchanting Smiles and reliable Hearts of those they love, an Auxilliary like Solomon's Abstergent Lotion, which admirably heightens their powerful Fascination, must certainly be a valuable Acquisition and Appendage to the Toilet."*

"Oh, Eamonn. Really."

"What, Mother?" He grinned. "Why should Ailís not be powerfully fascinating? So, what do you say, *mo cál bheag*? But a piddling four shillings sixpence for this valuable acquisition."

Unlike their mother, who was giving her son as disapproving a look as she could manage of a morning, Ailís was delighted with the whole advertisement. "Ah, well, reasonable as the price might be," she quipped, "I've neither tetters nor ringworm at present. Now you, you great peapod, have a smashing carbuncle right in the center of your forehead."

Even Anne had to laugh when Eamonn, vain as any handsome young man, slapped his palm to his head in search of the nonexistent pimple.

"Barnacle?" Thaddeus demanded. "What is the lad now? A sloop?"

"*Carbuncle,* Uncle," Ailís corrected, "though I daresay a barnacle might take a fancy to that hard head of his."

"Aye, aye. Now, your father"—Thaddeus's eyes were distant and fixed on the far wall again—"was as carbuncle-faced a lad as could be in his youth. 'Twas before you met him, of course, Annie. Oh, we worried for the lad. He had so many spots that the blackflies mistook him for a cream-and-red currant pie . . ."

At the mention of blackflies, Ailís sighed and closed her eyes. It was but a matter of time before she would have to answer for that one, she knew. With luck, the time would be long enough to have Lord Clane back in London before he ever saw the thing.

She did not expect the small, sudden pang in her chest at the thought of his taking himself back to England. Nor did she like it.

" 'Twas my dear sister-in-law, God rest her soul," Thaddeus droned on, "who covered young Thomas ear-to-ear with marigold and seaweed paste. Off went the spots, never to be seen again. And then you came along, Annie-girl, and gave him your heart."

Never to be seen again. Gave him your heart . . .

The cup slipped from Ailís's fingers, thudding against the table and spattering the remains of her chocolate over the linen cloth.

"Ailís?" Her mother was already on her feet, mopping at the spill with her napkin. "Ailís, are you unwell?"

"I . . . nay . . ."

Tilly appeared when summoned, damp cloth in hand, and promptly tipped Eamonn's coffee into his plate when her coughing made her arm jerk. In the act of moving away from the spill, Eamonn caught the edge of the tablecloth with his

knee. Thaddeus's plate went over the edge, followed by the
coffee pot. At the sound of the crashes, Sweeney came bustling
in from the kitchens, brandishing her wooden spoon, and pro-
ceeded to lambast the maid for clumsiness. Tilly burst into
tears, Eamonn began to turn red with laughter, and Thaddeus
loudly informed the room that percussion, as far as he was
concerned, was the splendid heart of music these days.

"It was just another morning with the O'Neills, Ailís
thought, as she stopped a rolling salt cellar from dropping into
her lap.

The loud banging at the front door seemed wholly appropriate. Fergus scuttled by the dining room to answer it. He was
back almost immediately, very nearly invisible behind the
charging form of the Earl of Clane.

Ailís had seen Christor annoyed, had seen him frustrated.
She had never seen him truly angry. Until now.

His eyes blazed blue fire from his stony face. His mouth
was a perfectly straight line. And his hair, when he whipped
off his hat and thrust it behind him in the footman's direction,
stood up in a pair of curving licks which were altogether too
diabolical for comfort.

"Why, Lord Clane . . ." Anne stood beside the table, a
serene island in the midst of chaos, wearing a mushroom trail
and dotting of egg yolk down the front of her dress. "Good
morning. Would you care for some . . . breakfast?"

His eyes slewed briefly in her direction. "Good morning,
madam. And no, thank you." Then, fiery gaze fixed on Ailís,
he stalked slowly across the floor. "I thought," he growled,
"that if I waited until this morning, if I refrained from charging
in here last night, I would be calm. Collected. Forgiving. Perhaps even a bit amused."

He stopped beside her chair, forcing her to tilt her head up
to see his granite-hard face. "I am not amused."

Ailís didn't think playing innocent would help much, but
since there was a chance, albeit a small one, that he had been
upset by something other than the caricature, she decided to
give it one try. "Not amused by what, my—"

"Don't even consider playing stupid, Ailís!" he snapped.
"You know full well why I am . . . am . . ."

"Not amused?" she offered helpfully. "Not calm?"

"Aaarrrhhh!" He actually thrust both hands into his hair and tugged. Now the two devil's horns were a half-dozen. That done, he reached into his pocket and yanked out a sheaf of rolled papers. He plunked them onto the table in front of her. "That. Is. Why."

Ailís thought she saw a familiar vole paw in the slowly uncurling papers. Before she could comment—and she wasn't certain what she should say anyway—her mother came and lifted the sheaf. Uncurling it, she studied the top image. It was the goosely Lord Castlereagh. Lady Carricknock as bat came next, then Drogheda the coot.

"I take it," Anne said slowly, "that these are your 'guide to Irish wildlife.'"

"Well, there will be a book . . . someday. I meant to tell you, Mama, truly I did."

"Oh, Ailís." Anne turned the coot into the light, examined it at length. "Oh, Ailís." Her lovely face broke into a brilliant smile. "These are absolutely wonderful! Eamonn, did you know your sister was doing this?"

Immediately, Eamonn and Uncle Taddy were by Anne's side, studying the caricatures. "By God, it's Clare," Eamonn exclaimed. "And to a bloody *T.* Well done, Ailís!" And from Thaddeus, "Always fancied the Wellesley boys looked a bit like foxes. Girls in that family look like weasels."

"Oh, Uncle Thaddeus, they do not!" But Anne was laughing.

"How did you manage it, Ailís?" her brother demanded. "I recall a painting of the bat, but it certainly was neither etching nor caricature."

"I do two paintings: one of the animal and then a caricature . . ." She gestured to Carricknock with his red vole nose. "I send both to London, someone there copies the caricature as an etching, it is printed and inked."

"Amazing," Eamonn murmured. "The fly. The fly is . . . Ah."

One by one, the O'Neills turned back to Christor. he had one hip propped against the table, arms crossed tightly over his chest.

"The fly," he ground out between clenched teeth, "is sorely tempted to swat back."

"My lord . . . Chr . . . my lord, please." Ailís clenched and unclenched her hands helplessly in her lap. "If you would but . . ."

"Up," he commanded.

"I beg your pardon?"

"Get up. We are going for a stroll, you and I."

"Wh-where?" Ailís did not like the look in his eyes. Not at all.

"Where do you imagine? Carlisle Bridge."

"Lord Clane . . ." Anne, still holding two of the prints, managed one of her hallmark, softly maternal smiles. "Please, have a seat." She glanced down the disordered table, then pointed— with the pigeon caricature—to one of the straight-backed chairs lining the wall. "There, perhaps. Please, sit down."

"Up," he repeated to Ailís. Then, "I assure you, Mrs. O'Neill, I will do my very best not to toss your daughter off the bridge and into the river."

Ailís, meanwhile, had seen Eamonn's jaw clench, had seen both him and Uncle Taddy reach for their sticks. As much as she appreciated their protective instincts, she did not especially want the three men going at each other like a trio of squabbling badgers. Besides, she did not think it would be a fair fight. Not only was Christor unencumbered by age or injury, but he appeared full angry enough to rout an entire army regiment.

"I'll go," she said, hoping her voice sounded steadier than her knees felt. "Tilly, if you would fetch a wrap and bonnet for me . . ."

The maid scuttled out of the room so quickly that she nearly left tracks in the carpet. Not wanting to give any member of the household the opportunity to do anything rash—for Sweeney had taken to swinging her spoon in a menacing manner and Fergus was now creeping stealthily toward the brass fire tools—Ailís rose to her feet and followed the girl out of the room. She could feel Christor not three feet behind her. In fact, when she halted in the foyer and turned, he nearly trod right over her.

"My lord," she said softly, addressing his cravat knot as she could not face the cold look in his eyes, "you must understand—"

"Later. I don't want to hear a word out of you just now."

"But—"

"Not a word!"

Ailís was beginning to have serious misgivings about her decision, was in fact ready to grab up her skirts and run for safety. But Tilly was back, wide-eyed and white-faced, carrying the wrap and bonnet. Ailís gave her a reassuring smile, spoiled somewhat by the fact that her hands were trembling as she accepted the items.

"Go!" was all it took from Clane to send the little maid scuttling away down the hall.

"You have no call to be frightening helpless . . ." Ailís's outburst faltered at his low growl.

She stood, unresisting as he himself tossed her wrap over her shoulders and plunked her bonnet onto her head. She did squeak when he propelled her out the door and down the stairs, but only because she was convinced she was going to trip over the ill-draped shawl and go nose-first into Fitzwilliam Lane. Of course, the iron grip he had on her arm would have kept her standing in a full force gale. Had there not been anger emanating from his touch, she might have found it rather nice.

They did not speak at all as they tromped past Trinity, past the denuded King Billy, and the bustling bank. Christor did not look at Ailís at all; he simply couldn't trust himself not to do something rash quite yet. He shot a brief glimpse into the window of Ross's Westmoreland Street shop as he hustled her past, then gave a terse wave when the jeweler's startled face appeared in the window. He supposed he would have to explain this appearance, as he had Ailís's presence earlier. Perhaps this time, however, Ross would refrain from pointing out his newest series of ladies' rings.

It was a glorious day in Dublin, Christor noted indifferently as they stepped free of the Westmoreland Street buildings and onto Afton Quay. Sunlight glinted off the Liffey, endless diamonds in the current. It was, too, one of the river's busy days. Ships arriving, departing, lining up for the quays and customs houses, filled the water nearly bank to bank, masts like a picket fence as far as the eye could see. It was Dublin at its very best. And Christor was suddenly, poignantly reminded of how much he loved this city.

He glanced down to the side. Ailís was gamely keeping pace with him, her lifted chin just visible beyond the brim of her bonnet. Every so often she would shove a bit of encroaching, worn silk wrap from her eyes or mouth, all without missing a step. Christor slowed, allowing himself a single moment of warm appreciation before reminding himself just why he was in her presence.

They stepped onto the bridge and followed its gentle arc to the center. Christor chose the western side, with its view down river of Essex Bridge's elegant stone arches and raised walkways. That sight, with the old Customs House in the foreground, the Liffey flowing steadily by, always calmed him. Today, with the sunlight, the ships, even a few pleasure boats slipping around the cargo vessels like persistent, eager infants, it was a magical scene.

He heard Ailís catch her breath, caught his own glimpse of her smile when he looked down. It vanished as soon as she realized she was being studied. When she turned her face away, hiding once again behind that infernal hat, Christor very nearly grabbed for the ribbons to send the thing flying into the wind and water.

Instead, he reached around her to grasp her far arm. Firmly but gently, he turned her to face him, his hands wrapped securely around both shoulders. She went rigid, eyes going wide behind her spectacles, soft cheeks losing a bit of their natural flush.

"I . . . I am not much of a swimmer," she stammered. "I once went straight to the bottom of my grandmother's pond, like a rock, and it wasn't more than five or six feet deep at the center. Eamonn had to fish me out and I promptly lost my breakfast all over him. As I've just come from the breakfast table and you are quite finely dressed, as always, I do not recommend—"

"Ailís, still your tongue, if you please. You are neither swimming nor sinking today as far as I am concerned."

"I am not?"

"Nor am I risking my apparel in any manner." He frowned down at her. "Did you honestly believe I would throw you into the Liffey?"

"I . . ." She gnawed delicately at her lower lip, all the while fumbling with the fraying, unwieldy edges of her wrap. Christor began to wonder if, as a matter of economy, she had chosen to swathe herself in old boudoir curtains. "Nay. I suppose I did not. I cannot imagine you lifting your hand against any woman, in any way. But then, I've little experience with you in a rage and could not be entirely certain."

"Trust me, I have more than once considered turning you across my knee and paddling you soundly."

"Aye, well, you and half of the men with whom I have dealings, I suppose. I seem to have that effect on some people."

Christor was in no mood to discuss the effect she had on men—one man, in particular. Nor did he much feel like contemplating any of the other Dublin men's desires regarding having her in their laps.

"Why did you do it?" he heard himself asking. It came out as a plaintive, wistful sound. "Dammit," he added to dilute any weakness. It wasn't particularly convincing, even to his own ears.

This time, she did not even attempt to play ignorant. "I'm sorry," she said simply. "I did not know you then as I do now."

"And what is that supposed to mean?"

"It means that I painted and posted that particular image a month ago, soon after you arrived in town and began hanging about the house. I . . . well, I know I found you a pest then, but I suppose I found you a threat as well."

That very nearly made sense. "A threat to Eamonn's future?"

"To that and . . . and . . . Oh, bother." She blew out a breath and frowned. "Let go of me, please. I cannot think properly without space between us."

He did. Not because he wished to, but because, just then, hearing her became more important than discomfiting her.

"Thank you." Ailís took unnecessary care in straightening her shawl, inching backward as she did until there was a good three feet of empty air between them. Then, pivoting so she was again in profile, her face hidden once more, she freed a length of wadded fabric from beneath her elbow, rested her forearms on the rail, and gazed out over the crowded river. "I've a comfortable life here, my lord—"

"Christor."

"Aye, Críostóir Rhys Próinsias Muiris. That's how I think of you now, you know. But then . . . then you were the grand Earl of Clane, and all I could think when you kept buzzing about . . . er . . . making yourself comfortable in Dublin, in our home, was that you were going to change it all somehow. Carry in all sorts of English nonsense and leave bits of it everywhere."

"Like fly-blow?" he offered with distaste.

"Yes, like fly-blow. It's awful, indeed, when one looks at it that way. I ought to have chosen another creature. I am so very sorry."

Christor did not know if it were the unfamiliar repentance, or the fact that it would take a stronger man than he to stay angry with Ailís O'Neill, but his fury had all but drained completely away. "You were doing what a caricaturist does," was his grudging admission. "And well."

She spun to face him so quickly that, for an instant, he thought he might be fishing her out of the river after all. Then, as unexpected as her penitence, she blushed, fiercely enough to make the scattering of freckles he so enjoyed disappear.

"You think so? You truly think my work is—"

"Clever." He sighed, resigned to his fate. "No, that is too ungenerous of me. Your work is brilliant, Ailís. Even Cruikshank does not have such a knack for capturing the essence of a person. I would very much like—"

The air went out of him in a whoosh when she suddenly lunged into his chest, wrapping her arms around him with impressive force for a not-particularly-large young lady who was tangled in yards of flimsy wrap. Then he realized she had just thrown herself essentially into *his* arms, and took advantage of the situation as best he could.

Slowly, expecting her to come to her senses and bolt at any instant, he eased his arms around her until they crossed over her back. Oh, how he wanted to kiss her, long and deep and hard enough to make them both see stars, but that was out of the question, if only really because she had her cheek pressed against his chest, her slightly wilted straw bonnet wedged beneath his chin.

The fact that they were standing in the middle of Carlisle Bridge, with a good part of Dublin's population passing nearby, had nothing to do with it. Had he been able, he would have kissed her right there and then, over and again until the sun set in the distance. Instead, he had to content himself with brushing his lips once, softly, over the straw-covered crown of her head.

The interlude ended altogether too soon. She dropped her arms from his waist and pulled away. He let her go. For the moment, he would let her go.

"Thank you," she whispered.

"For what?" *Not tossing you into the Liffey—or tossing you over my shoulder and carrying you back to my keep to ravish you on the solar floor?*

Just then, a quick dip in the cold Liffey did not seem like such a bad idea to him.

"For being so kind."

Ailís waited a beat before removing the edge of her wrap from her face this time. Her cheeks felt flaming hot and, she was convinced, were a matching fiery color. She was as mortified by her behavior as she was gratified by his praise.

Never in her life had she felt such an urge to throw herself at a man, and in public, no less. Nor could she have imagined that the sensation, the very bold power of the act, would be so overwhelmingly pleasant as to far exceed the consequences should her shamelessness be viewed. She had been bewitched by every second, thrilled from head-to-toe by the feeling of Christor's body against hers.

He, on the other hand, looked as if he had swallowed a beetle.

A new flush rose in Ailís's cheeks, even hotter than the first. Apparently it did not matter that he had flirted outrageously on several occasions, had *kissed* her, for God's sake, on the balcony at Dublin Castle. Had handled her, hefted her about as if she belonged to him.

Apparently everything changed when she was the one doing the lunging.

Anger and hurt battled within her. "My lord, I—"

He whipped a hand in front of her face, stalling her tongue. "Come along."

"What?"

"Come." Without warning, he seized her hand and, all but dragging her behind him, strode back down the slope of the bridge and into Westmoreland Street.

Thinking he was taking her home, imagining herself being dumped onto her own doorstep like an unwanted parcel, or, even worse, being delivered to her mother like a deviant child, she tried to dig her heels into the ground. This only caused her to skid along for a few steps, then nearly go tip-over-tail when her toes hit a cobblestone.

Clane did not pause, merely continued tugging her down the street. Ailís managed a weak smile for anyone who seemed to take notice of them, a weaker wave to an astonished-looking Edmund Ross, who was just escorting an elderly gentleman from his shop. Then they were rounding a sharp corner into bustling Fleet Street, and once again, into a little lane Ailís had never before noticed.

Christor did not slow until he was actually pushing through the door of a tiny shop with no sign other than a piece of fiddle-shaped wood swinging above the entry.

He stopped abruptly and Ailís thumped into his back. A quick glance around the little space showed four walls covered edge-to-edge with fiddles, wooden flutes, guitars, and a single old man seated behind a scarred work table. He had a glossy fiddle in one hand, a handful of strings in the other, and was staring at Christor as if he were a walking bear suddenly appeared in the middle of the shop.

"May I help you, sir?"

But Christor was already stalking toward one of the corners, still pulling Ailís behind him. It was not until he finally let go of her hand and stepped to the side that she saw his intent. As she watched, he ran a fingertip over the row of *bodhráns* mounted there, then lifted one from its hook.

"Have you a tipper?"

The shopkeeper wordlessly reached to the counter behind him and came back with the requisite wooden stick, bulbed at both ends. He handed it over, still a bit goggle-eyed. But there was more in his gaze now, Ailís noted: a skepticism and perhaps even some worry that his carefully crafted instrument was in clumsy hands.

The *bodhrán* Christor had chosen was lovely indeed. The goatskin was smooth, unblemished, stretched tightly over the shallow rim. Ailís watched as Christor traced a fingertip over the Celtic knotwork pattern lovingly carved into the wood, then deftly curved his fingers around the crosspiece in back. It was a large drum, easily twenty inches across, and a fine one.

The shopkeeper rose and, still without speaking, dragged two stools from beneath the table. He placed them in the center of the room. Christor nodded Ailís onto one, then took the second, propping one foot on the lower rung with all the ease and grace of familiarity.

He caught her gaze for a moment with his own, held it. And then he began to play.

It was a simple rhythm at first, single strokes with the tipper that thudded like a heartbeat. Then he added an upstroke, and another, like quickened breathing. Soon he was pounding a complicated rhythm that swelled, varied, and had Ailís tapping her feet while a reel played in her head.

From the corner of her eye, she saw the shopkeeper watching, arms crossed. Then, as Christor changed the tempo again, going from reel-time to jig, the man walked right out his own door and into the street. Ailís flinched, embarrassed for Christor, whose playing she thought marvelous. He merely quirked a brow and played on.

When the door opened again, a minute later, she shopkeeper was not the only one who entered. Behind him was a younger man, huge-necked and ham-handed, wearing the stained apron of a butcher. Behind him, a bit older, ginger-haired and wiry as a terrier, was a third man. His reddened hands and wax-spattered garb indicated he was a chandler.

Ailís half expected the new pair to haul Christor out of his seat and heave him into the street. Instead, they wordlessly removed their smocks and drew two more stools from the seemingly never-ending supply beneath the table. The shopkeeper handed the terrier a truly beautiful fiddle from the wall, choosing a second for himself. The ox pulled a sightly battered flute from his sleeve.

The trio waited a few beats, nodding in time to Christor's drumming. Then, one at a time, they joined in. In no time, the rollicking strains of "Lost Man's Jig" were filling the little shop. The old man whooped in delight; the young man thumped the floor in time with the music so hard that Ailís half expected his hobnailed boot to go right through the planks. And Christor, eyes flashing with a joy and fire unlike anything Ailís had ever seen in him, gave her a grin that was quick, wicked, and heaven to behold.

Her foot stilled its tapping as her heart caught firmly in her throat. Tears, unexpected and sharp, gathered behind her eyes. In that magical moment, sitting in the midst of a tiny music shop with four of Ireland's finest playing out their own hearts, she knew her life truly would never be the same. She would never be the same.

Chapter 14

Christor was still humming some eight hours later. If he closed his eyes and concentrated, he could feel the vibration of the *bodhrán* in his fingertips, could see Ailís perched atop her stool, eyes wide and glowing, her not-small foot tapping in time to the music.

He had not planned to take her to the music shop. He'd never been inside himself, only passed by on occasion. But she had brought out such a . . . he didn't necessarily care to think of his urge as *primitive,* but that's what it had been. The need to pound on something, preferably a drum, had been overwhelming. Had there been a big, hairy, prehistoric creature available, he would have stalked and thumped that, too.

Perhaps the interlude had not ended quite as planned. In the midst of the music, he'd come up with the idea to take Ailís driving, perhaps along the fashionable North Circular Road and into the nearby countryside. There, buoyed by a bottle of wine and a picnic lunch, a spreading willow for privacy, he'd intended to test just how deep was his connection to Ailís O'Neill.

He'd lost her in Fleet Street, not two minutes after waving the last farewell to his musical companions. Lost her to yet another Society dragon, as it happened. Lady Alderton had been prowling along Westmoreland Street, overladen footman in tow, when they had turned the corner from Fleet Street. Whether it was the concept of Ailís being in his company or whether the lady simply wanted another body to carry her parcels, Christor had no idea. Whichever, whatever, she had commandeered Ailís's company and whisked the girl into a mantua-maker's before Christor could mount an effective protest.

La Alderton's officious act, paired with the sight of the string of pearls she sported, had put him in devious mind of the stolen faux jewels he had in his desk. Cleary's gambit with the shoe had been amusing; there was still sport to be had at the Aldertons' expense.

Christor was not a vindictive man by nature. He did, however, find the Aldertons offensive in general, and Lady Alderton's treatment of Ailís especially vexing. He'd seen one too many Society matrons treating Ailís as a sort of scratching post, an old-maid-to-be whose purpose in life and in Dublin was to fetch, carry, and amuse. He was having none of that.

He was just reaching into his desk drawer when Figgis tapped at the door. The valet entered, bearing several freshly laundered shirts and an eager air. "Are you ready to dress for dinner, my lord?"

Christor glanced down at his pantaloons and shirt, waistcoat and cravat, and raised a brow. "I would consider myself dressed, Figgis."

"Certainly *not,* my lord!" The man bustled across the room, disapproval radiating from his narrow form. "You are attending the Fitzjohns, are you not?"

"I am."

"Well, then. This will never do."

Figgis promptly attacked the white silk waistcoat. Christor, given the choice of either batting the valet's hands away or submitting, opted for surrender. Not that he had any great desire to dress expressly for his hosts. Lord and Lady Fitzjohn of Artane were hardly the King and Queen of Connaught. But he supposed he could dress for Figgis—or rather, let himself be dressed for Figgis—and make the fellow happy. The valet had been dragging about the house of late, shoulders slumped and mouth pinched, and Christor knew it would not be such a hardship to make him feel useful.

He did balk at the formal black knee breeches and silk-bowed, patent leather shoes Figgis chose. Both had been intended for the requisite appearances at Almack's and, Christor thought, had been summarily shoved to the back of some wardrobe on his return to Dublin.

"I believe I shall remain as I am from the waist down," he announced firmly. Some lines did have to be drawn. "The rest is at your discretion."

Looking hurt but resigned to his employer's woeful lack of discernment, Figgis turned his attention to shirts. The batch he had been carrying all looked the same to Christor, but then, he was the one without vision, apparently. The valet discarded one for having too informal a cuff, the next for being too white a white. He actually allowed Christor to don and button the third before deciding the button-on collar was too low.

Five minutes later, Christor was back in the shirt he had been wearing when the valet arrived. "It will do, I suppose," was Figgis's gloomy pronouncement, "with the correct waistcoat."

The correct waistcoat was not the fawn brocade. Nor was it the white-on-white striped silk, nor the dove silk plush. A faint growl from Christor sent the ghastly embroidered ecru he could never recall purchasing back into the wardrobe with the breeches. In the end, he found himself garbed in white silk whose only discernible difference, so far as he could see, from the one he had originally donned, was that it possessed silver buttons rather than ivory.

Figgis took his time with the cravat, abandoning two before he was satisfied with the *orientale* he fashioned. Christor, never one to bother with either a pattern that took more concentration than calculating rates of the 'Change or so much starch that one was in risk of cutting one's jaw, bore the process with fading grace. Had he not already known what waistcoat the valet had chosen, he would never have been able to tell the difference. His chin was now destined to point skyward for the foreseeable future.

"Black, my lord?" Figgis queried, proffering a coat with one hand. "Or black? Of course, there's always the Weston black from last Season, or the new Hamberton—"

"Black. The first will do."

The first, as it turned out, did not do. "The left lapel has lost its shape," Figgis declared. And the Weston did not "do any sort of justice to the *orientale*." Christor could not be certain which of the other two he ended up being buttoned snugly into; they looked precisely the same as each other—and the two discarded.

Having been poked, prodded, and prompted for more than a half-hour, and looking very much as he would have that half hour earlier under his own ministrations, Christor quitted the room. Cowardly, perhaps, but he did so, and quickly, when the valet vanished into the depths of the dressing room in search of a more suitable watch chain.

Christor had made it down the hall and had his foot on the top stair when Figgis came scuttling after him. "My lord."

Christor turned, resigned to disapproval and clanking chain. "Yes, Figgis."

He did, in fact, jingle somewhat when he was finally able to descend, and had acquired a diamond cravat pin, replacement pocket handkerchief, and a quizzing glass, which Figgis had repeatedly thrust on him and which he could only assume had once frequented Dublin soirees with his departed father. Philosophical under the circumstances, he thought perhaps he could make use of it to read the hallmarks on the bottom of his hostess's silver.

The Alderton fakes would have to wait. He wasn't taking any chances on remaining in his rooms, where Figgis might suddenly decide his shirt was not white enough, necessitating the removal of coat, waistcoat, and cravat. One torture by *orientale* was sufficient for the evening. He'd dismissed the valet for the night, not wanting to face a debate later over nightshirts, which he rarely if ever wore.

He still had a good quarter-hour before he had to leave the house. He contemplated lounging by the fire with the day's copy of the *Journal,* but thought better of it. The less he had to sit and rise in his fitted coat, the better. So he contented himself with gazing out the library window onto the street.

Dublin was on the move, setting out for whatever entertainment the evening was to provide. A herd of overdressed young bucks strolled by, flasks and walking sticks flashing. Lady Ferrisett bounced by in her sedan chair, a gauzy tail of her wrap flapping alongside where it had been caught in the door. And old Major O'Doul went trotting youthfully up the steps of the tidy, narrow house that Christor knew belonged to a lady who was neither friend nor relation of either the major or his heiress wife.

Christor watched in surprise as Séamus Cleary came striding up the street. Moments later, the door knocker clacked. Cleary had not been expected; they had arranged to meet after midnight. Beyond that, the man started complaining almost before the butler had closed the library door behind him.

"I've better things to do of a night than follow the Scannals up and down all over Town again."

"So do something better, then," was Christor's mild reply.

"Sure and I'm going to forget that some loutish sod is riding our roads in our name, frightening innocent folk and doing God knows what else."

Christor refrained from commenting that they had a very good idea of what the sod was doing—they'd started this whole trend in robbing coaches, after all—and that the fellow was about as frightening as week-old oat porridge. Instead, he asked, "What were you planning on doing?"

Séamus eyed the liquor decanters hopefully, all but leaping across the room when Christor gestured for him to help himself. "We'd thought to ask about for that monster of a horse." He drained a glass of brandy in a swallow, then poured himself another. "Someone in Boot Lane must know something."

Christor winced at the thought of his three young confederates bouncing from pub to pub within shouting distance of the New Gaol, asking questions about a highway robber's horse. None of them were either inconspicuous or particularly subtle. "Perhaps," he suggested, "you might resume your search of stables in the area instead."

Cleary groaned and, lifting one brilliant green-clad arm, thrust a hand through his flaming red hair. "Oh, grand. Excluding the stables you've made use of, the one I do, and the dozen-odd we've already visited, we've only . . . oh, twenty or so left in Town and easily that number nearby."

"I know. Far more enjoyable to make inquiries inside, with a tankard in hand. I do hate to spoil the evening, so . . . here." Christor crossed the room and removed an unopened bottle of fine Tullamore Irish from a cabinet. "Take this along. Just be certain Pól doesn't start spinning tales with a loose tongue."

"Aye." Grinning, Séamus tucked the whiskey under his arm. "For all that the fellow spends most of his time shut up like a clam, he's a rare one after a bit o' the Irish." When Christor's eyes went back sharply to the bottle, he chuckled. "Don't fret yourself. I'll keep watch over him."

"Fine. I'll see the three of you with Declán Clancy and Milo Muldoon at Ross's shop later. And no," Christor muttered when Cleary's eyes glinted, "we're not riding the roads tonight. We agreed already. Tonight we plan."

Belatedly realizing Figgis might have something to say on the matter of his hat and greatcoat, Christor hurriedly followed Cleary out. They parted at Stephen's Green, Séamus off to inform the Scannal brothers that they would not be working from a pub bench that night, Christor heading toward Ely Place and the Fitzjohn House. He paused for a minute to gaze over the wrought-iron fence that surrounded the Green. Inside, among the dark paths and darker clumps of trees, he imagined there were a handful of cutthroats and pickpockets. One of these days, the city would bother to put in better lighting. For now, only the brave and the foolish strolled at night in the eight or so acres that were so bright and welcoming in the day.

He was forced to admit that London did have its benefits, the seemingly endless expanses of Hyde Park among them. But he would gladly take his exercise inside a Hoby's boot box if it meant being in Ireland. He could not imagine Ailís being happy in London, nor much more so on his Surrey estate, and as each day went by, he had an increasingly difficult time imagining being happy without Ailís O'Neill.

With that in mind, he continued on his way. He knew Ailís, Eamonn, and Anne would be among the guests at supper. He had made certain before accepting. Quite probably, the baroness would have been more than happy to exclude the O'Neills, but Christor had a strong suspicion that Gerry Fitzjohn had made his own request. And there was a decent chance that, in her scheming to keep Ailís away from her son, Lady Fitzjohn would be seating her next to Christor himself.

He whistled and rattled his stick along the Green's fence as he went.

Ailís had been waiting for him. As far as she was concerned, she had been doing a very good job of not looking as if she were waiting for anyone or anything, save perhaps to be fed, but of course, her mother was not fooled.

"Watched pots . . ." she quipped as she drifted past, nodding toward the drawing room door at which Ailís had been staring intently.

"Never burn," Ailís shot back, but quickly dragged her gaze away.

Gerry Fitzjohn, playing the overly attentive swain, bounded back from his trip to the sideboard. "Punch!" he announced, and shoved his fist into her face.

"Thank you, Mr. Fitzjohn." She accepted the glass before he could spill its contents all over her white dress. "You are very kind."

"Not at all. Not at all. There must be something else I can fetch for you."

Lord Clane, she said silently. "Nay, I am quite content with this, thank you."

He was not to be deterred. "Well, I'll just stay right here, then, should you think of anything. And if not, I shall be in just the right place to escort you in to dinner."

"I believe your mother intends for you to escort Miss Reynolds."

Gerry's eyes drifted to the giggling blonde who was holding court at the opposite end of the room. Miss Caroline Reynolds was a recent addition to Dublin Society, having suddenly arrived to spend the autumn with cousins in Howth. Looking into the vapid if beautiful face, it was hard for Ailís to imagine the young lady doing something so improper that she would be hustled out of England. Of course, she might not have done anything at all, but . . .

"Twenty thousand pounds," Philly Lorcan announced, having recently been in the lady's circle, "and whatever else Reynolds decides to throw into the settlement pot."

"Did she tell you that?" Ailís demanded. Not that she was in the least ashamed of her own meager dowry—she had no intention of handing it over to some man, after all—but she certainly would never discuss it in public. She already did not like Caroline Reynolds, nor the fact that Eamonn seemed quite entranced by the creature. Or by her twenty thousand.

"Her cousin told my mother," was Philly's response. "Don't think she meant to, though. Seemed most distressed that I might slight the chit as a result. As if I'd sneeze at twenty thousand."

The cousin, Ailís speculated, had probably been most distressed that Philly might *not* slight Miss Reynolds. Young ladies with twenty thousand pounds, after all, could be counted upon to set their sights somewhat higher than the son of an Anglo-Irish knight.

Ailís's present concern was that Miss Reynolds might not sneeze at Eamonn O'Neill. If a young lady, twenty thousand pounds notwithstanding, had somehow removed herself from the running for a needle-nosed, chinless English peer, a clever and handsome future Member of Parliament might look rather tasty indeed. And the last thing Ailís wanted for her brother was to see him swallowed by an English family with more money than sense.

"Here's Clane," Gerry exclaimed, jolting Ailís from her thoughts. "Splendid. We ought to be able to eat soon!"

Ailís's stomach promptly did a familiar flip, her fingertips sizzled, making dinner a wholly unimportant issue. Who could think of food, after all, when such a man as the Earl of Clane was about?

"Dia is Maire," she whispered, stunned. It had happened, unbidden and sly, and just as her moonstuck friends had described.

She had fallen in love with him.

When his eyes met hers, she shivered. And thought she might cry. She did not want this, this certainty that for the foreseeable future, if not aeons more, her heart was no longer hers alone. It was his, she thought, to tuck in his pocket or fling about like an India rubber ball.

"Why, Lord Clane!" As Ailís watched, Caroline Reynolds detached herself from her admirers and glided across the carpet, hands extended. "How delightful a surprise to meet again! And here in Dublin. I would never have imagined . . ."

Christor looked surprised indeed, but not in the least displeased as he lifted one of the lady's hands to his lips. "Miss Reynolds. What happy chance."

If Caroline were in the least surprised to be encountering Clane, Ailís would eat her shawl. She might well have imagined it, but the lady was looking a wee bit smug.

"And what," Christor was asking, "has brought you to Ireland?"

A flying broomstick, Ailís thought waspishly, *and perhaps a boot in the posterior from the ton.*

"Oh, I have always longed to visit my cousins here in this lovely country. When they tendered an invitation this year, I simply could not refuse."

"Was it a footman, do you think? Or perhaps a groom?"

Ailís spun to find Maria Farnham at her elbow, mouth pursed, looking slightly green about the eyes. "I beg your pardon?"

"It must have been something. I would wager a week's pin money she was caught rolling about with some spotty footman."

Ailís suddenly had a very clear mental image of the devil and the deep blue sea. To be befriended, even temporarily, by a smutty-tongued Miss Farnham, was no gift, even if it were at Miss Reynolds's expense. In that moment, she could not despise Maria, no matter how intent the creature was on snaring the earl. She could only pity her. And feel rather dramatically sorry for herself.

This English beauty with her fortune was, after all, just the sort of woman with whom the Earl of Clane would be expected to ally himself.

She was saved the effort of speaking by Lady Fitzjohn's announcement that it was time to move into the dining room. As expected, Miss Reynolds went in on Gerry's arm. Ailís found herself well down the line of thirty-odd people, escorted by Philly Lorcan. Worse, she was seated between Philly and Christor's pompous friend, Lyndhurst. And Christor himself was almost directly across the table—where she could see his every expression, hear his every word, but could not speak to him.

Silently cursing her hostess and silly protocol, she steeled herself for a very long meal.

"So we meet again, Miss O'Neill."

Ailís sighed, brushed Philly's hand away from her thigh when he took rather too long to settle his napkin, and replied, "So we do, Mr. Lyndhurst."

Across the table, occupying the seat between Gerry and Christor, Miss Reynolds smiled prettily into her soup. Christor and Gerry smiled prettily at Miss Reynolds. Ailís tried to take comfort in the fact that Eamonn was further down the table, smiling graciously at the elderly Lady Louisa Conolly.

"What is the word of your hero bandit, Miss O'Neill?" Apparently Lyndhurst had already ascertained that Mrs. Balch, seated to his left, was stone deaf. "Does he still hold a lofty place in your esteem?"

The debate between discretion and satisfaction was weak and short-lived. "Among the loftiest," Ailís replied tartly. "There is nothing quite so admirable, is there, as a noble cause and a man who practices it?"

"You consider crime a noble cause. How . . . interesting."

"Crime, sir? I do not speak of crime, but of being certain that the welfare of the people is seen to by those with the means and opportunity. As a matter of fact, is that not the purpose of Parliament? My goodness, Mr. Lyndhurst, I have only just realized that you and our An Cú are intended for much the same purpose! How . . . interesting."

She glanced about at the sound of a muffled chuckle, but could not find its source. Christor was not looking at her at all, staring soberly instead into the bowl of his spoon.

Lyndhurst, it seemed, was speechless. He was also, when she looked back, a bit purple in the face. She wondered if perhaps she ought to summon a footman to thump him upon the back. She did not particularly want to touch him.

On her other side, Philly brushed her breast with an encroaching elbow and announced, "Wouldn't it be splendid to have the Hound at this very table! The questions we could put to the fellow . . ."

Protocol quickly vanished to the winds. And it became rather windy in the dining room. "Foul, base creature!" Lady Fitzjohn declared. "Why, he quite spoiled the Lady-Lieutenant's ball!"

Lyndhurst made an unfortunate choking sound. "His continued presence is testimony to the need for effective, old-fashioned English martial standards here in Ireland. Such heinous acts against good citizens would never be countenanced in London."

Ailís bit her lip, thinking of all the tales she heard from London of gentlemen being assaulted near their clubs, of ladies' carriages being stopped by thieves on their way home from the opera. Effective martial standards, indeed.

"What we need are a few good Bow Street runners," was Lord Fitzjohn's comment. "Demmed clever fellows, those chaps."

"Their cleverness commensurate with their reward, I believe," Eamonn said mildly.

"What we need"—Sir John Alderton pounded the table with a meaty fist—"are a few good guns and a pack of hounds. Tree the blackguard and let fly with the lead. That would see the end to his thieving days."

"I've a jolly pack," offered Mr. Balch. "Noses to beat the best of them."

"My pointer bitch would see the deed done," from Sir Edward Lorcan.

Before long, a slavering pack fifty strong had been assembled at Lady Fitzjohn's dining table. Had the creatures not been spread out over the bulk of Ireland, it might have been a serious matter. But Ailís knew the ladies present would sooner invite An Cú himself into their homes than countenance the presence of hounds from their country estates.

"Curious tale about all the false gems floating through Dublin Society."

The gentlemen and their hunt talk were no match for the ladies when jewels were mentioned. One by one every female face turned to Christor. "False gems?" Lady Lorcan demanded, her hand going to the jade collar at her throat.

"Mmm." Christor twirled his wineglass between thumb and finger and nodded. "Have you not heard? Part of the Hound's booty ended up in the hands of an honest jeweler. And half of it was fake."

"How did you hear this?" Ailís's mother asked, clearly fascinated.

"All rubbish!" was Alderton's grunted pronouncement. "No such thing as an honest jeweler. Probably cried fake and pocketed the whole lot."

The elderly Lady Louisa, draped as always in multiple jewels and ever eager for a good bit of gossip, leaned forward in her seat. "What were the pieces?"

"Rubbish," Alderton repeated. No one so much as looked his way.

"Well, I did get the tale third-hand from my tailor," Christor announced, taking a lengthy pause to drain his glass and wait for a footman to refill it. "But I do believe he said it was sapphires, large pieces, set in gold with diamonds. A complete set, if I'm not mistaken: necklace, bracelet, ear bobs. All paste."

Christor could see the wheels spinning behind the eyes of most of the ladies present. Then, slowly, Lady Fitzjohn's gaze slid toward Lady Alderton.

"As I heard it," he continued, "there were several man's rings in the same group, and those were quite genuine." He pretended to think for a moment. "A large ruby, I believe, and a diamond. There might have been a cravat pin among them as well, and a sapphire watch fob. Of course, I could very well be mistaken. I take so little interest in such matters . . ."

Now no one save perhaps Miss Reynolds was paying any attention whatsoever to him. Those persons not looking at the pale Lady Alderton and puce-faced Sir John were staring into their laps, their plates, or empty space.

Christor willed Ailís to meet his gaze, if only so he could look into her eyes for a moment. Oh, she was lovely, certainly, in near-profile; he could easily spend an hour admiring the curve of her cheek, the arch of her brow. Well, he amended, amused with himself, a quarter-hour. But he was firmly convinced he could pass weeks of his life happily staring into her eyes.

"What lady," Caroline Reynolds suddenly demanded, jolting everyone from their silent contemplations of one lady and her purple-jowled husband, "would possibly want to wear fake sapphires when there are such lovely real ones to be had? What ninnies you must have here in Dublin!"

"Well said, mademoiselle," Christor murmured, and tucked cheerfully into the terrine of goose that had followed the soup.

While the remainder of the meal never quite returned to the entertainment level to which it had risen, it was not an utter waste. Christor was reasonably diverted by the whiteness of Lady Alderton's knuckles where she gripped her meat knife, and by the dagger-sharp glances she kept darting at her husband.

He was not so amused by Philly Lorcan's constantly disappearing hands, but was prevented from flinging his own cutlery across the table when the fellow yelped, jumped, and lifted a reddened paw to his mouth for an instant. Ailís, Christor imagined, would be an excellent pincher if forced into it.

Mrs. Balch, who nodded off during the dessert, was prevented from going nose-first into the blancmange by the fact that her turban was caught in the fussy design at the top of her hostess's chairs. Gerry Fitzjohn did manage to plop his elbow into his plate, sending a cream-drenched strawberry rolling quickly across the table toward Miss Farnham. And Sir John's innards commenced a distressed rumbling that brought Lady Fitzjohn's wheezing pug scampering out from under that lady's chair.

All in all, Christor decided, it was as enjoyable an evening as a fellow could have when the company was mostly comprised of fools and the woman he desired was out of reach.

She remained that way till the end, whisked into the drawing room with the ladies so the gentlemen could have their requisite—and ultimately abbreviated—encounter with the port decanter. It was not long before the combined serenade of Sir John's rumblings and Pug's yapping sent the men fleeing from the dining room.

Ailís, Christor soon discovered, was all but hidden on a settee, bracketed by the Ladies Louisa Conolly and Lorcan as the assembly listened to Miss Reynolds taking Haydn to new lows at the pianoforte. Opting for the most pleasant alternative, he took a seat beside Anne O'Neill, who promptly patted his hand and handed him a biscuit.

The Aldertons, he noticed during a pause when Miss Reynolds finally ceded her place to a sullen-faced Maria Farnham, were nowhere to be seen. And finally, when the inter-minable-evening ended and the guests were spilling out the door and into their various conveyances for their respective two-minute drives home, he realized that, not only had young Fitzjohn and Lorcan vanished, but that Eamonn was nowhere to be seen.

"Well, Clane"—Lyndhurst's hand landed heavily on his shoulder—"another provincial affair survived. What do you say we trot over to Daly's for a brandy and roll or two of the dice?"

"I . . ." Christor cursed under his breath as he watched Ailís and her mother roll off in Lady Louisa's carriage. "I am afraid I must decline."

All the things he wanted to say to Ailís, and he firmly believed in addressing important matters at the earliest possible moment, would have to wait. He hated waiting.

"You have other plans, do you?" Lyndhurst gave a prurient chuckle. "Well, enjoy her, and should it not be an exclusive arrangement, pass her on to me. You've always possessed a marvelous eye for the bit of muslin."

Jonathan Lyndhurst, ever the striving and tally-keeping competitor, had no idea just how close he came that night to being first among every single person of his current acquaintance to meet his Maker.

Chapter 15

"Miss O'Neill, would you do me the honor of . . . Miss O'Neill, allow me to tell you how ardently I worship and . . . Ailís, my love, my heart, marry me . . . Oh, blast it all!"

It was useless, of course. A reverie, a pipe dream. No amount of fantasizing, of pacing the bedchamber planning his proposal, was going to make it come about. Ailís let out a wretched groan and flopped face-down onto her bed, startling the hedgehog who had been snuffling about its cage. The little creature promptly rolled into a tight ball and sat atop the straw-strewn cage bottom like a quivering pin cushion.

"Ah, Turloch, I am sorry." Abandoning her own woes for the moment, Ailís coaxed the animal out of its spiny ball with a piece of apple. "I know precisely how you feel. This entire situation makes me want to curl up and vanish, too."

She'd never asked to fall in love, could even recall more than one occasion when, in church, surrounded by friends who could not quite control their moonish grins and wistful sighs, she had prayed *not* to be struck with that particular affliction. To be fair, she supposed God had far better things to do than to be constantly protecting her from her own stupidity.

She'd spent the better part of the day *not* thinking about Christor. At breakfast, while Uncle Taddy muttered and groused about the dismal performance of *The Battle of Vittoria* at the Rotunda, she had not thought about him playing his *bodhrán* for her. She had not seen his impressive height and breadth of shoulder in every man she had passed while running errands in Grafton Street for her mother. And she certainly had not thought of him while watching Turloch munch on the supper Fergus had reluctantly provided him of garden worms and blackflies.

Christor would be returning to England soon, she thought glumly. Or perhaps he would simply retire to his Kildare estate, which could be China for all the difference it would make. Either way, she'd not be seeing him. If she were fortunate, her Tullamore relations would invite her for an extended stay, as they often did. There, in the comfort of her grandmother's home, she would not have to pass every day on the streets where she had first gotten to know—fallen in love with—the Earl of Clane. She would not think of him at all.

And next they'd be selling sandy lots in the Wicklow hills.

"Bleagh," she moaned, and buried her face in the coverlet.

Her life, she mused with no small amount of helplessness, was not meant to take such dizzying turns. Nay, she'd always been so in control, so sure of herself and her desires. Painting, reading, a bit of money for the family coffers, a bit of extra pleasure for her family. Oh, she'd thought occasionally of children, of a home of her own. Somehow, though, she'd managed lately to paint that particular picture without a man in it. Foolish creature or not, even she knew it was all but impossible to beget without some help. There had never been anything immaculate about her character or person in the past, and it wasn't likely she was going to attain perfect Grace now.

Sacrilege aside, she was a sorry mess.

She was no better suited to self-pity than to idiocy, but she was presently up to her eyeballs in both, and sinking fast. Why, she thought, would a man like Christor consider choosing her for an instant? Oh, she was clear enough on her appeal; she had as much brains and beauty as was necessary for an ordinary life. She was proud, too, of her heritage, of the hard-working men and women her ancestors had been and the more scholarly gentlefolk they had become. But she also knew she was contemptuous on occasion, stubborn as a matter of principle, and about as well suited to the life of the Earl of Clane's countess as an Ulster banshee.

"And I loathe painting landscapes!" she moaned into the pillow. Cruel fate, she concluded, had, from the very beginning, blasted any aristocratic aspirations she never knew she'd had.

Well sunk in her gloom, she did not move at the sound of a tap at her door, but merely uttered a muffled invitation to enter.

"Miss Ailís?"

"Aye?" She turned her head just enough so she could see the cook's sturdily-shod feet in the doorway. "Oh, Sweeney, forgive me, but I've no appetite for a sweet tonight. Supper quite filled me."

"Nay, nay. I've no sweet for you, Miss, but news."

"Aye?" Feeling some interest was warranted, Ailís rolled over onto her back.

The cook trundled into the room and bent over the bed. "He struck again last night. Our Hound. On the road to Clontarf this time. Took a carriage belonging to some wine merchant. Shot a piece off one of the wheels, too, as it rolled away."

Startled, Ailís pushed herself up onto her elbows. "That does not sound like An Cú. He's not known to take from those who earn their living, nor to shoot at them once he lets them go."

Sweeney shrugged ample shoulders. "Word has it the merchant rubs elbows with the likes of Sir John Alderton and his fancy lot. As for the shot, I've no idea, but we can be sure our Hound had his reasons."

"Aye. I suppose . . . Aye, I'm certain we can. Thank you, Sweeney, for the news."

"But there's more to tell, Miss, and not so pleasant."

Ailís had her own opinions as to the pleasantness of gunshots, but held her tongue. It was An Cú, after all, noble and good, a far better man than Sir John or his wine-swilling associates. "Yes, and . . . ?"

Now the cook was twisting her apron between her fists, eyes bleak. "There's something brewing about Town, miss. Fergus was passing a group of soldiers in the market today and heard them speaking of the Hound, of plans they had for him. They've an intent to put extra men on the roads, secret-like, dressed as farmers and such. They mean to take the Hound, Miss Ailís, and not without some blood-letting."

Ailís's own blood chilled. "Oh, God."

"Aye. Pray, Miss. Pray hard." Sweeney was offering her own pleas to the Saints Colmcille, Finnén, and Máel Muire as she left.

It was not long after, when the lights were out and Ailís had spent a twitchy hour in bed, that she decided prayer was not enough. She needed to *do* something. Flinging back the covers, she rose and paced her chamber, mind whirling.

She needed to find Séamus Cleary, for his own safety and for that of the Hound. The problem, of course, was that she had no idea where to even begin looking. Séamus led a merry life, often where he was not meant to be and rarely where he was expected. He might well be in Town, swilling ale in some pub. But he might also be out riding the roads, following An Cú in their endeavors—and perhaps into the waiting jaws of the militia.

Eamonn. As she had for most of her life when troubled with matters better kept from their mother, Ailís thought of her brother. Eamonn might be able to help. He could go places she could not in search of Séamus, knew of other men who could find Cleary if he could not. Aye, if Eamonn were still home, he would help. He had to.

Grabbing up her dressing gown, Ailís rushed across the hall. She tapped at his door, and got no response. Peering inside, she saw the room was empty, the bed unruffled and fire dead. For once, unlike most nights in recent memory, she had not heard her brother leave the house after supper; he must be about somewhere.

All was quiet downstairs. Chewing fretfully at her lower lip, Ailís checked the parlor, the little library, even the dining room. No Eamonn. His smart silk-plush hat was on its hook, the fashionable greatcoat he had recently taken to wearing was hanging below it. She mounted the stairs again, desperate for any inspiration. It did not take her long to decide that she was going to have to go out in search of . . . anyone who might help.

Her heart was hammering in her chest as she dug through the limited clothing in her wardrobe. Deeper she went, nearly to the very back, and breathed a sigh of relief. The coat was there, with the shirt, boots, and breeches, old clothes of Eamonn's that she had worn in the country years before. They had been far too large then; with luck they would be a better fit now. With more luck, she would not look like an hourglass draped in sacking once dressed.

Knowing what she had would not be enough, she crept back to Eamonn's room, careful to miss the creaking floorboards and squeaking hinges that might wake her light-sleeping mother. From her brother's decent supply, she took an unstarched cravat, an older hat that she hoped wouldn't slide down to her nose. Then, struggling with unfamiliar buttons and knots, she dressed.

As it turned out, her feminine shape was not totally obvious inside the men's garb, but neither was it completely hidden. She had seen plenty of men with projecting paunches, none whose bulk rested above their waist. The coat was still large on her, however. As long as she kept it buttoned, slouched a bit, and stayed out of bright light, she might pass for a young man. The ensemble would have to do. The other option, going out in a dress, was not an option at all.

She was struggling into the first boot when she heard the front door thud shut. Hopping, muttering, she hurried to the landing window. Just in time to see her brother strolling away down the street. *The kitchens.* She had forgotten to check the kitchens. Eamonn and Fergus occasionally shared a bottle of stout when the rest of the household was asleep.

"*Fool!*" Ailís cursed herself, slapping at her forehead. "Stupid, stupid!"

She rushed back to her chamber, crammed her foot into the second boot, shoved Eamonn's hat onto her head, where it promptly slid down to rest on her ears, and crept as quickly as she could down the stairs. Eamonn was nowhere to be seen when she finally reached the street, but she thought she knew the direction he would be taking. All nearby entertainment, she knew, involved heading toward the Liffey and, she supposed in somewhat hysterical glibness, sometimes falling into it. Trying to imagine how a man looked running—and finding herself feeling more like an ape—she hurried past Merrion Square.

She was approaching the Trinity College grounds now, and was soon weaving in and out among groups of cheerful young men who, clearly freed from their studies, were either strolling toward their favorite drinking spots or weaving aimlessly from them.

"Wasting your parents' funds, are you?" Ailís muttered under her breath at a clutch of particularly well-dressed, especially drunken boys. "Get back to your books and out of my way!"

She spied a tall figure, stick in hand, that could only be Eamonn entering College Park. Eying the dark rows of trees with some misgiving, Ailís took a deep breath and followed, only to come up short when her brother disappeared through a stone entryway.

"Blast!" she hissed aloud.

It was one thing to traipse around Dublin at night dressed as a man, quite another to stride boldly into Trinity's halls. She might be desperate, but she was no idiot. Her disguise would last all of a second inside, and she could guess what sport a bunch of sotted students would make of a woman who tumbled into their midst.

She bounced impatiently in place for a minute, mental wheels churning. Eamonn had no reason she could think of to be inside the college. The most likely scenario was that he was meeting a friend, and would be coming out sooner or later. Hoping it would be sooner rather than later, and that he would choose the same path, Ailís decided to wait.

She had done far wiser things in her life than hang about one of the darker spots in central Dublin alone at night. Then, again, she thought philosophically, she had done far more foolish ones, too. Falling head over heels for the Earl of Clane ranked highly among them. If she could survive that, heart and soul intact, a bit of nightly creeping should be a stroll in the park.

Ailís winced at her own slightly crazed, certainly pitiful wit, and prepared to wait for her brother to reappear. Eyes fixed on the entryway through which Eamonn had vanished, she took a few steps backward into the shelter of a dense cluster of field maples. And came up abruptly against a very solid object that most certainly was not a tree.

She tried to scream, but the only sound to emerge from her throat was a muffled whimper as a massive hand clamped over her mouth. Whatever as-yet-untested instinct for survival she possessed took over, and was quickly quashed. Her struggles were as easily subdued as her voice by the arm that wrapped like steel around her ribs, lifting her off her feet. She squirmed, kicked, tried to bite, then added fervent prayer to the mix when her attacker dragged her further into the trees.

There was a satisfying hiss from near her ear when her heel made solid contact with what felt like a kneecap, then, "For God's sake, Ailís, be still!"

It took a few seconds for the words to reach her panicked brain, another for her to recognize the voice. *Christor.* She went limp with relief. When she did, he removed his hand from her mouth and set her down. She promptly spun on somewhat shaky legs to face him.

"God help us, woman, you nearly crippled me!" Christor bent over to massage his leg.

"What are you doing here?" she demanded breathlessly. Then, "You were following me!" The idea sent a thrill down her spine.

"I was following your brother," came the terse retort, sending her airy heart sliding downward toward the pit of her stomach. "You got in the way."

She swallowed, then recovered enough self-possession to ask, "Following Eamonn? Why?"

"I might ask you the same thing."

"He's my brother. I was curious—"

"Ailís." Christor was in no mood for games. He was tired from having gotten precious little sleep the night before, stiff from having spent a full hour crouched in a bush near Leinster House, waiting for O'Neill to make his appearance, and now his leg smarted like the very devil where Ailís had smacked him. "You know damn well why we're both here, so don't waste my time blathering rubbish."

Her chin went up. "And just what is it I am supposed to know?"

He could just see her eyes in the shadows, wide and unblinking. So perhaps she didn't know, or didn't want to. But something had sent her running after Eamonn in the night, something had her worried enough to dress herself in absurd clothing and barrel into the Dublin streets. Christor sighed, counted five. "I can help him, Ailís, but he'll have to stop his night rides. There is too much interest right now, too many soldiers and civilian patrols on the roads. If he doesn't shoot someone first, they'll put a hole in him—or in some unfortunate soul who happens to be riding in the wrong place at the wrong time."

There was a long pause. Then Ailís laughed. It was a short, harsh sound, but a laugh nonetheless, and it pricked at his pride. "You believe Eamonn is An Cú."

"No," he corrected crisply. "I believe he is impersonating An Cú, riding on his own and putting all rightful highwaymen at risk. I am certain of a good many things, *cailín,* but none so much as that."

"Have you gone daft? Rightful . . . impersonating . . ." He heard Ailís take a deep breath, felt the brush of her breasts against his coat. "My God. It was you. On the road, in the carriage. An Cú. It was you all along."

"Clever girl."

"Nay." Suddenly she was shoving him back, pounding her fists against his chest. "Stupid girl. I should have seen it, it was right there in front of my nose, ringing in my ears. How could you! Why would you—"

He did the one thing he could think of to silence her and explain at the same time. Grasping her two fists in one of his, easily halting the assault on his already pummeled person, he pulled her tight against him and covered her mouth with his own. She resisted for several heartbeats, very nearly pulled free. But then, as his lips slanted over hers, hard and insistent, she went still. Then, with a soft, throaty sound, she melted into him, both lips and lush form.

After allowing himself a few heartbeats to savor the sensation, he released her, hard as it was, and drew his own slightly shaky breath. "That," he said gruffly, "I wanted that, Ailís. And with you gone starry-eyed over An Cú, I decided . . . Oh, it doesn't matter. Not now." Her head was still tilted to the side, and he had the distinct impression she wasn't hearing a word he was saying. Gratifying as that was, it wouldn't do. He gave her a slight shake. "Ailís. Listen to me, *muirnín*. Do you know why Eamonn went inside the College?"

"Nay. Nay, I . . . You wanted . . . ?"

"I still want, but it will just have to wait. Damn. I loathe waiting." Opting for feeble patience, Christor stepped away from Ailís and mused, "He'll have to come out sooner or later." With that, he let out a low whistle. In seconds, Séamus Cleary appeared from the shadows. "You'd best watch from Dame Street. If O'Neill comes out, bring him here."

Ailís tugged at his sleeve. He placed a hand over hers and continued, "If you stand at the east corner of the Bank, you'll be able to watch Westmoreland and Bank Streets as well." Now Ailís was tugging with her free hand at his lapel. "I'll keep watch from here."

"Fine." Cleary glanced at Ailís, shook his head, and vanished again, this time through the portal Eamonn had entered.

"What?" Christor demanded of Ailís, more harshly than planned, but her hand was sliding down the front of his coat and he decided he'd best stop it before it did some delightful damage.

"There are extra patrols on the roads tonight. Everywhere. Sweeney told me. Men disguised as—"

"Farmers, party-goers, travelers. Yes, I know. I have more men of my own out, as it happens, and they're a damned sight more adept than any half-cocked hired gun."

"You've an entire band of merry men, haven't you?" Ailís demanded, and Christor realized she was utterly awed by the concept, rather than mocking him with her choice of words.

"Comrades," he corrected sharply, "and there is nothing merry about this bloody situation. I'm putting a dozen good men at risk here, for the sake of one who might not deserve the consideration."

"Oh, you don't mean that! You are An Cú: noble and generous and—"

Christor grunted. "Don't push me, Ailís. I've had a dismal day and it might well be a dismal night. Catching your brother here will save us all precious time and our most precious hides."

"I still don't believe Eamonn . . ." She stomped one foot, an impressively audible sound. "Oh, ploid on it all! On all of you crock-headed little boys who think to behave like fools in search of adventure! I have no idea why you hatched this ridiculous scheme, riding about the countryside at night, putting yourself in just the right circumstance to be shot, behaving—"

"Ailís."

"Aye?" she snapped.

He was tempted to remind her just how highly she thought—and spoke—of the Hound's behavior. Instead, he commanded, "Go home."

Her spectacles glinted faintly like owl's eyes. "What was that?"

"Go home," he repeated wearily. "I'll walk you to the street. You'll be fine from there. Yes, yes, I know you want to hear the whole tale of my feckless search for adventure, and I'll be more than happy to spend the next ten years telling it to you, but for now, I want you home."

It occurred to him when she crossed her arms over her chest and did not budge, making it clear he would have to pick her up and bodily move her out of the copse, that she did not want to go home. "Ailís," he growled, voice lowering dangerously.

"Ailís, Ailís, Ailís," she shot back. "It's not a command, my name, and I'll not be taking any of your officious Earl of Clane rot tonight, regardless."

"You will not? You think you will not?"

"Nay, I will not. I'll have some answers, thank you very much, and right here, right now will do nicely."

"Ailís." When he took a menacing step toward her, fully intending to get her out of the area by whatever means necessary, she shot one palm toward his chest.

"I'll scream if you come a step closer. We'll see how you talk to a group of drunkenly chivalrous young men. Stop right there. I mean it."

"Empty threats do not suit you, *mo muirnín*," he muttered, taking that forbidden step, "especially foolish ones. Whether or not I were to have my face creased by said swains, the tale would eventually get out that you were caught wrapped around a gentleman in a dark park, and you might well find yourself rusticating indefinitely in Tullamore. Neither of us would much like that."

"As if I care about . . ." Her hand dropped, fisted on her hip. "And I am not wrapped around anyone!"

"You will be."

She squeaked when he reached out and grasped each lapel of her coat, but she did not scream. Nor did she scream when he pulled her toward him, fast. She did give a single little gasp when she bumped gently against his chest, but made no noise at all as he hauled her up onto her toes by her coat—a sweet and familiar situation—until they were nearly nose to nose. In fact, she went so still that Christor thought she might have stopped breathing entirely.

He wasn't particularly concerned with air at the moment, his or hers. He was far more interested in silencing her chattering—and satisfying his wanting.

He'd meant to be gentle, was telling himself to be gentle even as he took her mouth with his. But, as seemed to happen every time he touched her, his noble intentions lasted only until his skin was against hers. Once he tasted her, he forgot everything he had ever known about the graceful art of seducing a lady. His mind promptly drained of all thoughts of anything save for what he wanted to do to the woman in his arms.

He certainly forgot all about Eamonn O'Neill.

Ailís didn't need coaxing this time. As soon as their lips met, hers parted. She opened for him, warm and welcoming, and he felt the contact like lightning. Her arms slid upward to wrap fiercely around his neck, pushing his own hands aside. Not one to pass up such a delightful offering, he made short work of her coat buttons and wrapped his hands around her waist, covered now by only a thin layer of soft linen.

It had never occurred to Christor that there might be an advantage inherent in making love to someone else wearing clothing like his. He soon learned better. As his fingers clenched in Ailís's shirt, bunching up the fabric, it began to rise from the waistband of her breeches. A few more gentle tugs and suddenly his knuckles were brushing at bare skin.

"Dear God," he whispered against her lips, and flattened his palms against her back.

She felt like warmed silk. He pulled her that scant inch closer, all the while running his hands over the exposed expanse of her skin. Then, with a growl, he wrapped his arms all the way around her ribs until his fingertips were brushing the taut sides of her breasts and the wind would have been hard put to find a space in which to flow between their bodies.

Mine, was his only clear thought as he drew her down to kneel with him on the hard earth: a simple, single word that expressed everything.

All Ailís knew at that moment was that she had never fit anywhere in life as well as she fit in this man's arms. There was no question, no surprise at the intimacy of his hands on her bared skin, certainly no shame or fear. She wanted the kiss, the embrace to go on just as it was forever And she wanted it all to be different.

She pulled her mouth from his and unwound her arms from around his neck. When his grip tightened and he tried to follow her, she braced her palms against his chest and pushed. *"Ailís,"* he groaned, but he relaxed his grip.

It was difficult to see nuances in the darkness, but she got a glimpse of his clenched jaw and tortured eyes. She could see what releasing her cost him, knew somehow that his scruples were engaged in a mighty battle with something less noble— but far more exciting. And she was overwhelmed by the gift of it all.

"Oh, God. Ailís . . ."

"Shhh." She stretched to plant a kiss on his tense jaw. Then she sat back on her heels and set to work on his waistcoat.

So many buttons, she thought, and her fingers were clumsy in their haste. At last the heavy silk parted and she was free to explore the wide expanse of his linen-covered chest. He was hard, hot, and wholly unlike anything she had ever touched before. Beneath her exploring fingers, muscles twitched and leapt. The very difference between his form and hers was amazing. Where she was all soft hills, he was granite planes.

"You feel like David," she whispered, awed. And suddenly found herself being thrust an arm's length away from those wonderful, unfamiliar lands she had been so happily exploring.

"Who," Christor snapped, "is David?"

His whole face was hard now, shadowed stone. "I . . . he . . ."

"Dammit, Ailís how many have there been?"

"How many what?" she asked shakily.

His fingers clenched on her upper arms, viselike but not quite painful. "How many men before me? *Daman don diabhal, cá mhéad?*"

And suddenly she understood. "You're jealous." So much so that it had driven him to Gaelic. Ailís grinned broadly. "You are jealous!"

"I warn you, Ailís. I will not take—"

"Jealous. Jealous. Jealous!" she sang in delight, then broke free of his grip to hurl herself at his chest.

In an instant, they were both horizontal, her body stretched atop his, one of her thighs nestled between his. She felt wicked, suddenly, wholly beyond propriety and care. It was marvelous. Quite as marvelous as knowing he was angered by the thought of some unimportant man named David.

She propped her elbows on his chest. "Green throughout. And of a plaster statue, no less."

"What was that?" Slowly, as if he was not certain he wanted to touch her, Christor clasped her waist.

"David," she said, rubbing her palms against the sage-smelling linen of his shirt. "Auntie Ursula's husband brought back a small plaster copy of Michelangelo's David when he visited Florence. I used to love to play with it when I visited. It quite gave my aunt fits."

"I can well imagine why," came the dry retort. "Oh, Ailís. You will be the death of me."

"Not for a long while yet, I hope," she whispered.

"Hmm?"

"Oh, nothing of import. Christor?"

"Yes, Ailís?"

She lowered herself till they were chest-to-chest again. "Will you kiss me again now, please?"

"I will do anything to you that you wish, Ailís O'Neill."

She never got the chance to even ponder the possibilities. Just as her lips were about to meet his, the sound of footsteps came crashing through the trees. Christor rolled into a crouch in a single, smooth motion, taking Ailís with him and bracing her behind his arm.

"Clane! Damn it, Clane, where are—" Séamus Cleary cursed as he stumbled around the last tree, then came to a staggering halt not five feet away from where Ailís was furiously trying to get her shirt back into her breeches. He did not even spare her a glance. "He must have gotten past one of us."

"Who?" Christor demanded, rising to his feet, then, "O'Neill." The string of curses that followed included several Ailís had never before heard. "What has happened?"

Séamus's face was ash-pale in the faint light. " 'Twas young Timmy Muldoon who came running for Milo. They've got him trapped, Clane, inside Phoenix Park."

"Milo?"

"Nay, nay. Milo's doing what he can there." Cleary let out a long breath. Ailís felt her own go still in her chest when he continued. "O'Neill, riding as An Cú. The militia has him cornered like a fox."

Chapter 16

Christor cursed fluently, then hauled Ailís to her feet by one arm and thrust her in Cleary's direction. "Take her home. I'll see to having horses readied at Farrell's."

"Nay." She was standing between the two men now, Christor holding her by one arm, Cleary by the other. She shook both off and plunked her hands onto her hips. "I am going with you."

"Don't be ridiculous, Ailís!"

"Don't you take that tone with me," she shot back. "And don't think that simply because I enjoy having your hands all over me I'll turn all soft and malleable now."

"Ailís—"

"And there you go again with my name. It isn't nearly so effective as when you sigh it into my ears, you know."

"Ailís!" Christor darted a sharp look at Cleary, who was suddenly looking far too interested in the exchange. "That is quite enough. You are now going to show me your pert backside as you walk away with Séamus. And you are going to walk quickly, *muirnín*. Your idiot brother is on the verge of finding himself at the wrong end of a gun, and if it's all the same to you, I would like to make certain he does not come away from this evening peppered with lead."

He nodded to Cleary. "Take her home. Carry her if you have to."

"You're a bully, Clane!" she snapped. Then, as Séamus bent and easily hefted her over his shoulder, "Get your hands off me, you carroty behemoth! I mean it, Séamus. I'll be having words with your grandmother, and don't think she won't come after you with a shillelagh . . . Clane . . . Ouch! Touch me there again, Séamus Cleary, and you'll be walking like a duck till Judgment Day. Christor . . . *Damnú air, Críostóir Rhys Próinsias!* Eamonn is my brother . . ."

Christor waited until he was certain Cleary had matters well in hand, so to speak, then set off for the Denzil Street stables at a run. Matthew Farrell, now Dublin stablemaster for the Duke of Clonderry, had ridden with him in the early days of An Cú, then fought under him in Portugal. He currently kept several of his own animals among the duke's. He would hand two over with speed and no questions asked.

As it happened, Christor did not even have to wake the man. Farrell was pacing the street outside the stables, his cannon-blast-shattered leg dragging as he stalked and turned. At the sight of his former captain, his eyes lit. "Thank the Lord. I'd heard they had you! Took ten years off my life, it did. Timmy Clancy woke me. I thought—"

"They have the wrong man," Christor grunted. "I need two horses, Matt. Now."

"Aye. Of course. Aye."

Together, they hurriedly saddled a pair of bays. Cleary appeared at last, hat askew and bruise already blooming on his jaw. Apparently Ailís had put up quite a fight. Had Christor not been in a generally foul mood, he might have been impressed. As it was, he was thinking only of the hard ride to Phoenix Park and the uncertainty of what waited for them there.

"What else can I do, Captain?" Farrell pleaded. "There must be something."

"Ready any other horses you can. If the other lads come by, send them to Phoenix Park. And tell them to be bloody careful."

Farrell nodded eagerly. "I'll do that. Godspeed, Captain!"

As he and Cleary galloped off, Christor knew it was Eamonn O'Neill who needed God with him just then. Phoenix Park, a pleasure garden and Dublin's even larger equivalent to London's Hyde Park, was more than two miles west of the city center; every minute was of utmost importance.

They'd covered half the distance when Christor's well-honed ears picked up the sound of rapid hoofbeats behind them. Keeping his head down, he turned to look. He was not certain, but it appeared to be the third of Farrell's horses. Shouting to Cleary, he slowed his own mount slightly, then reached into his pocket. If it were an ally, he would be welcomed. If not, he would find himself face-to-face with a readied pistol.

The rider gained on them, came even. And rode right past with a flare of rippling cloak and wave. Blinking, Christor stared after the figure for a moment, then urged his horse back into a gallop. It was Farrell's horse, no question about it, but the rider was not a member of An Cú's band. Christor had gotten little more than a fleeting view of a pale face beneath the hat and a pair of ungloved hands.

When a long curl slipped from beneath the hat to whip in the wind, his uneasy suspicion turned to full-blown fury. *"Ailís!"* he bellowed.

Her head jerked toward him for an instant. then she was leaning low over her mount's neck, urging the animal into greater speed. And ordinarily it might have worked. She weighed a good five stone less than either Cleary or himself, enough to make a real difference to a horse. But Christor was a masterful horseman, and he had rage on his side. As if sharing the surge of emotion, his mount leapt forward and gained ground, soon running neck-and-neck with hers.

"What in the hell do you think you are playing at?" he shouted. She did not respond, didn't even look his way. "Dammit, Ailís, you'll get yourself killed!"

"Not unless you're the one to shoot," she yelled back.

Furious, uncertain, Christor tried to decide what to do about this bloody awful turn of events. He could reach out, grasp her reins, and haul both animals to a halt. But he didn't think Ailís would meekly turn about and ride home at his command. In the time he would spend tying her securely to a nearby tree, her brother could be lost.

Deciding he had no choice but to allow her to accompany them to Phoenix Park—and tie her to something there—he muttered several of his favorite oaths and rode on.

They reached the wall surrounding the huge park some ten minutes later. Not wanting to ride through the main Park Gate and hence take the chance of running into military or militia, Christor led the other two along the wall to a smaller entrance a quarter-mile further along. Inside, lantern lights bobbed and an occasional shout rang out. He swung from his blown mount. Cleary and Ailís followed.

As soon as both of her boots touched the ground, he was looming over her. "I ought to turn you over my knee right here and paddle you until you can't stand."

He was momentarily flummoxed when she replied, "Perhaps you should do. But you won't."

"Dammit, Ailís—"

"Please, just hear me out. I will make a bargain with you. I have an idea. If it does not sound viable, I will turn around and go home. You'll never have to speak with me again."

She found herself holding her breath while she waited for his response. When he finally snapped, "No deal. Séamus and I are going in. You will stay here. *Quietly.* Until one of us returns to see you home."

"Christor, please!"

"Shut up, Ailís. Now, Cleary, I'll ride to Knockmacoon Gate. I believe it's another quarter mile in this direction. From there, I believe I might be able to—"

"I have spent far more time in Dublin than you in the last several years." Desperate now, Ailís grabbed at his sleeve. "And I know the Park. I've bullied Eamonn into bringing me often enough, for even a brief respite from city life."

Christor shook off her hand. "I can't hear you, Ailís. Again, I believe from the gate, I might be—"

"Perhaps we ought to listen to her, Clane."

Ailís's jaw dropped. She turned slowly. "Thank you, Séamus."

He shrugged. "You were clever enough to sneak out of your house after I left you there and hare after us."

It hadn't been so difficult, really. She'd simply grabbed a cloak, gone right through the house and out the back, trailing Séamus to the stables, where she'd overheard Christor telling the stablemaster to mount anyone who came along. There, she had swaggered in on shaky knees, mumbled little more than "An Cú," and ridden out almost immediately on a horse.

She didn't think either Christor or Séamus wanted to hear just how easy it had been. And Christor appeared to be listening for the moment, so she said instead, "I've been here often enough at night with Uncle Taddy for his dismal musical performances. There are few trees spreading or dense enough to hide, but I know many of the thickets and shrubs, as well as the only hillocks large enough to shelter a man for long."

When she got no response, she pressed, "They haven't found him yet; we'd be hearing it if they had. Now, the pair of you can trot in and try to find him while dodging those lanterns, or you can trust me to lead you."

"You truly know the Park that well?" Christor's tone was hard enough to pound nails. "I swear, Ailís, if this is but a crackbrained scheme . . ."

"I know the Park," she said simply.

"Very well then, but I require a promise from you."

"Aye?"

"If anything goes awry—and I mean *anything:* if either Séamus or I goes down, if there is gunfire, if you stub your *toe . . . anything*—I want you to get out of here the fastest way you can and ride back to Town. Promise me that."

"You cannot be serious!"

"Promise me, Ailís," he growled. "If anything were to happen to you, I would run mad. Promise me."

"Aye." She could no more have refused him just then than she could have flown. "I promise."

"Good." She thought she heard him exhale. "Then lead on."

They secured their horses behind a rowan thicket nearby, then crept through the park gate. Ailís did know the park; she'd dragged her brother over every path and hillock enough times in search of escape from Dublin's crowded streets and drawing rooms to know it from corner to distant corner. She was not quite as certain of herself at night, despite what she had told Christor. Walking alongside her uncle to some musical event or another by the light of countless lanterns was one matter. Groping about in the middle of the night was quite another.

Taking a deep breath and willing her heart to cease thundering in her ears, she pointed up a low rise. "There. There is a sort of pathway among the shrubbery. It will take us to the north border of the Park. Anyone wanting to hide would be best to do it there, where it's least open."

They found the opening in the shrubs easily. Navigating the thorny path without light was not so simple. The moderate moonlight helped somewhat, but not enough. Ailís, still in the lead, walked straight into several bushes, earned glancing scratches from countless others. Not twenty yards away, on the intended pathway, they could see lanterns, hear the stomping and muttering of mounted and foot patrols.

Ailís's thoughts rolled and twisted around themselves. Phoenix Park was nearly three miles east to west, more than a mile north to south. They could walk in helpless circles all night and still not cover half the ground. As they approached the main road bisecting the park, she stopped suddenly. Christor came up hard against her back and promptly wrapped his hands around her to steady her. His aim had probably been lower, Ailís thought slightly hazily, as his fingers splayed intimately over both breasts. She caught her breath, his hands dropped away.

"God help me," she heard him mutter, then grunt as Séamus bumped into him.

"Shhh." She peered through a break in the shrubs, looked as best she could in all directions. "All the lanterns seem to be on the east side." She thought hard. "If he's evaded them this long he must be . . . Ah. Ashtown Castle. It must be."

Certain of her direction now, she turned west. There was a large clearing ahead, but no sign of anyone there. Ailís's knees shook, threatening to fail her. Then Christor's hand was around hers, large and strong. "Hold fast," he murmured, and she did.

The three ran, fast and quiet as they could, across the clearing, through more shrubs, over several hills. Then suddenly, looming ahead of them in the dark was the craggy outline of Ashtown Castle. Ailís had always loved the partially restored tower house, with its mellowed stone and seventeenth-century lines. Now it looked as grim and forbidding as an ancient keep.

Christor took the lead, keeping Ailís's hand in his and Ailís herself safely between him and Cleary as they skirted the edifice. His free hand slipped once again into the pocket of his greatcoat to close around the pistol there.

It was Ailís who spied the figure first. Crouched behind a tumble of fallen masonry, it would have been easy to miss. But she did not miss it. Christor stopped at her fierce tugging, followed the line she pointed. In the moonlight he could just see the hunched line of a coat, a dark hat. Gesturing for Ailís and Cleary to stop, he crept forward.

Apparently the man had neither spied nor heard them approaching. He did not move as Christor came up behind him. He did, however, jerk like a stringed puppet when Christor leapt on him, one arm pinning him to the ground, the other clamping over his mouth. In a matter of seconds, An Cú the Wrong was caught as effectively as a hare in a trap.

The fight went out of him quickly, almost as rapidly as Christor realized it was not Eamonn O'Neill beneath his elbow. The masked figure was too small, too slight. Christor impatiently tugged off the mask to expose . . . spectacles. He bent low, got a good look, and shook his head as if he could change what he was seeing.

"Figgis."

He slowly removed his weight from the valet's prostrate form, lifted his hand. Figgis pulled himself up slowly until he was leaning against the stones. He adjusted his spectacles, retrieved his hat which had been knocked loose in the brief scuffle, and carefully settled it back atop his head.

"Good evening, my lord."

"Good evening? Good *evening*?"

Christor thrust his clenched fingers out. Figgis squeaked and pressed himself back into the masonry. Christor had every intention of throttling the man then and there, and might well have done it had not Ailís suddenly inserted herself between him and the cowering valet.

"Get out of the way, Ailís," he snapped. "I don't care about honor and forgiveness and nonviolence. I am going to kill him."

"Fine," she replied tartly, startling him into some semblance of sense. "But do it later. There are lanterns coming this way. We need to move."

She scooted aside then and he rose to his feet. Grabbing Figgis by the coat collar, Christor hauled him upright. "Why?" he demanded harshly.

"I will be more than happy to tell you, my lord, but perhaps not—"

"Now."

The valet's entire frame slumped. "Uselessness is the quickest road to death, my lord. When you left for the Continent, left me in Dublin with no purpose, no work, I could not bear it."

"So you pawed through my belongings, discovered the remnants of An Cú . . ."

"I discovered nothing." Surprisingly, Figgis's chin went up with that. "I always knew what you did, my lord. And was proud of you for it."

Even before Ailís stepped in again, tugging at his sleeve, Christor felt his fury beginning to wane. "God help us all, Figgis," he sighed.

"I meant only good, my lord."

"Good such as mowing Miss O'Neill and me down with my mother's old Town coach?"

He remembered now, both the old coach, long since stored away, and the horse, one of his father's last purchases. It was little wonder neither had been uncovered on any of the searches. They'd been tucked away in his own property.

Figgis flinched. "I am sorry for that, my lord, more sorry than I can say. I only intended to alarm you, perhaps send you back to London. I am very much afraid I have little experience with the ribbons, and my eyesight is not what it once was."

Christor wearily closed his own eyes. "Whose is?" Then, "Come along. We'd best leave before Dublin's bumbling finest appear."

It was too late. As they stepped around the corner of the tower, they could see lanterns approaching from two sides. Tension curling like a cold fist in his gut, Christor searched for any solution. The one that came was chancy, certainly dangerous, but it was all he had.

"Where is your horse?" he asked Figgis.

"There"—the valet pointed shakily to the north side of the tower—"tied behind the wall. But it will never carry—"

"See them both home, Cleary." Christor was already gauging the distance to the wall—and to the approaching patrols. "Then return the horses to Farrell."

"Clane . . ."

"Christor." Ailís's hands were on his chest now, clenching in his coat. "What are you going to do?"

"When you speak of me, speak well, *cailín*." He winked, grinned, and kissed her, hard and fast. "Stay here till it's safe to move."

Then he spun and loped northward into the darkness. As soon as he was clear of the Castle, he tore off his hat, raised it into the air, and let out a loud whoop.

"An Cú!" he bellowed, then again as he ran toward the park wall. *"An Cú go bráth!"*

Seconds later, he heard the shouts and hoofbeats of the horde behind him. Summoning resources he had not tapped since that last battle on the Peninsula, he bellowed again and sprinted toward the wall.

Ailís was still shaking when Séamus walked her to her door an hour later, her heart still skittering in her chest.

"He will be fine, Séamus, won't he?" She grabbed desperately at his sleeve. "Won't he?"

"Aye. Sure and he will. He is An Cú. 'Twould take more than a few paltry soldiers to bring him down." But he did not meet her eyes. "You go on inside now, Miss Ailís. When there's news, I'll see you get it."

"Thank you, Séamus." She paused with her hand on the doorknob. "Don't be too harsh with Figgis. Please. He is right in saying uselessness is—"

"Don't worry. I'll not harm him . . . not yet, anyway."

"Séamus . . ." But he was already walking away.

Shivering, Ailís opened the door and let herself in the house. It was dark, utterly still. Knowing she would not sleep, but not wanting to face the empty parlor, she headed for the stairs and the solace of her chamber.

A faint light beneath the library door caught her eye as she mounted the first step. Curious, she crossed the hall and opened the door. Eamonn was there, seated at their father's battered old desk. He had removed his coat and cravat, rolled up his shirtsleeves, and was bent over a sheaf of papers, a glass of amber liquid at his elbow. He glanced up as she entered.

"Ah, did I wake . . ." His smile faded as he took in her appearance. "Good God, Ailís. What happened to you? What have you been up to?"

She could only imagine how she looked: garbed in his old clothing, mud-streaked, bearing the marks of countless thorny branches. Bone-weary, cold as ice with fear and desperation, she took a few steps into the room. "Don't ask me questions just now, Éamonnán. Please, not just now."

And bless him, he did not. Instead, he sprang from behind the desk, crossed the room, and plied the brandy decanter. Returning, he pushed her, unresisting, onto the worn leather sofa with one hand, then passed her the glass with the other. He lowered himself to sit beside her.

"Drink that. You look like utter hell."

The brandy burned like fire on its way down. When she began to cough, Eamonn took the glass from her hand and thumped her gently on the back. Once she'd gotten her breath back, he wrapped her fingers again around the glass.

"Better?" he asked.

She thought for a moment, nodded, then burrowed into his side. It was a familiar spot, a comforting one, and she realized how long it had been since she'd been able to run to her brother with her woes.

"Where have *you* been, Eamonn? So many nights . . . Where were you?"

"So you're allowed to ask questions and I am not?" He draped an arm over her shoulders and rubbed the top of her head. "Fine, then. But you'll talk to me later?"

"Tomorrow," she replied. "I promise."

"As it happens, *cál,* I've been making my fortune."

Ailís lifted her head. "What do you mean?"

"Just what I said. I've long had need of funds, for my Parliamentary stand, for you and Mother. So I went out and . . . Well, I suppose you can say I earned them."

"How? Forgive me, Eamonn, but you've no training for anything save the army."

He grinned down at her. "And grand training it was. There's no place like the barracks for learning how to manage a hand of cards. Remind me to thank Clane when next we see him for teaching me *vingt et un* so well as he did."

Ailís resolutely ignored the painful clutching of her heart at the sound of Christor's name. "You've been . . . *gaming*?"

"I have been winning. There's a world of difference, you know. And I've just received word that some investments I made not a month ago have brought in rather delightful returns. God bless something called a gas-main." Clearly delighted with himself, Eamonn stole a swallow of her brandy. "You have the great honor of being related to Dublin's newest fortune, whose noble genesis came at the tables."

"Daly's . . . ?"

"Daly's, Blackrock, Fingall's, a place or two in Howth."

"Oh. Oh, Eamonn."

"Aye. We're wealthy folk now, sister mine. What do you say to a slew of new dresses, a horse of your own, a Season in London?"

She reflexively wrinkled her nose at that one. "I'd sooner have a summer in the netherworld." Her gaze slewed to the desk, to the papers, and the pile of bank notes she could now see among them. "Tonight's spoils?"

"Five hundred pounds," Eamonn replied delightedly. "Old Lorcan will never miss them, nor the other hundreds he has so graciously surrendered to me in past weeks, but it's manna for us."

"How much, Eamonn?" Ailís was struggling to get this new information into her already overwhelmed head. "How much have you won, in all?"

"Well, I was just doing some calculations when you came in, but"—he leaned back and crossed one leg negligently over the other—"as best I can tell, between the tables and wonder-

ful world of gases, I now possess something in the region of
twenty-five thousand pounds."

"Twenty-five *thousand* . . ."

"Breathe, *cál.* In and out. In and out. Good girl." Patting her
head again, he mused, "You've a decent dowry now, Ailís. Not
that a man wouldn't love you without it—one would be a fool
not to—but now you've the means to marry just about whoever and however you please. That is, if you *want* to marry, of
course. Good lord, Ailís. What on earth is the matter?"

Ailís couldn't help herself. Letting the brandy glass thud to
the floor, spilling what contents remained over the threadbare
carpet, she threw both arms around her brother's waist, buried
her face in his shirtfront, and sobbed.

Chapter 17

She had stopped crying eventually, courtesy of her own strength of will and Eamonn's liberal hand with the brandy. Now, as she sat in the sunny parlor, hunched miserably in the chair farthest from the window, she allowed herself a whimper or two. Even the recent church bells announcing afternoon services had pounded painfully inside her head.

She clapped one hand over an ear, the other over her mouth as her mother bustled into the room and plunked a laden tray onto a nearby table. "Please," she mumbled between her fingers. "Please take it away."

Anne ignored her. She poured something from the tisane pot into a teacup and thrust it in her daughter's direction. "Drink," she commanded, settling herself gracefully in her chair.

Ailís sniffed suspiciously at the cup. "What is it?"

"Hemlock," her mother replied tartly. "We all agreed to put you out of our misery."

"Mama . . ."

"Meadow-sweet, chamomile, and black horehound to settle your stomach, lavender for your head."

Ignoring the fact that her entire body tensed to the word *hound*, Ailís took a tentative sip and, when her insides did not rebel, another. She soon drained the cup and accepted a second. She balked somewhat at the dry biscuits her mother pressed on her, but managed to nibble on the corner of one. "I am dying," she announced eventually.

"You are not dying, Ailís. You are suffering, aye, but I have always thought the effects of overindulgence were the only consequences in life truly commensurate with the behavior. Rather tidy, actually."

"Bleagh," said Ailís, and slowly lowered her head to rest against the chair back.

"What could Eamonn possibly have been thinking, plying you with brandy?"

"He meant to . . . comfort me, Mama."

"Ah. Men. They believe spirits are the solution to whatever ails a body." Anne sighed. "Perhaps they are correct. Oh, Ailís. I have no idea what to do when what ails my daughter is one of them."

"What was that?"

"I have no tisane to ease lovesickness."

Ailís stared at the ceiling. "Would it do any good for me to insist I am not lovesick?"

"Good for whom, dearest?" her mother replied mildly. "But I'll not press you on the matter."

They sat in shared silence. Ailís, now that her head and stomach felt better, was left with only her fear to contemplate. Eamonn had done quite right to get her foxed. Had she not gone face-down on the library floor, dead to the world as he hefted her upstairs and settled her in bed, she would have spent the night in restless, agonized pacing.

There had been no news at all, not from Séamus, nor from any of the sources who could usually be counted upon to bring tidbits of interest. Nothing.

She tried to take heart in that. Had something terrible happened to Christor, the news would have been all over Town by now. Then again, she mused miserably, if it had been discovered that the Earl of Clane was the notorious An Cú, all efforts would probably have been made to quash the tale.

"He should have come by now, Mama," she whispered, and turned her face to the wall.

Anne was halfway out of her seat when Eamonn came bounding through the door. He looked impossibly, annoyingly hale and handsome, Ailís noted, recalling the rather frightening view she'd had of herself in the looking glass earlier. He was also sporting a brand-new, deep green coat and boots so glossy she could have gotten yet another frightening view of herself had she possessed the energy to bend over.

"It is," Eamonn announced as he dropped cheerfully onto a settee, "a marvelous day out there. Come have a walk with me, Ailís. The air might do you some good."

She could see the concern in his eyes and silently thanked him for it. He had not pressed her the night before, merely let her cry herself dry into his shirtfront, then gotten her blind drunk. All in all, a perfect brother.

"I don't think so, Éamonnán. I'll be better for just sitting."

"Ailís . . . Ah, as you wish. I dropped into Hodges' as you asked, Mother. They've sold out of Lady Morgan's *Wild Irish Girl* yet again, but expect to have more within the sennight."

"Thank you, Eamonn. I ought to have known better than to lend mine to Ursula."

"By the by," he continued, "I ran into Clane in Grafton Street. . . ."

Ailís jerked to attention. "You saw him? You truly saw Lord Clane?"

"I just said so, didn't I?"

"How did he appear, Eamonn. Did he seem . . . well?"

Her brother gave her a brief, appraising look, then replied, "Well as ever, I suppose. He was placing an order for a portmanteau at Brightwell's."

Ailís's heart, which had soared airily only moments before, came down with a thump. "Is he . . . is he planning a journey, then?"

"I didn't ask, but one could assume so. I daresay he's heading back to London and decided to have a new case."

"Oh." Ailís's fingers clenched hard around the arms of her chair. "Oh."

"He asked after you, *cál*. Being the splendid sibling I am, I refrained from telling him you were nursing a bear's head today."

He was well. He was well, Ailís repeated silently. *That must be enough.*

It did not matter, of course it did not, that he hadn't come to her with news of his successful flight from Phoenix Park. He was well: free of chains and apparently uninjured. And leaving. She rose shakily to her feet, forcing a nattering Eamonn to his. "Nay, don't get up. If you will excuse me, Mama, I believe I will . . . go . . . upstairs."

"Ailís. Dearest—"

"Nay, be easy. I am fine, merely a bit woozy. No more brandy for this bear," she said to Eamonn, managing a weak smile. "I believe I will . . . go. . . ."

She had reached the first landing by the time her mother came hurrying out of the parlor after her. "Ailís, is there anything I can . . ." Anne frowned, turned toward the front door. "What on earth is that noise?"

Ailís heard it, too, a faint tattoo-like sound in the street. "Colonel Ellsworth marching his troops again, no doubt. They've that favorite pub near the Canal Docks."

"I do not believe it is marching at all." Anne trotted up the stairs to join Ailís on the landing. Together they peered out the window and into the street. "Oh, my. How nice."

That, Ailís thought as she surveyed the scene below, was an understatement of epic proportions. Striding a bit haphazardly down Fitzwilliam Lane, quite blocking the street, was a full Irish band.

There were pipers, tin whistlers, fiddlers, and more, easily a dozen, and all garbed in the various uniforms of their trades. Butchers, printers, stevedores. She spied the aged music shop proprietor, fiddle beneath his chin, sawing away and hopping as he went with the rhythm of the song. The oxlike flautist was there, too, and the wiry fiddler.

And there, at the front, drumming on a massive *bodhrán,* was Christor.

"Help me, Mama."

Together they lifted the heavy window just as the motley orchestra halted in front of the house. The lovely notes of *"Caisleán Uí Néill"*—"O'Neill's Castle"—trilled to an end.

"Mathái!" Ailís hissed as her decorous-to-the-marrow mother actually leaned out the window.

"Good afternoon, gentlemen," Anne called down.

From her vantage point, hidden by the curtains, Ailís watched as Christor doffed his curly-brimmed hat and bowed low. "Good afternoon, Missus," he called back in that wild Wicklow brogue that set Ailís's heart a'thumping. "We're here to serenade a Miss Ailís O'Neill. Is she to be found at home today, by chance?"

"She is indeed." Anne withdrew and, with all the love and care of motherhood, hauled Ailís out from behind the curtains, shoving her all but right out the window.

Below, Christor let out a loud sigh and clapped his hat over his heart. "There she is, boys, the fairest of all in Ireland. Isn't she breathtaking, Malachy?"

The shopowner stepped forward and scratched for a moment at his beard. "Aye, sir, that she is. Comely as they come. Billy?"

The ox tipped his cap and gave Ailís a beautiful grin. "Stuff of dreams, I'd say. Pádraig?"

The wiry chandler nodded. "A face as inspired the troubadours of old," he announced. "A damsel of exceeding grace and singular magnificence. The epitome—"

"Aw, leave off, Paddy!" someone called from the back. "Ye'll make us all dizzy."

Christor grinned and turned to his companions. "So what song do we have worthy of this beauty?"

He struck a few beats on the *bodhrán* and the rest soon joined in. "The Rogue's Reel" swelled through Fitzwilliam Lane, sliding easily into "The Nobleman's Wedding."

Ailís stood, breathless, heart aloft, as they played. Around the street, other windows opened, hands began clapping to the tune, breaking into applause when the last note was played.

"Clane?" was heard from several houses down. "Lord Clane, is that you?"

He flashed his stunning grin and came to stand right below the window. "Come down to me, Ailís O'Neill!"

And she did, at a run.

He tossed drum and tipper to a waiting Billy and caught Ailís up as she came flying out the door. Swinging her in a dizzying circle, he found himself laughing aloud. This was what he wanted, all he'd ever wanted: a fine Dublin day, music, and a beautiful woman in his arms.

"You'll be marrying me now, Ailís Mary O'Neill, the very first morning possible."

The eyes she raised to him were sparkling, sparking, and unobstructed. Her spectacles were dangling from one ear. She fumbled to get them back on her nose. "That is your idea of a proposal, Christopher Rhys Francis Moore?"

"Ah. I do beg your pardon, mademoiselle." He promptly set her on her feet, steadying her when she wobbled noticeably, then dropped to one knee. "Miss O'Neill, would you do me the great honor of—"

"Aye," she said tartly. "I will, but only if you tell me how ardently you admire and adore me first."

As he rose, brushing every inch of her soft body on the way up, he kept his eyes fixed steadily on hers. "I admire you, Ailís, your wicked wit and clever mind. I adore your freckles, your clefted chin, your noteworthy feet." He grinned when a pair of adorable frown lines appeared between her brows. "I love you, Ailís, for all that you are, with all that I am. Will you marry me now?"

"Nay."

He blinked, stupefied. I—"

"I've an appointment with a hedgehog this afternoon. But I'll marry you any day after."

Laughing, body warm with pleasure unimagined, Christor pulled her close. "Tell me how you admire and adore me."

"I love you," she said simply. *"You."*

He wanted to kiss her, was desperate to kiss her right there and then, for the next several hours or so. But she rapped a finger against his chest.

"Who is the portmanteau for?" she demanded. "Eamonn said you were choosing one and I was terrified you were sailing for London as fast as the wind would carry you."

"Never," he said fervently. "Well, not until the next Parliamentary session. I must, Ailís," he insisted when she frowned again, then grinned with her. "You might find you actually like London. I'd hope so, as I won't be going without you."

"As long as we always come home again soon."

"I promise."

"So, the portmanteau . . . ?" she repeated after a long, soft moment.

"For Figgis. It's the only way I seem to be able to convince him that I'll not leave him behind again."

"You are a good man, Lord Clane. It will be my honor to marry you." She gave him a blood-stirring look then, a slow flutter of eyelashes that registered down to his toes. "I know exactly what to give you as a wedding gift."

"Oh, Ailís."

"And precisely what I want from you."

The possibilities were endless. And very pleasant. "You do, do you?"

"Aye." Ailís leaned up on her toes, placed her lips just below his earlobe, and whispered, "I want a complete set of etching tools. I've a personage or two of Ireland yet to paint."

Christor groaned, then decided he would buy her every bloody etching tool in Ireland as she whispered just what she planned to give him.

Epilogue

From **The Freeman's Journal,** *28 November, 1813:*

FANTASTICAL SATIRICAL PRINTS

Presently in their fifth Printing in London, now to be found here. No Person of Taste and Discrimination yet Unsatisfied should Despair, but should make a Perusal of these Extraordinary Images of Personages of Ireland. Represented in full Detail and Color are to be found the most Illustrious Figures of Ireland today. The Vendors of these Singular Works frequently cannot get supplied so Quick as the Demand is for them; and it is a Fact, worthy of Remark, that they are sold nearly as they arrive on Hand, most of the Series being Bespoke before they are Ordered.

Sold by Holyfield's Repository of Arts, 33 Grafton Street.

MARRIAGES

On Thursday last, the Honorable Jonathan Lyndhurst, of London and this city, in Christ Church Cathedral, to Maria, only daughter of Richard Farnham, Esq., of this city.

On Saturday last, the Earl of Clane, Captain of the 88th Division Connaught Rangers, in Tullamore, Queen's County, to Ailís, only daughter of the late Thomas O'Neill, Esq., of Queen's County, and niece of Thaddeus O'Neill, distinguished music critic of this publication. The bride was radiant; the orchestra local, enthusiastic, and somewhat rough.